Little Black Girl Lost 3
Ill Gotten Gains

Also by Keith Lee Johnson

Sugar & Spice: A Novel
Pretenses
Little Black Girl Lost
Fate's Redemption
Little Black Girl Lost 2
The Honeymoon is Over

Little Black Girl Lost 3
Ill Gotten Gains

Keith Lee Johnson

URBAN BOOKS
www.urbanbooks.net

Urban Books
10 Brennan Place
Deer Park, NY 11729

ISBN-13: 978-1-893196-78-0
ISBN-10: 1-893196-78-x

First Printing February 2007
Printed in the United States of America

10 9 8 7 6 5 4 3

This is a work of fiction. Any references or similarities to actual events, real people, living, or dead, or to real locales are intended to give the novel a sense of reality. Any similarity in other names, characters, places, and incidents is entirely coincidental.

Submit Wholesale Orders to:
Kensington Publishing Corp.
C/O Penguin Group (USA) Inc.
Attention: Order Processing
405 Murray Hill Parkway
East Rutherford, NJ 07073-2316
Phone: 1-800-526-0275
Fax: 1-800-227-9604

Dedication

To my aunt Darlene Grier
And to all the fans of Johnnie Wise
Thanks for reading all the novels!

Acknowledgments

To Him, who is able to do considerably more than I can ask or think, I give You thanks.

To my mom, thanks for teaching me to tell the truth from a very early age. It has been invaluable over the years.

To Dr. Frederick K.C. Price of Ever Increasing Faith Ministries, thanks for being bold and for having the courage to speak the truth in Love. Your series on Race, Religion, and Racism was truly excellent!

Special thanks to Joel A. Rogers for his eye-opening work in *Sex and Race*, volumes I, II, & III.

Special thanks to Martha Weber for your contribution to the content of this novel. Were it not for you, this work would be woefully less than it is.

Special thanks to Carl Weber for taking on all the *Little Black Girl Lost* novels and being a man of integrity.

To my man, Phillip Thomas Duck, author of *Playing with Destiny* and *Grown & Sexy*, in stores now, thanks for all the laughs you provide and the invaluable wisdom. Remind me to write that story we talked about at BEA 2006 in Washington, DC.

To my good friend, Kendra Norman-Bellamy, author of *Because of Grace* and *More than Grace*, in stores now, thanks for letting me know about the Circle of Friends gathering in my hometown, Toledo, Ohio, June 2007. I hope to see you there.

To Alisha Yvonne, author of *Lovin' You Is Wrong* and *I Don't Wanna Be Right*, thanks for being such a gracious and accommodating host when I signed in your Memphis Urban Knowledge Bookstore, February 2006. You definitely know how to get people to come to signings. Hopefully more authors will come to Memphis and see how the women in the South do things.

Special thanks to Tabitha, manager of borders Bookstore in Toledo, Ohio. Thanks for always looking out for me from the beginning. I won't forget you.

Special thanks to OOSA Book Club for your tremendous support and for recommending my controversial novel, *Fate's Redemption*, in *Upscale magazine*.

Special thanks to Schylar Meadows of Juice Talk in Toledo, Ohio.

Special thanks to Sherry Springs of Winston-Salem, North Carolina. Thanks for featuring me on your Easterbaby's blog.

To Trisha Olsby and Roshaundra Ellington, two sweet women and faithful readers of all my novels, thanks so much.

To all my coworkers who *bought* and read every single book, I can't thank you enough and I appreciate each of you.

To all my fans, thanks for all the emails, and thanks so much for buying and reading *Little Black Girl Lost 1 & 2* and making it a perennial Black Expressions Best Seller.

To all the beauty salons in Toledo, Thanks for allowing me to put stand-up posters in your shops.

And last but not least, special thanks to my man Fletcher Word of the *Sojourner Truth Newspaper* in Toledo, Ohio. BIG, BIG THANKS for all the articles and publicity.

Book 2

The End

Christmas Eve 1953

Someone was knocking on Johnnie's front door. She was still wrapping the last minute gifts she had purchased, putting them under the tall Christmas tree she had carefully selected in Zachary, Louisiana, where the trees were grown. Most of the presents were for Sadie and her kids, who were coming over for dinner. They planned to sing Christmas carols, drink eggnog, and spend the night. This would be Johnnie's first Christmas without her mother, who she now had mixed feelings about. She missed her now that she was dead. Were it not for Sadie, it would have been a very lonely holiday season with Lucas still 135 miles away at The Farm in Angola.

As she walked to the front door, Johnnie wondered why Sadie and her children hadn't come to the backdoor as usual. She opened the door and her mouth fell open when she saw Earl Shamus standing there. Madame DeMille, the fortuneteller who performed her abortion, had told her he would arrive when least expected. Ironically, it was two years had passed to since the day that he had stripped her of her virginity.

The fulfillment of another prediction scared Johnnie. Her heart was pounding. Anxiety saturated her mind. There she was, looking at the man who had ripped away her innocence, humbling her, removing her purity, turning her into a woman long before her time.

Madame DeMille said I had to confront him and I will. I guess it's time for me to take care of this shit now. She told me I would experience many hardships and obstacles, but I would triumph over all my enemies because my hardships would open my eyes. I wonder what that last part means.

Johnnie opened the screen door. "Long time no see."

"Can I come in?" Earl asked respectfully.

"I'm expecting company. How long is this going to take?" she asked, having made up her mind to make every effort to speak proper English from now on. She looked at her watch.

"You expecting that boyfriend you deceived me with? Or are you expecting Martin Winters, my former friend?"

"Come on in, Earl. I see we've got some things to say to each other."

Earl walked in and closed the door. "So you don't deny sleeping with Martin?"

"I only did what you and my mother taught me to do *when she sold me to you.* Are you really going to stand there and blame me for what *you* did?"

"What did I do besides get you this wonderful house, and put beautiful clothes on your back? What did I do besides get you stock in a company that was flourishing? What did I do, Johnnie, besides love you the best way I knew how? And how did you repay me? By fucking my friend!"

"How dare you come to me, blaming me for some shit *you* did?" Johnnie shouted. "I was fifteen goddamn years old, Earl! FIFTEEN! Don't come into my house yelling about all the shit you did for me. You should have done that and more. As a matter of fact, they should lock your ass up for raping a minor! What you did is called statutory rape, Earl!"

"But I—"

"SHUT UP! I don't wanna hear your bullshit! You're not getting out of this! You came over here! You came to *my* house!" She folded her arms. "So I'm going to tell you the truth about you, Earl! The truth is you didn't just want some pussy, did you? You wanted to fuck a child, didn't you? How would you like it if somebody fucked all three of your daughters, huh? Would it be okay if a sex-crazed insurance man fucked Janet, or Stacy, or Marjorie? Oh, and on Christmas Eve at that! Do you even remember what you did two years ago today; that you fucked me in my mother's bed? Do you remember me saying the Lord's Prayer while you pumped me?

"So yeah, I got what I could get out of you! Yeah, you bought me this house! You bought me just about everything I own. But guess what? None of it, and I mean none of it, can replace what you took from me!"

"I'm sorry, Johnnie," Earl offered without contrition, which was indicative of a conscience that had long since been abandoned.

"I'm not finished, Earl! You know you're partially responsibly for my mother's death, don't you?"

"What? How can you possibly blame me for that? I had nothing to do with that, Johnnie! You're being totally unfair to me!"

"I can and I do blame you, Earl, because you gave me a taste of the good life."

"Are you fucking kidding me? I took you out of a rattrap Marguerite called a house and you blame me?"

"You're too blind to see your own bullshit," Johnnie said, calming down. "My mother was trying to blackmail Richard Goode because you had given me so much. Don't you see? A mother's jealousy often overshadows her love. By doing all you did, by giving me all you gave me, by helping me make some real money, my mother saw her own failure as a whore. Like you, she was blind to her own bullshit, too. Now she's dead, Earl . . . dead and gone, all because you wanted to fuck a child."

"What can I do to make it up to you?" Earl said sincerely, finally coming to grips with what he'd done.

Johnnie shook her head in disbelief and compassionately said, "Do you really think you can make it up to me, Earl? Do you really? People are dead because of you—lots of them."

"You mean the riot? You're blaming me for that too?"

Enraged again by his need to deny his complicity in the murders, Johnnie screamed, "You goddamn right I blame *you* for the riot! But I don't just blame you for that. I blame you for the death of my white uncle and his two sons. See, *your* sin has spread through the whole damn town. You corrupted me, and now lots of people are dead." She stopped short of telling him about the murder of Sharon Trudeau, the stockbroker who was murdered by Napoleon's hitmen after she stole $250,000 of Johnnie's investment money. Tears formed and dropped. "I watched my cousin Blue kill his brother Beau in a fit of rage. Then I watched Blue put a gun to his head and blow his brains out.

"After that, my uncle tried to choke the life out of me, and my aunt, Ethel Beauregard, shot him in the back of the head and blew his brains and blood all over me. All of this because my uncle Eric didn't know he was calling his half sister, the woman you knew as Marguerite, a whore that got what she deserved. When he called my mother that, when he talked about her like she wasn't even a human being, I told him about the whores in his own family, and that's when the killing began. So yes, you caused their deaths too."

Crying now, Earl asked, "What can I do? How can I make this right?"

Calm again, Johnnie said, "Go home, Earl. Go home to Meredith. She loves you and only God knows why. Don't ever come here again. If you return to this place, I won't be responsible for what happens to you. If you see me on the street, act as if we are total strangers. And in time, perhaps I can forgive you for all that you've caused because you didn't have enough self-control to keep from fucking a defenseless child, a fifteen year old church-going, Bible-believing Christian girl."

She walked past a whimpering Earl Shamus, whom she had completely dismantled with her truth, and opened the door. "Get out," Johnnie said in a genteel voice that would otherwise be soothing. "You can cry out there if have to. But this is Christmas Eve, and I won't let you ruin another one for me."

Earl turned around and walked out. He stopped in his tracks and turned around to say something, and Johnnie slammed the door in his face. Feeling good in her soul for the first time in two years, she walked over to the sofa, sat down, picked up the phone and called her best friend, Sadie Lane, and cheerfully said, "Everything's all set! Bring your kids over. This'll be the best Christmas they ever had!"

After she hung up, Johnnie realized it was time to visit Marguerite in her mausoleum. She had a number of things to say to her too. Earl Shamus was wrong, but so was her mother. The things she had to say to her mother could wait. Christmas Eve was supposed to be fun and when Sadie and her children came over, fun, was what they were going to have.

Book Three

Ill Gotten Gains

Part 1

The Sentinel Article

"The heart is deceitful above all and desperately wicked." Johnnie thought he was talking to her as he spoke, like he was standing right next to her, speaking directly in her ear. "Some of us are so self-righteous that it's going to take a lifetime to discover the truth of this verse so that we might be truly saved."

Reverend Staples
Little Black Girl Lost
Book One

Chapter 1
Day 1

"Until the End of Time."

Move on? Did Lucas really say that? Did he mean it? Those words occupied Johnnie Wise's mind as she drove back to New Orleans. She could hardly believe it even though he'd said it a number of times. It was Christmas, and she had driven 135 miles to see him so he would have a good holiday even though he was in prison. She had taken him a hearty meal, which consisted of candied ham, navy beans, cornbread, macaroni and cheese, potato salad, Cole slaw, sweet potatoes, peach cobbler, and a gallon of sweet tea. On top of that, she bought him so many presents that the guards had to carry them in for her, which they were more than happy to do, hoping and probably praying for a chance to bed her. In her mind's eye, she could see it all now as she neared her Ashland Estates home.

She excitedly watched Lucas open his presents, but he showed no enthusiasm. He was just going through the motions, like he was trying to please the woman he still loved; besides, she had driven a long way. She thought it was because he couldn't keep anything she'd brought to the prison, which she knew before she drove nearly three hours to show them to him. The whole point was to give him something to look forward to when he came home. She had spent hour upon hour looking at expensive suits, ties, shirts, handkerchiefs, watches, and shoes that would make him look like a successful businessman. She had spent a small fortune on him, and he barely smiled when he saw her.

Initially she thought he was embarrassed to be wearing prison dungarees, but quickly realized he was very unhappy. *Why wouldn't he be unhappy?* she'd thought. *He is in prison, isn't he?* She was going to cheer him up and give him something to look forward to, but no matter what she said, no matter what gift he opened, his expression barely changed, and it began to irritate Johnnie. Nevertheless, she tried to remain upbeat for his sake and grabbed the large picnic basket, but even the food did little to change his stolid mood.

Finally, she angrily said, "What the fuck's wrong with you? It took a long goddamn time to make all this for you. I shopped for hours getting you these presents. I meticulously matched every piece in every ensemble to make you look good, you ungrateful so-and-so."

He continued eating his food heartily, as if he hadn't eaten in the three weeks he'd been there.

"Lucas, I know you heard me!"

He finished off what was on his plate and gave it to her, expecting her to fill it again. She took the plate, set it on the table, and stared into his depressed eyes, silently waiting for him to acknowledge her magnanimous gifts, the time it took to select them, and her culinary expertise. Time stood still as they stared at each other without the interruption of words or the intake of food. At some point, Lucas looked away as tears welled.

Realizing he was in pain, she reached out and touched his hand, which he withdrew when he felt the warmth of her touch. Immediately, she thought he knew about the Las Vegas trip. *What else could it be?* She had slept with Napoleon again. *But how does he know?* As far as she knew, no one knew about the tryst, not even Sadie.

It occurred to her that perhaps Marla Bentley had told him about the affair. As far as Johnnie was concerned, Marla was the one person who would tell him, even though she didn't have any evidence because she didn't go on the Vegas trip. Marla would have to have assumed it all and told Lucas, but Johnnie couldn't ask him about it, just in case she was wrong.

"I love you, Lucas," she managed to say. "And I always will."

"Don't."

"Don't what?"

"Don't love me no more," Lucas said, looking at her with watery eyes.

"Huh?" Johnnie heard herself say.

"You heard me," Lucas said without malice, still looking into her brown eyes. "It's time we moved on with our lives, Johnnie. Me into the Army and you and your new big words . . . wherever good fortune takes you."

She was glad he had noticed the growth of her vocabulary, but she was also stunned by his heartfelt words. "You want to break up again?"

"Yeah," he said confidently, like he'd given the matter lots of thought. He picked up his plate and piled it high with more of the delicious food she'd brought with her. "Since this is your last time coming here, I figure I better at least enjoy your cookin' one last time."

On the verge of tears, her lower lip quivering uncontrollably, she said, "You're serious about breaking up?"

"Uh-huh," he said and continued devouring her food.

A tear fell.

She sniffed and looked around to see if anyone was paying attention to them. "Tell me why, Lucas. What did I do this time?"

"Nothing at all. I know it hurts, baby. I'm hurt too, but—"

"Then why?" she pleaded.

Tears fell from both her eyes.

"I got three months," he said and took several generous gulps of the sweet tea. He put the jar down and looked at her again. He could tell she was waiting for something more than what he offered as an explanation. "After that, the Army owns my black ass for three years, Johnnie. Three goddamn years. Are you gonna sit there and tell me you're gonna wait for me that long?"

"Yep," she said confidently and without hesitation. "I'll wait for you until the end of time. I'll wait for you until I see Jesus coming in the clouds. Don't you know that? Don't you know I would do anything for you? Three years is nothing." She leaned in and whispered, "Bubbles found Sharon Trudeau and got me my money, so I can afford to come and visit you wherever they send you."

Lucas kind of chuckled when he heard that. "I've been here three weeks, and married men that rode the bus in with me are getting what they call Dear John letters. They found a guy this morning—dead. He hung his self. They found a letter from his wife saying she couldn't wait three years for him and that she was going to move on with her life. The guards say that shit happens all the time. Grown men can't deal with prison life, and they definitely can't deal with their girlfriends and wives fuckin' other men. I know I couldn't. And I can't live my life wondering when you're going to send me a letter telling me the same thing. The guards say it happens to all the men sooner or later, and I might as well expect one sooner or later too. I know you love me, and believe me, I love you too. But it's better this way. This way I can live with no expectations of you. You're smart and you're tough. You gon' be somebody one day."

Johnnie pulled into her garage and turned off the ignition, still thinking about Lucas' last words to her. And there, in the quiet, in the dark, she wept for about an hour. She wept because deep down, she knew Lucas was right. She had already betrayed him with Napoleon twice. Unlike the first time when he blackmailed her, there was no threat to kill Lucas. As a matter of fact, the way she saw it, Napoleon had done his best to leave her alone, and she pursued him because she couldn't get him out of her mind or out of her system. Truth be told, she wanted to bed him again, but she would never admit it to herself. She couldn't because it would be clear evidence that she was indeed a third generation whore.

She had gone to Napoleon's suite at the Sands Hotel. He let her in to have a drink and then went to the bathroom to relieve himself. When he returned, she was in his bed, completely nude, allowing him to gaze at her magnificent body. As he amorously stared at her breasts, which were 38Ds, she told him he knew he wanted her, when in fact, she wanted him. They had great sex without the comfort of love, which left her feeling like the inside of a doughnut—empty and alone.

As the pain of losing her man deepened, an emotional song rang in her mind. She got out of Lucas' new 1954 Chevy, closed the garage door and went into her home. She remembered what Reverend Staples, her piano teacher and mentor, had told her. "Always get the music and the words on paper," he'd said. She sat down at her kitchen table, closed her eyes, and placed her hands on the table as if they were on the keys of a piano, and visualized the melody. That's when she realized she needed her own piano and music sheets to create. Once she had the melody, she wrote the words of a song she would call "Until the End of Time."

Chapter 2

"Thirty minutes."

"Hello," Johnnie said after lifting the receiver from its cradle. She was still in the kitchen, working on the song's bridge.

"Merry Christmas, Johnnie," Napoleon said. "I hope yours was better than mine."

When she thought about what he said, sadness resurfaced and covered her like a dark cloud—thick and threatening. Solemnly, she said, "It was okay, Napoleon."

"Okay? Just okay?"

"Just okay," Johnnie said, exhaling as she spoke.

"Oh, I see. You spent the day alone, huh?"

"Not really. Sadie and her kids spent Christmas Eve with me. We stayed up 'til midnight and watched them open their presents. Later, when we all woke up, I made breakfast for them." Earl Shamus' unexpected appearance came to mind. "Oh, and my old lover came by, accusing me of doing him wrong. I told his ass off, too. Then I put him out of my house and slammed the door in his face."

"Good for you, Johnnie."

"What about you, Mr. Gangster? What did you do today? Something exciting, I hope."

"Not really. I've been here all alone for the most part. I had dinner with a couple of my bodyguards. I bought 'em all presents, and watched them open them."

"You mean Marla's not there with you?"

"Marla left me, Johnnie."

Sarcastically, she said, "Really? I *wonder* why."

"I guess I deserved that, but I'm wondering why she stayed as long as she did. I mean, I'm no angel. I know that."

"She was probably afraid you'd kill her if she left. Isn't that what you Mob guys do? Kill anybody that gets in your way?"

"You sure know how to hurt a guy, Johnnie. You make me sound like Lucifer himself. I'm nowhere near that bad, am I?"

"Are you, Mr. Gangster? You tell me."

"No, I'm not. I'm really a nice guy who has to do some bad things sometimes, ya know? I mean . . . let's look at. Richard Goode beat your mother mercilessly and he needed to be dealt with, didn't he?"

"Uh-huh, and thanks again for dealing with that good for nothing cracker!"

"You're welcome. Now, what about Sharon Trudeau? She stole all your dough, and she needed to be dealt with, too, didn't she?"

"She sure did. Right again on both counts, Mr. Gangster."

"Lucas got himself in a whole bunch of shit and I did what I could. I mean the guy was caught with heroin in the trunk of his car. Good thing the judge owed me some serious money, otherwise Lucas would have had to do the whole stretch. I got him a damn good deal considering the charges levied against him, didn't I?"

"I guess so."

"Wait a minute! You guess so! He was looking at fifteen fuckin' years, Johnnie! Give me some fuckin' credit! I had Bubbles warn him not to do that shit months before he got caught, didn't I?"

"Yes."

"I gave him a brand new car and—"

"Now you hold on there, Mr. Gangster. You gave him that car because you knew you were wrong for blackmailing me into sleeping with you, right?"

"Well, okay, but I gave him a fifty dollar a week raise. I was paying the guy a hundred bucks a week. I never paid any kid that kinda dough when all he had to do was collect my money and run my wife on a few fuckin' errands. After all I did for him, he went against my orders by selling smack, and I still called in a favor or two to get this guy a good deal. Am I right or am I right?"

Johnnie smiled. "You're right, Mr. Gangster."

"All right then. I'm glad I could put a smile on your face even though you had such a shitty Christmas."

"How do you know I'm smiling, Mr. Gangster?"

"I can hear a distinct change in your tone."

"You can, huh?"

"Yes, I can."

"I guess you like putting smiles on all the girls' faces, don't you?"

Napoleon flashed his devilish grin. In just a few short minutes, he had created an opening for more romance. Johnnie had a disappointing Christmas, which was by design. He wanted her vulnerable to his wiles at this critical time. Lucas was in jail, her mother was dead and gone, her brother, Benny, was in San Francisco, and she was still dealing with the role she played in the deaths of the Beauregard men. On top of that, he'd heard about the abortion she had. With all of that on her shoulders, she still came to his room in Las Vegas and made sweet, satisfying love to him. He wanted her again and believed he could get her.

"Let me put it this way: whenever I can put a smile on a beautiful woman's face, I do my best to oblige. Now, am I so wrong for that?"

Johnnie remained quiet for a few seconds, thinking about their lovemaking. She particularly thought about that first encounter at the chic Bel Glades Hotel, when Napoleon had tantalized her with his very active and very knowledgeable tongue. The thought of him doing that again moistened her secret place and raised her temperature a bit. Feeling so alone, she didn't try to reject the images that now bombarded her young, but experienced mind. Her body wanted attention; the kind of attention she'd gotten at the Bel Glades Hotel that night a few months ago. The strange thing was, when she was in Las Vegas, she had promised herself she would never let Napoleon lap at her secret place again, and now she wanted him to do that very thing for hours. Nevertheless, she had no intentions of going through with it; she just wanted to get close to the flame without getting burned. After all, she couldn't do what Lucas thought she would eventually do and then send him a Dear John letter. She couldn't do it just a few hours after he told her she would, but she could flirt with Napoleon a little; no harm in that.

In a breathy voice, she began the tease saying, "When you put it that way, I guess not."

Napoleon sensed more than vulnerability from those words. He sensed opportunity, an open door to a house where lewd acts were condoned and encouraged. Confidently, he said, "You remember that first time we did it?"

Weakened by desire, vulnerable due to circumstances, and sensing the brilliant flames of lust as they beckoned, softly she said, "Uh-huh."

When she responded that way, without a hint of discouragement, he surged forward and said, "Do you remember how good it was?"

Johnnie closed her eyes and let the memory of him lapping her like there was no tomorrow wash over her. She could hear herself sigh in rhythm with each delicious stroke. Her legs began to open and close as the heat down there intensified.

She whispered a breathy, "I remember."

Napoleon's erection was as hard as a diamond, but still, he managed to stiffen a little more each time she responded to his flirtatious stroll down paradise road.

He said, "I enjoyed licking you down there."

"So you did get something out of it, huh?"

"Well, to be honest, I'd much rather give than receive. It's more blessed, they say."

Johnnie was totally into the sex play now, moving ever closer to the edge of surrender, where the thoughts and intents of the heart could be played out in seclusion. "Um, so you wanna give me some more?"

"Would you let me if I did want to?"

"It depends."

Napoleon's heart was pounding now. His hunger for her

edged him forward, telling him he was only inches away from having the young beauty again. He wanted her more than anything; more than being the Boss of New Orleans even. He had lied to have her. He had set up her boyfriend to do prison time and afterward, a stint in the Army. He had killed for her on more than one occasion. He felt like she was on the verge of complete surrender, unlike their first time, when she acted as if she had a gun to her head.

In a nearly desperate tone, at the point of begging for her fulfillment, he said, "It depends on what?"

"On what you're going to do *if* I let you."

That was all Napoleon needed to hear. He was going to get a piece that night. As far as he was concerned, after tonight, after he had taken her to paradise, she was going to give it up repeatedly, which was what he'd wanted all along. This was the moment he had waited for, and he knew he was almost there, almost home.

"What do you want me to do?"

"I want you to tell me what you're going to do if I come over to your place tonight."

Napoleon swallowed hard. He wasn't expecting that response at all. He wondered if she was really willing to drive out to his place so they could satisfy their heated appetites.

"Are you serious, Johnnie?" He panted.

"Are you?"

"Don't play with me," he begged.

"I'm good at that. Playing with you, aren't I? Didn't I prove that in Las Vegas? The question is can you duplicate what you did to me at the Bel Glades? Was that luck or can you do that each time out?" Johnnie surprised herself when she said that. She liked the way her efforts to increase her vocabulary and speak well made her sound—intelligent and refined—like her mother Marguerite when she spoke to white folks on the phone. "So, can you?"

Without a second's hesitation, he said, "That and more. All night long, baby. That's what you want, right?"

"All night long?"

"All . . . night . . . long."

"Um . . . sounds good to me."

"And it will be, believe me."

"Tell me what you're going to do."

"Why talk about it when we could be doing it, baby? Meet me at the Bel Glades in about thirty minutes and I'll tell you everything I'm gonna do."

"I want to hear it now." She had gone too far, and now she was going to give in to the temptation of being fulfilled by the gangster who had never failed her.

"Right now?"

"Right now."

"Are you wet?"

"Very."

If it were possible, Napoleon's erection stiffened even more.

"When we get to the room, I'm gonna start by kissing those juicy lips of your. I know how you love kissing. And while I'm kissing you, I'm gonna slide my hand up your dress, into your panties, so I can feel your wetness. Then I'm gonna massage you there."

"Sounds good so far. Then what?"

"Then I'm gonna get you outta your clothes and do what you want me to do."

"Lick me?"

"Uh-huh."

Both nipples hardened; her special instrument swelled, in much need of attention Napoleon was more than willing to give. "What time do you want me to be there, Mr. Gangster?"

"Thirty minutes."

"Okay. I'll see you then."

"Don't play with me, Johnnie. Are you gonna be there or not?"

"Are you going to be there?"

"Yeah. I'm leaving right now. Don't keep me waiting too long. I'm about to bust."

"I won't. This is something we've both been fighting, and I'm through fighting it. I just have to pack an overnight bag."

"All right then. I'll see you there."

"Thirty minutes."

Chapter 3

Where would she be going?

Napoleon told his bodyguards he was going to bed then slipped out of his mansion and arrived at the Bel Glades Hotel in record time. He checked in, went to the suite, undressed, and got in bed. After the first half-hour of waiting, he appeased his impatience by rationalizing that a woman had to pack a bag, fix her hair, put on the appropriate amount of makeup, and find just the right outfit. He knew she couldn't leave her home until she looked at herself in the mirror and saw perfection. Then and only then could she leave feeling sexy and desirable; not a second before.

After an hour and fifteen minutes had passed, he became antsy, wondering where she was and what was taking so long. He wanted to plow her territory and plant his seed in her fertile soil. He waited another fifteen minutes and called the front desk, believing he knew what had happened. It occurred to him that some racist desk clerk wouldn't let her up because he forgot to tell them the lady he was expecting was a Negro. After all, the Bel Glades didn't allow Negroes in the lobby, let alone in a hotel suite without the proxy of a guest whose financial statement warranted that particular perk. In Napoleon's case, he was the resident Mob Boss and with that title, people did what he told them or they took a fierce professional beating. In some cases, people got killed. It was that simple.

To his surprise, the desk clerk told him no one had come in the hotel after him. He called Johnnie's home and let the phone ring twenty times. No answer. He called back a couple more times and still got no answer. He smiled because it had occurred to him that she had skillfully teased him and left him waiting in an expensive hotel suite with only his plow for company.

He began to wonder if she had figured it all out. *Is that what the tease was all about?* Had she figured out that Lucas was in jail because of his lethal orchestration? After a few moments, he rejected the notion because she wasn't the type of girl to hold her cards close to the vest. If she suspected that he had cold-bloodedly set up the man she loved, she would have said something about it. For that reason, he knew she didn't know anything. Another possible reason for the no-show entered his mind. He thought he had offended Johnnie by soliciting her on Christmas night while Lucas was languishing in prison. That had to be her reason for leading him on. Undeterred, he laughed to himself, got out of bed and dressed. It was going to take a little longer, but he was going to have her all to himself, he thought, and left the room.

As he made his way to Riviera Heights, where he lived, for some reason he couldn't explain, he found himself headed over to Ashland Estates. As a made Mafioso, he knew better than to be in the company of Negroes, let alone be seen in their neighborhood, at the house of the woman who for all intents and purposes had started a race riot. Mafia rules notwithstanding, Negroes were the only people he trusted. There was no way he'd ever trust anyone in the Mafia because treachery was a way of life with those guys.

Negroes, on the other hand, were simple folk. If you did right by them, treated them with respect, they would be totally loyal. Nevertheless, it was still dangerous because people talked too much about things they didn't think mattered. If someone saw him going to Johnnie's house, it wouldn't be a big deal; lots of white men had dalliances with Negro women, but gossip would never be muzzled. Someone could say something to the wrong person, and he could be killed without hesitation.

It felt a lot like Christmas seeing all the decorative lights on every house in Ashland Estates. Fake snow covered the front yards in the upscale parish. Nativity scenes, angels, Santa Claus on a sleigh led by the most famous reindeer, Rudolph, were common fixtures in virtually every yard.

As he approached Johnnie's house, he noticed that her kitchen light was still on. He remembered the first time he'd come to her home, meeting her friend Sadie in the kitchen, eating pie, and overhearing an outrageous tale about Johnnie's secret life. That's when he realized why his lovely date hadn't shown up for their much anticipated rendezvous. He figured that Sadie had come over at the last minute and Johnnie couldn't leave that late in the evening without an explanation. Lucas was in jail. Where would she be going?

He was about to drive past her house and go home, but for some reason, he was compelled to see if he was right. After pulling into her driveway, he shut off his Cadillac, got out, and looked around nervously, hoping everyone in Ashland Estates had stuffed themselves with food and drink, and had fallen into a deep slumber. Satisfied that he wasn't spotted, he made his way around the side of the house, careful not to step on anything that might alert whoever was in the kitchen to his presence. With his back against the house, he peeked in quickly, but didn't see anybody in the kitchen. Feeling more comfortable, he took his time and looked in again. This time he saw Johnnie on the floor, naked. It never even crossed his mind that something terrible could have happened to her.

Chapter 4

"You did, didn't you?"

Johnnie's House
Two hours earlier

After the steamy sex talk with Napoleon, thoughts of Lucas' incarceration coursed through her vulnerable mind. Even though he had broken the relationship off and she was free to pursue a relationship with Napoleon, sexual or otherwise, a pang of guilt stung her good-girl conscience. Just a few hours earlier, Lucas had said she would do what she was about to do, and here she was hot and bothered, literally marinating in her own juices, about to parttake in an interlude she'd wanted for quite a while. She wasn't sure what it was about Napoleon that drew her to him in that way. It was like a vampire had locked his penetrating eyes on her and with the power of his stare, hypnotized her, drawing her to him, compelling her to be his sex slave without her permission.

Well, I might as well get it out of my system now. Then when

Lucas gets out, I won't think of Napoleon while I'm doing it with Lucas. Besides, what he doesn't know won't hurt him. It'll just be a few times, I'm sure. If it wasn't Christmas, if Lucas was here and I wasn't all alone, I wouldn't be doing this.

Now that she had justified the act she was about to commit, she composed herself, and was about to go upstairs to pack an overnight bag when she thought she heard a noise outside. She looked through the kitchen window and thought she saw someone. *Is someone watching me?* Startled, she tentatively walked to the window over the sink and looked out to see if someone was there. As she had hoped, she saw no one, and turned to go upstairs again. However, just as she was leaving the kitchen, she heard gentle rapping on the door. She assumed it was her best friend and next-door neighbor, Sadie Lane.

Johnnie had forgotten they were supposed to have coffee later that night when she returned from Angola Prison. Upon remembering this, she concluded that Sadie's lover, benefactor, and father of her children, Santino Mancini, had left. She pulled the curtain back to make sure it was Sadie before she opened the door, a habit she learned at home from her mother, who told her time and again to check to see who it was prior to opening the door. Utterly surprised, she saw her longtime nemesis, Billy Logan, who Lucas had beaten up for taunting her in front of a group of students while she was on her way home from school.

Her face twisted a bit when loudly, she said, "What do you want, Billy?"

"You, baby. Been waitin' for a long time, too. It's my turn to ride. I told Lucas. Told you too. 'Member? I said I was gon' be fuckin' you at Walter Brickman's that day I kicked his ass, 'member? I'm here to back up what I said. Open the door, bitch!"

"Fuck you!" Johnnie shouted and left him standing there as she made her way toward the phone to call George "Bubbles" Grant, who she hoped would be at a French Quarter nightclub called Napoleon's Bayou. She would have called Napoleon first, but she didn't have his home number. Besides, she assumed he was anxiously on his way to the Bel Glades Hotel with no way of reaching him until he arrived.

Billy Logan kicked in the door and entered her house. "My turn tuh sample the merchandise, you little whore. You gon' gimme some tuh-night! Its gon' be good, too. I just know it."

"Get out of my house," Johnnie screamed defiantly.

"Sure, bitch," Billy said matter-of-factly. "As soon as I get finished fuckin' you, I'll be glad to leave. And satisfied, too."

By this time, Johnnie had reached the phone, had it to her ear, and was calling the nightclub, desperately trying to dial the last two numbers.

Billy grabbed her and snatched the receiver out of her hand, then the phone out of the wall. "I'm fuckin' you tuh-night and that's all there is to it. You can give it up, or I'ma take it." He smiled wickedly. "I prefer to take it."

Twenty-four hours earlier, Earl Shamus, who had forced himself on her, had come over, which reminded her of the first violation. Now, here was Billy Logan, threatening to do the same thing a little more than two years after she'd submitted to Earl's licentious demand for her virginity. She looked at Billy, who looked like he was possessed by the essence of evil, his lips turned upside down, clown style, his forehead wrinkled, his eyebrows coming together, attempting to meet each other in the center.

Johnnie snatched away from him and turned to run.

Billy reached out and grabbed her shoulder length hair and said, "Where you goin', bitch? We gon' fuck tuh-night!" He pulled her close to him, her back against his chest. He grabbed clumsily at her considerable breasts and squeezed hard. The thrill of having her thick hills in his hands threatened to hasten his coming eruption. His heart thumped hard. Her resistance was like a powerful electromagnet. It forced his lust to the surface, exposing what was in his heart, and fueled his tool's voracious need to enter her incredible body and pound her slippery sheath like a jackhammer breaking up asphalt.

Johnnie broke free and turned around. Without thought, she slapped him as hard as she could. The stinging blow didn't have any effect on him. It was like she never even touched him; like his face became a slap sponge, able to absorb the fury and the harmful intent it promised. As a matter of fact, slapping him served as a stimulant and made his erection stiffer. Fighting him, denying him only furthered his cause, making him more aggressive during the act of taking what she wouldn't freely give. Upon seeing his determination to have her, she turned to run again.

He grabbed her again and pulled her close to him, laughing uproariously, like a drunken sailor at a burlesque show. One hand was around her waist, the other alternately squeezing her inviting breasts, sending more pleasure impulses to his evil mind, spurring him on, making him continue toward the edge of sexual insanity. Once there, he would force himself inside her, pump her recklessly, and spill his seed into her unwilling pleasure-giver.

As Johnnie fought for her life, struggling relentlessly to break his vise-like grip, she heard Billy whisper in her left ear,

"Did you suck his dick? Remember when I asked you that two years ago? So answer me! Did you suck the white man's dick? You did, didn't you? You did suck his dick!" Again she remembered that Earl Shamus had ruthlessly taken her virginity and taught her how to do the nasty things Billy had just asked about. All that was done to her and all that she had done was seared in her mind, but this time she wouldn't cry. This time she was going to fight for what was hers to give and hers to deny.

She stopped struggling and said, "You want it that bad, Billy, that you have to take it?"

Chapter 5

"You can lick 'em."

When Billy realized that she was no longer struggling, he turned her around and looked at her. "You shouldn't be so goddamn pretty and I wouldn't have to take it." With his strong hands, he snatched her closer and kissed her full lips hard. To his surprise, she wasn't fighting the kiss and relaxed. He kissed her even harder as his erection began to poke her stomach. It felt good to kiss Johnnie, and it felt even better when he gripped both halves of her pear-shaped rump.

He moaned as the sensations he received overwhelmed him. Soon after, he began to grind her stomach, and even that pleasured him. When Johnnie gripped both his cheeks, when she opened her sweet mouth and slipped him her wet tongue, he removed his right hand from her rump and placed it on her left breast, which added even more erotic pleasure. Placing both hands on her shoulders, he pushed her back a little, caught his breath, and desperately said, "You gon' give it up?" He said it like they were long lost lovers, like he really believed she was just as aroused as he was.

She smiled seductively and screamed, "No!" and kneed him in the balls—twice, which dropped him to one knee. "I would never give it up to you."

While Billy struggled to get to his feet, Johnnie hurried over to the place where she kept her cutlery, violently snatched opened a drawer, and grabbed a butcher's knife. She turned around and shouted, "I'ma cut you every way but loose! Ya hear! Every way but loose, goddammit!"

Determined to do exactly what she threatened, she rushed at Billy, swinging the knife, but slicing only air. As he backed away, still attempting to recover from two blows to his family jewels, she moved toward him, intent on killing him. She sliced again and again, but he was able to evade her, barely avoiding the lethal weapon. She sliced again, but this time she opened up a deep gash in his arm.

Billy screamed and grabbed his wounded flesh. He looked at his hand and saw his own blood. He was afraid now, but the thought of running through the door he'd kicked open never even entered his mind. He was set on having Johnnie, and he would not be denied, not by a sliced arm, not by two knees to the balls, not by anything; as a matter of fact, her determination to defend herself not only intensified his desire to have her, but made the thought of being inside her more delicious.

Johnnie became more aggressive. She had seen blood and she wanted to see more—a lot more. She had seen Bubbles kill Richard Goode, the Klu Klux Klan leader who had brutally killed her mother. She had watched Lucas and Bubbles beat Goode mercilessly. She had even seen Napoleon Bentley slice his balls off. And that's what she was going to do to Billy Logan. She was going to slice his balls clean off, which was what her brand of justice demanded.

Johnnie wasn't aware of it, but as she edged ever closer to her would-be rapist, an evil grin crept across her lips, evidence of the glee that bubbled within. She sliced at him again, slower this time, giving him the time he needed to move his arm, but leaving his leg vulnerable. She sliced through his thigh.

"Ahhhh, shit! You bitch! You cut my thigh!"

Relishing every moment, having had men take advantage of her for so long, and finally taking control of what belonged to her exclusively, she screamed, "If you don't get outta here, and I mean now, your balls are next! I'm sick of this shit! If you want some pussy that bad, buy you some! But I'm through letting you bastards have your way with me. Through, do you hear?"

When those words resonated in Billy's ears, he forgot the sharp pain he was in and his oozing blood. He was smiling now, backing up, keeping his eyes on Johnnie the entire time. With his eyes still on her, he reached back, searching for the door, and when he found it, he closed it gently and moved toward her to finish what he'd started.

Johnnie smiled. Hubris forced her to say, "It's your balls then."

"I don't think so, bitch! I'm fuckin' you tuh-night. You can believe that shit! Sliced arm, sliced thigh, I don't give a fuck. I'ma stick it in you and you gon' like it!"

"Come get it."

Billy moved forward, let her slice, but as the knife neared him, he dodged it, grabbed her wrist, and slammed it hard on his knee. The knife spun and then clanged when it hit the tiled floor. Then he slapped her so hard it looked like her eyes crossed two times before straightening out again.

Even though she was dazed, she continued to fight as best she could, swinging wildly like she was in a swim meet, racing to the finish line. When he slapped her again, her knees buckled and she staggered to the right, attempting to maintain her balance.

He punched her in the stomach and she doubled over, clutching her midsection as the wind left her body. He heard her wheeze when he hit her there a second time. It sounded like she was hyperventilating. Grabbing her by the hair, he forced her to look at him. Calmly, almost serenely, he said, "Now . . . what was that about my balls, whore?"

Smack! He backhanded her.

"Oh, nothing to say now, huh?"

Smack! He slapped her again.

"Didn't I tell you I was fuckin' you tuh-night?"

Smack! He backhanded her and threw her on the floor. Maddened by lust, he grabbed the front of her dress and ripped it down the center like it was made of paper, exposing the white bra and panties she wore. The sound of buttons hitting the floor rang out. Wanting to see the two melons on her chest, he picked up the knife. Slowly, like he wanted to enjoy every minute of the assault, he placed the knife under the center of the bra and cut until the burgeoning cups snapped off. Her exquisite breasts shook like jelly before becoming quiescent.

"You said you were gon' cut off m'balls." He put the knife under her left nipple. "How 'bout I slice off your nipples? Both of 'em? How'd you like that? Seems fair tuh me."

Weak and still dazed from the pummeling, but cognizant of what was happening to her, feeling the cold stainless steel threatening her means of feeding her future children, she said, "Please . . . don't."

Billy smiled. "Don't what, bitch?"

Tears rolled from the corners of both eyes. "Don't," was all she could say.

"Don't cut your nipples off? Is that what you want?"

She managed a surrendering nod.

"Hmpf! Well, that must mean I can suck 'em, huh? Is that what that means?"

Again she nodded.

Billy relished every mouthwatering moment and taunted her further. He remembered when Lucas made him apologize to her on his knees after giving him a fierce whipping in front of her and a crowd of onlookers. He remembered how embarrassing it was to have to repeat words he didn't believe, yet repeat them or take more bone-jarring punches to an already bruised and swollen face. She had to answer for that too. "Tell me I can lick 'em."

Through trembling lips, she said, "You can lick 'em." And then she began to cry. The humiliation was just too much. The sound of the degradation she felt in her soul found its way out of her mouth. Helpless, she wailed loudly like an infant would for its mother.

Billy laughed. Softly, he said, "Don't cry now, bitch. Just a little while ago you wanted to slice my fuckin' nuts off, didn't you?"

She nodded, afraid not to answer, yet still aching inside.

"Tell me you want me to suck 'em. Say that's what you like."

She managed to repeat the words he needed to hear, hoping he would have mercy, hoping he would come to his senses and realize what he was doing to her. She hoped he would realize that not only was he violating her, he was violating himself and the Negro race itself.

But that wasn't to be.

"Now, let's get these panties off."

He grabbed her white undergarment and pulled until they stretched. With the knife, he cut them from each leg opening and snatched them off her, leaving her completely naked, vulnerable. His mouth watered as he scanned her chiseled body. He looked at the ripped panties in his hand, put them to his nose, and inhaled like it was the last breath he was ever going to take. Suddenly, hungrily, he lapped at her breasts, slurping, growling, ignoring her trembling body, ignoring her shrill-like wail of defeat that echoed off the walls. As he lapped at her nipples, he imagined that they looked and tasted like luscious black berries. The sensation of having them in his mouth fueled his passion as it raged out of control.

Sadistically, he put the knife under her left nipple again, threatening to slice through it. With a knee on either side of her, looking down into her beautiful face then deeply into her eyes, he said, "I'ma stick it in. Is that all right with you, Johnnie?"

She closed her eyes and nodded reluctantly, surrendering.

He slid his pants and underwear down to his knees as he stared at her upside down triangle. "Open yo' legs!"

She closed her eyes and did as she was told, but her legs barely moved.

His eyes winced. Grabbing her legs, he parted them roughly, throwing them like they were in his way. He didn't realize it, but as he gazed hypnotically between her legs, a thin drop of saliva dangled from the corner of his mouth, sliding ever downward like a spider spinning his web. Then he climbed on top of her, handled his thick tool, guided it to her opening, and forced in the tip.

"Damn, girl! You wet as hell! I knew you wanted me. I knew you was enjoyin' this shit too. Well, I'ma give it to you good. You gon' love this."

He pushed forward until the head was in, and continued pushing until the long shaft was all the way in.

He pumped her.

As Billy forced himself in and moved inside her, Johnnie could hear her sticky lubricating fluid deploy without permission, enveloping her rapist, making the incursion easier to accomplish. All she could do was weep as her vagina betrayed her, moistening, consenting, against her will, and taking part in the encroachment. She blamed herself for having a sexually explicit conversation with Napoleon, believing she would have been dry, which would have at least made it difficult for him to enter her. If she was going to be raped, she wanted him to work for it; instead, the fool actually believed she was aroused and getting pleasure from a man she despised.

The humiliation was complete when Billy began to whisper in her ear like he was her adoring paramour, thrusting deep inside her like he was trying to hit bottom.

Thrust! "Didn't I tell you I was gon' fuck you tuh-night?" *Thrust!* "I told yo' boyfriend too." *Thrust!* "Now I'm doin' it." *Thrust!* "I'ma fuck you all night, girl! All fuckin' night!" *Thrust! Thrust! Thrust! Thrust! Thrust! Thrust! Thrust! Thrust! Thrust!*

As he pumped her, he remembered the nasty things he said, the words he made her repeat. All of this aided the pleasure he received, satisfying his uncontrollable urge to have his seed travel up his shaft as if they were being powered by retrorockets into a new frontier.

Billy Logan ravaged Johnnie savagely three times before the monster that controlled him no longer raged. He pulled his glistening tool out of her, stood, pulled up his pants and zipped them, looking down at her triumphantly, sweetly satisfied. He turned around and took a couple steps toward the back door, stopped and turned around. He walked back over to her, looked down at her menacingly, and kicked her vulnerable vagina—twice.

"Now we even, ya whore!" he screamed then left her on the floor weeping, holding her brutalized private place.

Chapter 6

"You're not coming with us?"

It was all very clear to Napoleon now, and he rushed into the kitchen and found the raped and traumatized young woman he was planning to bed two hours earlier. Seeing her like that, beaten and violated, stirred his emotions and made him vulnerable. He hadn't felt so unguarded since he'd met and married Marla, who had left him to pursue a life of her own. He never liked feeling vulnerable; it made him weak and put his life in jeopardy, he believed. But still, he couldn't help himself. He was falling for the young coquette, and he was powerless to stop himself.

On his knees now, he looked at Johnnie, who was lying on her left side, facing the wall, curled in a fetal position, sobbing softly, cradling her wounded pleasure center. Blood was starting to puddle. His eyes watered and he sniffed.

Hesitantly, he touched her shoulder and said, "Are you okay?"

Johnnie turned her head to the right and looked at him,

staring deeply into his eyes. In them, for the first time, she saw his heart and knew how he felt about her. But she was in so much pain that all she could utter was, "Get Sadie. She lives next door."

"Okay," he said as he stood up and ran out the back door.

Moments later, Sadie, Napoleon, and Santino Mancini rushed to Johnnie's side.

When Santino saw her on the floor, battered and bruised, he said, "Sadie, you need to get her to the hospital. I'm sorry, but I can't be a part of this." As he backed out of the kitchen, he shook his head at the horror of it all, wondering who would do such a thing to such a beautiful young woman. Seconds later, he was in his car and on his way back to his wife and legitimate children.

On her knees now, Sadie said, "Let me see, Johnnie."

When she wouldn't move her hands from her vagina, Sadie gently moved them for her. She cringed when she saw Johnnie's clitoris. It looked liked it was partially detached.

"Napoleon," Sadie said desperately, "she needs a doctor! Now! Can you take her to the hospital?"

Without hesitation, Napoleon took charge. "Get her some clothes and a blanket."

Sadie rushed out of the kitchen and up the stairs.

Napoleon said, "We're going to get you to the hospital, okay?"

Johnnie didn't respond.

"Where can I get some towels? We've gotta put pressure on the wound."

Weakly, she said, "There's a bathroom near the garage."

Without a word, Napoleon ran to the bathroom and grabbed a couple of thick beach towels and put one over her wound. He draped the other one over his shoulder in case she needed it. "It's going to hurt, but you've gotta put some pressure on it, sweetie. You want me to do it?"

"I'll do it," she said and groaned as more throbbing pain surged through her. Bravely, she continued the pressure.

Napoleon knew he was exposing himself to his enemies by taking her to the hospital where lots of people would see him, but he also knew she needed his help. He had to get her proper medical attention as quickly as possible.

"You ready? I'm going to carry you to my car."

She nodded.

When he reached the Cadillac, he opened the back door and gently eased her in.

Johnnie forced a short, grimacing smile and with sincerity said, "I'ma get blood all over your nice seats. When I'm better, I'll clean it up, okay?"

"Don't worry about it right now, sweetie," Napoleon whispered lovingly. "Let's get you taken care of."

Sadie opened the garage door and rushed to the car. She handed Napoleon some clothes and then she placed a blanket over her friend.

"I'll be there as soon as I can," Sadie said to Johnnie.

Angrily, Napoleon said, "You're not coming with us?"

"I have to get someone to stay with my children, but I'll be there as soon as I can. I swear."

Chapter 7
Day 2

Baroque Parish Hospital
Early the next morning

I hope it's not too late.

Clicking heels echoed down the quiet corridors of the Dr. Charles Drew Hospital as George Grant, better known as Bubbles, who seemed to be as tall as the walls, made his way down the hall. He was looking for his friend and white Mafia Boss, Napoleon Bentley, who had called him from a payphone. The two men had met in an Illinois prison, where Bubbles saved Napoleon's life during a riot. Napoleon never treated him or any other Negro like he was better than they were. And for that reason, George and most blacks loved him.

"How she doin'?" Bubbles asked.

"I don't know, man," Napoleon replied. "The doctor said they had to operate immediately."

"Okay, I understand," Bubbles said softly. "But listen, we gotta get you outta here, man. Too many people know you, and that could be trouble for us."

"Yeah, I know, but I don't care. I've gotta make sure she's all right, man. Besides, this is a Negro hospital. These are my people. They would never hurt me."

Bubbles looked at his friend and realized that he was in serious trouble because Napoleon's romantic interest in Johnnie had become something else; his feelings for her were no longer just a devilish delight. Johnnie had become more than forbidden fruit; she had become their undoing, their living and breathing Helen of Troy. And if Napoleon continued to pursue her, if he reached out his hand and partook of her alluring nectar one time too many, the sentence would be death. Everyone in their organization was at risk—Johnnie too. Unlike death row inmates, there would be no appeals, no last minute stays of execution. The Mafia Bosses would meet, decide his fate, and carry out his sentence immediately.

"We'll get the word, man," Bubbles pleaded. "I promise you . . . we'll get the word."

They stood up.

"Where we goin', ol' friend?" Napoleon asked.

Bubbles looked at his watch. It was five o'clock in the morning. "Walter Brickman's should be open. How does a stack of hot pancakes and freshly brewed coffee sound?"

"Sounds good to me. Let's go."

As they walked to the exit, Bubbles said, "It's still dark outside and that's good. We can meet out in the open. If anybody's watching, which I doubt, I've got the envelope right here." He patted his breast pocket twice. "I'll pass it to you, and it'll just be me passing you your end of the policy racket. But we even gotta keep that shit to a minimum because you're the Boss of New Orleans now, and those bastards up north are just lookin' for an excuse to rub you out and put one of their own in. You're gonna have to start sending one of them crackers you brought down here for the money from now on. Agreed?"

"Agreed."

Thirty minutes later, Bubbles and Napoleon were quietly stuffing themselves with pancakes, neither of them saying what was so obvious that a blind man could see it. Billy Logan had raped Johnnie and they both knew it, or at least that's what they believed. He had bragged about having sex with her in Napoleon's office at the Bayou a little over a month ago. As far as they knew, Billy didn't know about Napoleon's secret relationship with Johnnie; otherwise, he never would have touched her.

Nevertheless, Napoleon thought deeply about the matter and how he would handle it. He hoped Billy wasn't stupid enough to brag about raping Johnnie because if he did, he'd have to take care of him immediately. He wanted him to suffer first, and then he would kill him personally. He also wanted Johnnie to be there, so she could see her rapist humbled and then shot to death. But if Billy kept quiet, he might not run. After all, if he didn't know about Napoleon's relationship with Johnnie, and he didn't, why would he run?

Napoleon looked at Bubbles and said, "You know who did this shit, don't you?"

"Uh-huh."

"Where the fuck is he?"

"Don't know. Let's see if he comes to work today."

"You think he will?"

"Probably. The damn fool probably doesn't even realize what he's done. The dumb bastard probably thinks all he did was fuck her and slap her around a little. Probably don't even know he damaged her pussy. With her being a Negro . . . and since she has a reputation with that insurance man, Logan probably thinks she didn't have a right to refuse him. Probably told himself she wanted it as much as he did."

"And that's why he beat her like that?" Napoleon asked, full of incredulity. "Because she wanted it?"

"I hate to say this shit, man, but this is the God's honest truth. We black folk don't give a fuck what we do to each other. We really don't. We'll fuck over each other and not even feel bad about the shit. Doin' what he did to Johnnie, as far as I'm concerned . . . is proof of that shit. Ain't no way in hell he would have done that to a white woman. And fuckin' up her pussy like that? No fuckin' way. Knows better than that shit. The white man would cut that nigga's dick off and he knows it. Now watch . . . this muthafucka will bring his ass to work like he didn't do shit."

"He's not going to get away with it!" Napoleon shouted. "I promise you that!"

The patrons in Walter Brickman's stopped eating and looked at the two men.

Bubbles stopped eating, leaned in, and whispered, "Let's keep our heads about this shit, man." He looked around to see if anybody was paying attention. They were. He shot them all a menacing stare and they turned away and resumed eating. He looked at Napoleon again. "I say we play the shit the same way we played Lucas. I say we give him a promotion, more responsibility, to make sure we know where the fuck he is when we're ready to put our hands on him."

"Fine. You see to it, Bubbles. Let's keep this shit quiet, too. Just between us. I don't want to take a chance on somebody fuckin' this shit up. I'm sure Johnnie will want to be there when we take care of him."

"I'm on it, man. I'll keep you up to speed on the girl. And I'll make sure she knows not to say anything to anybody, okay? You just make sure you stay away from her."

Napoleon stared at Bubbles, showing no expression, yet his eyes fired lightning bolts for a couple of seconds. "You givin' me orders now, ol' friend?"

"Naw, man, but think about what you're doing. All of our asses are on the line. Why continue to expose yourself like this? It just ain't smart, man."

Napoleon looked out the window, mulling over the advice of his best friend and right hand man. It occurred to him that he had fallen for Johnnie, but he would never, ever admit it. He knew Bubbles was right. The best course of action was to allow him to handle *all* the Negro business.

He looked at Bubbles again. "As usual, you're right. I'll go back to consorting with lots of women. They'll distract me. So look, man, I'm gonna disappear for a little while. I gotta get my head straight on some things. I'll be in touch."

And with that, he walked out of the restaurant without saying good-bye, thinking, *There's no way in hell I'm gonna give Johnnie up after all I've done to have her. I've killed three people, stole her money and returned it, set up her boyfriend to get rid of him, and I'm divorcing my wife. Besides all that, she wants to see me too. We'll just have to be real careful. When she's well again, maybe we'll go somewhere together—Paris, maybe.*

Bubbles watched his friend leave the restaurant. He knew and understood what Napoleon was feeling and how a made man could long for the love of a woman, but could never allow himself to be weakened by its brilliant flame. He wondered if he was too far gone. Was he already in love with Johnnie Wise? If so, Napoleon would need more than a few weeks to get his head straight because once a man fell in love with a woman, especially a man who couldn't afford to fall in love, it would be years before he got his head straight.

I'ma hav'ta run some serious interference for both their sakes. Mine too. I hope it's not too late.

Bubbles pushed his plate to the side and pulled Napoleon's over in its place and finished off his pancakes. He drained his cup of coffee and said, "Hey, Walter, another stack and another cup of coffee!"

Chapter 8
Day 2

Beauregard Mansion
Breakfast

True gratification.

Ethel Beauregard was still outwardly mourning the deaths of her two sons, her father-in-law, and the subsequent murder of her husband, which she herself committed. The dining room was such a painful memory that she closed it off and forbade anyone to go into the room or even open the doors. Whenever she ate, she had Katherine, her faithful Negro cook and friend, bring her meals to the east terrace, which faced the Mancini mansion. The memory of the day they had all died like actors in a Shakespearean play haunted her dreams and continued the pursuit during her waking hours.

A little more than a month had passed, and as far as she was concerned, that was sufficient time for a refined Southern Christian lady to get past her feelings over the profound loss of her favorite son, Beau.

She and Beau had a special bond from the moment she birthed him. Even though he and Blue were identical twins, Beau had always been her pick, just as Blue had always been her husband's pick. Beau had been such a precious kid. Unlike Blue, he was obedient to a fault and did whatever she asked, with one exception—he married Piper Carrington, whose reputation for being easy was legendary among the blue blood New Orleans aristocracy. She had begged Beau not to marry the rich tart, but she knew there was no chance of him ever giving her up the day she heard them making love in the bed she slept in.

While she had never known sexual pleasure other than by self-stimulation, Ethel was very familiar with the throaty sounds that touched bedroom walls everywhere. It always puzzled her that other women received what sounded like indescribable pleasure when she never did. Not one time. The first time she'd heard a woman's howl was when she was six years old. Nearly every night, her mother's moans found their way through the walls and echoed in her ears. She didn't know what her father was doing to her mother at the time, but she knew her mother enjoyed it nevertheless. So when she heard Beau's throaty sighs that day, she knew her boy would never give up whatever Piper was doing to him in her bed.

Ethel had tried to disrupt the relationship from the very beginning. It all started in church one Sunday morning after Beau had delivered a particularly stirring sermon about the evils of fornication, and how far reaching its destructive force was. After the concluding prayer, an invitation to become one of Jesus' disciples was extended, and Piper Carrington sauntered down the center aisle. She was wearing a white dress and veiled sunbonnet when she gave her life to Jesus. The members of Grace Holiness Church applauded politely, but no one believed her conversion was sincere.

Ethel thought Piper was seeking respectability, something that true believers like herself received as long as they demonstrated their conversion with righteous living. But when she warned Beau of her suspicions, he rejected her motherly intuition and wisdom. The more she tried to steer him away from the Jezebel, the more he was drawn to Piper's seductive wiles. Piper constantly maneuvered Beau into having church picnics and barbeques, and a myriad of church functions she created: All were carefully constructed to elicit his presence, where she could worm her way into his heart.

Ethel was so troubled by Beau's decision to ask for her hand in marriage that she decided to do some maneuvering of her own. She knew of Blue's ability to seduce silly women, and began speaking glowingly of Piper in his presence, knowing full well that Blue was rotten enough to bed her, which was what Ethel wanted. When she saw how Piper looked at Blue when she thought no one was looking, Ethel knew he was close to bedding her, and set up a situation where Beau could walk in on them. Once Beau caught her howling with his brother, she believed that revelation would turn his blind heart from Piper and back to her. Ethel had already picked a lovely young Christian woman who would be the perfect wife and mother her favorite son needed. And it didn't hurt that the woman came from a refined, well-to-do family of aristocrats with old money.

Ethel's plan worked marvelously. Blue had bedded Piper. She noticed that during family gatherings, of which she made sure there were plenty, the secret lovers tended to disappear for twenty minutes or so, and then all of a sudden, they were both back at the family gathering, smirking like honeymooners who had saved themselves for marriage. Ethel let it go on for a couple of months, long enough for them to get stupid and take crazy chances to be together. She let them believe they were smarter than everybody else.

On a particular Fourth of July weekend, Ethel made sure Piper would have to be in the house by assigning her the task of baking the potato rolls. She believed they would think it was a providential opportunity to devour each other. When she saw them sneak off to the house, she knew what they were up to. After waiting for what she thought to be sufficient time to begin the sordid intertwining, she sent Beau into the house to get her fan, which was in the basement—their supposed love nest.

But as Beau approached the house, Ethel saw Morgan, their college educated Negro butler, coming out the back door. She watched Morgan and Beau talk for more than ten minutes, laughing about something Morgan was saying. While the two men continued their exhaustive chattering, Piper came out of the back door. Ethel watched Beau say something to Piper, and she went back into the house and later came out with her fan.

Ethel often wondered if Morgan knew what was going on and thought he was doing Beau a favor by stopping him from catching the two lovers in the act. She never found out if Morgan knew about the affair, but it made no difference because Piper and Blue never tried to sneak off again at a Beauregard family function. None of it mattered now, though. All the Beauregard men were dead—Piper too. And while she would never acknowledge it aloud, with the exception of Beau, she was glad they were all dead because they were all good for nothing fornicators that got what they deserved. *True gratification.*

Chapter 9

"It's begun."

"Can I get you anything else, Mrs. Beauregard?" Katherine said, handing her the morning *Sentinel* newspaper.

Ethel looked at her and said, "Sit down and have some of your delicious breakfast with me."

Floored by the invitation, Katherine, using her very best English, knowing how much Ethel hated to hear the English language butchered, said, "Ma'am? Are you feeling okay this morning?"

"Katherine," Ethel began, "from this day forward, I want us to have our meals together."

"Ma'am?"

"You heard me. I want us to have our meals together from now on. Morgan too, if he's willing to listen to two women enjoy life without men interrupting the tranquility. You two are just about all I have left in this miserable world. And I want you to call me Ethel when we're on the Beauregard grounds. When we're out, we have to remember our places, okay?"

Still stunned by her sudden transformation from a haughty aristocrat to a meek human being, which was nothing short of a miracle, Katherine repeated, "Ma'am? Are you feeling okay?"

Ethel smiled for the first time since the Beauregard men died. "Why, I'm wonderful, Katherine. Just wonderful."

"What will people say, ma'am?"

Ethel's smile vanished. "This is my house now, Katherine. And I'll do what I damn well please in it! Now . . . get some breakfast and come out and eat with me."

Puzzled, Katherine did as she was told, albeit hesitantly, thoroughly questioning all she'd heard as she went back into the kitchen. *Hmm, what's come over Mrs. Beauregard? Has she finally lost her mind like so many of the other women in the Beauregard family? Is she on the verge of killing herself like they did? She's always been so refined, someone to be looked up to. On the other hand, I might as well enjoy this while it lasts. I always wanted to be treated like family.*

Meanwhile, on the east terrace, Ethel opened up the newspaper and thumbed through it, occasionally stopping at an article, reading the first line or two. Seeing nothing interesting, she moistened her thumb and continued to work her way to the society section where she read the following headline: PROMINENT BEAUREGARD LEGACY EXTENDS ALL THE WAY TO SABLE PARISH.

As Ethel read the blistering article, the words seemed to leap off the pages. The scandal was coming, she knew, but still, to be blindsided like this with no warning was unforgivable.

The article read:

Flagrant miscegenation! There seems to be no end to the revelations concerning the Beauregard and Wise families, if you can call them that. This reporter isn't sure the word "family" applies, however. So let's begin this piece with a question: What do the super wealthy Beauregards and the dirt poor, nearly indigent Wise families have to do with each other? Apparently a lot! It appears that the recently deceased Nathaniel Beauregard is the father of Marguerite Wise. If the name (Marguerite Wise) sounds familiar, it should, folks, as this poor, unfortunate Negress was murdered last summer and her killer was never brought to justice.

Miss Wise, a resident of dilapidated Sable Parish, was found a couple of miles from a Cajun restaurant, ruthlessly beaten beyond recognition. By whom, we still don't know. However, this reporter told you nearly six months ago, prior to the riot, that several days after, notorious Klansman, Richard Goode, was murdered in like manner, and that the two murders seemed to be linked, due to their marked similarity. Well, it looks like I was way off the mark, folks. I thought I was on to something, and I was apparently wrong. I apologize profusely. Here's my new theory. (This time, it's not just conjecture and speculation as our friends over at the Raven, the Negro newspaper, asserted shortly after my first article.)

It turns out that Marguerite's daughter, who, according to a confidential source, was brutally raped last night, Christmas night, to the shame of her rapist (not that there's a good time to rape, mind you) was working undercover as the maid for the affluent Beauregard family. If you haven't just skimmed this article, you now know what that means. It means that Marguerite's daughter was working for her white relatives, and they had no idea who she was. Friends, are the hairs on your neck standing tall? Mine are! Did the Beauregard family somehow learn the wicked truth? According to my source, Marguerite's daughter dropped the proverbial atomic bomb that faithful Thanksgiving Day when all the Beauregard men met their maker.

Let's reexamine these cases, shall we? Marguerite Wise, murdered on a lonely road in the middle of the night. Richard Goode, murdered at his farm—castrated! All the Beauregard men, dead—one right after another.

The common link, you ask?

Marguerite Wise's daughter!

Another common link—no one ever gets arrested in either family.

Why?

*If all the players in this ridiculous play were rich white folk, well, you know how that goes. But Marguerite Wise and her daughter are Creole (that's what we call them when they're mixed. *wink*wink*).*

Folks, if that isn't enough, how is it that Sharon Trudeau and an innocent bellhop are murdered down in Fort Lauderdale and no one is arrested in that case either? What's going on? Now, some of you smart folks who have been paying attention to this entire article are thinking, what does Sharon Trudeau have to do with any of this? Well, friends, I'll tell you. Sharon Trudeau was Marguerite's daughter's stockbroker!

It turns out that all the money was recovered except for two hundred and fifty thousand dollars. And guess who lost that much money—nearly to the cent? You guessed it! Marguerite's daughter!

Again, friends, I ask you, why hasn't this seventeen-year-old been at least questioned? But before we even ask that question, let's ask this one first: How did a Negro teenager get that kind of money in the first place? And how on God's green earth was she able to purchase a home and live among the so-called Negro elite in Ashland Estates, where the homes start at fifteen thousand dollars? Let's not forget that Marguerite lived in rundown Sable Parish.

I could be wrong, but I think we can safely say Marguerite didn't leave her daughter much of anything. Otherwise, why would Marguerite live in Sable Parish if she had the means to move to a better neighborhood? What then? Insurance money? Please! I've seen the policy. It was worth fifteen thousand, but Marguerite's daughter had moved uptown before her mother's death. Call me stupid, but I don't think you can collect death benefits without a death certificate.

Where did this Negro kid get two hundred and fifty thousand dollars?

More important, who had that kind of money to give her?

Further, who would be motivated to give it to her?

You see where I'm going with this, friends?

The super rich Beauregards are the only people who have that kind of money and the motivation to pay off the mother to keep her quiet. However, that raises a whole lot more questions, doesn't it? Who really killed Marguerite Wise that night? Was it Richard Goode? If so, was he paid to do it? If so, it would explain the fierce whipping he gave her first, wouldn't it?

Again, why no arrests?

How does the woefully inept New Orleans Police Department explain why the daughter hasn't been arrested or at least questioned? They don't, folks. Mum's the word over there. I know because I asked them. Sounds to me like a lot of money has been passed out in those thick yellow envelopes mobsters get from the shop owners they extort in The Quarter. Did I say mobsters? J. Edgar Hoover said there is no Mafia. And we know Mr. Hoover can't be wrong, can he?

The last time I questioned what was going on, one of the bloodiest riots in our nation's history ensued. White women and children were killed, and no one was arrested. Friends, the bodies are piling up. Who's next?

Just as Ethel finished the article, Katherine returned to the terrace with her breakfast and sat next to her. Feeling like a kid on Christmas morning, Katherine heartily ate the food she cooked, enjoying every delicious mouthful. But in her periphery, she noticed that Ethel wasn't eating and was no longer reading. She was just sitting there, staring over tall shrubs into the next yard, where Mrs. Mancini was staring back at Ethel and holding up a copy of the *Sentinel*. Mrs. Mancini was gleefully smiling, unable to contain the immense pleasure that bubbled within.

Ethel exhaled loudly and said, "It's begun."

The article might start a series of events that would lead the police to my front door if Johnnie ever told the police I killed my husband and would have killed her too. How I missed that little bitch I'll never know. I pointed the gun right at her head and pulled the trigger. Now all my fears are about to be realized. That's the real reason I wanted Katherine and Morgan to have breakfast with me. I might need them to testify on my behalf if this thing ever sees the light of day.

Still confused about Ethel's generous offer, her previous ebullient demeanor and now her sudden silence, Katherine thought it best to continue eating quietly.

Chapter 10

"I don't think so, Charlene."

Ethel Beauregard stared unflinchingly at Mrs. Mancini, seething as the flame of anger blazed within. *How dare she gloat in my time of tragedy? I don't care if I did look down on her for allowing her husband to not only bed Sadie, but produce three bastard children with her. There's no way any part of this article's true. None of it. Not one line. Not a goddamn syllable. It never happened. Grandpa Nathaniel would never have a baby with Johnnie's grandmother. No way in hell! I don't care what anybody says—not even him! I should've known something was wrong with Johnnie the day she stepped foot in this house. From the very beginning, she thought she was too good to work for me. Now I'm the laughingstock of the Garden District. So you go ahead and smile now, Mrs. Mancini. She who laughs last, laughs best!*

By now, Ethel supposed that the article had been read by all the women in the prestigious New Orleans Chapter of The Southern Christian Ladies Social Club. She knew this moment was coming, but hoped it never would. Now, as she continued to gaze unflinchingly at Mrs. Mancini, Ethel knew she had to do what she'd been contemplating for more than a month. Without realizing it, slowly the corners of her mouth edged upward; little, by little they crept until a bright, beaming smile burst forth and revealed the inexplicable joy she was now feeling. She had a contingency plan for this revelation, knowing her family secrets could become fodder over ice-cold lemonade and fresh beignets.

Ethel knew all of her so-called friends were already on the phone, talking incessantly about the article. She suspected they had been talking about her behind her back since the deaths of the Beauregard men. Each one of them had called the mansion and offered a sensitive but disingenuous ear, a sympathetic yet treacherous shoulder to lean on in her time of incomprehensible tragedy. She knew their tricks all too well because she was guilty of the very things they were doing. She had perfected the art of solicitation without appearing to pry; she was the architect of it. And now the seeds she had sown over the years had taken root and threatened to spring forth and choke the life out of her.

It was only a matter of time before the phone rang. The call would be coming from whichever of her *caring* friends had gotten the short stick when they drew straws a day or so after the Beauregard men died. It would all be so carefully orchestrated by the woman who came up with the best idea to elicit the desired information. If successful, the woman would take all the information she learned back to the inner circle of the club, which was why Ethel would be sure not to surrender any information at all, ensuring maximum curiosity about the whole matter.

While she thought on these things, Morgan brought a phone out and said, "Mrs. Beauregard, you have a call of the uttermost urgency from Sister Charlene of your social club. Do you want to take the call?"

She looked at him and nodded.

Morgan placed the phone on the table, plugged it in, and left quietly.

After lifting the receiver to her ear, Ethel forced herself to smile warmly and offered an inviting, "Why, hello, Charlene. So good of you to call."

"Ethel," Charlene began with pseudo sincerity and manufactured contrition, "I was truly appalled by this morning's article in the society page. I've never read such rubbish in all my days. It's slanderous, I tell you. Slanderous! Why, the man ought to be jailed for implying that the Beauregard family would allow themselves to be blackmailed by niggers. And then to infer that you all were involved with Richard Goode, who he originally thought had murdered your maid's mother, and that your maid is your niece by law? Why, it's enough to call for the hangman's noose. That's how the men handled things in the old days."

After she finished speaking, Charlene could hardly contain herself. She almost believed in her sincerity as she waited with baited breath for the president of the social club to respond. This was the opportunity for which she'd waited years. This was her chance to oust Ethel as president and replace her. As far as she was concerned, the article in the *Sentinel* would be the springboard from which she'd move up from vice president to the coveted leadership position.

Ethel remained quiet for a moment or two, having listened to Charlene's long-winded rant, taking in her recitation of the article. She knew her *secret* ambition. She also knew that Charlene was making sure she knew what the article said, just in case she hadn't read it, leaving no room for denials. To this, Ethel simply said, "I'll explain all at our next meeting."

"Ethel, there won't be another meeting until after the New Year. Do you *really* think this can wait that long?"

"I don't see why not, Charlene. You said it yourself, summing it up with one word: slander. I'm sure the rest of the ladies will come to that conclusion also, don't you?"

"I don't know, Ethel. You know those women believe every word of the society page. To them, it's almost like the Bible itself. I don't think this can wait. I think you need to call a meeting tonight and let everybody know that this article is full of falsehoods."

"I don't think so, Charlene," Ethel said, lying. "I think the women in our social club are a lot like you. They'll draw the same conclusions you've drawn. I'll see you after the New Year and I know you'll quell any tongue on fire with gossip, won't you, dear?"

While Charlene was still speaking, Ethel pleasantly said, "Good day," and hung up the phone.

After delicately handling that situation, she smiled broadly. She knew that by denying them her version of the truth, they would all be at the next meeting, if for no other reason than to hear whatever ridiculous explanation she came up with, so the gossip could begin anew. And that was exactly what she wanted. She wanted them to be comfortable with the idea that they had her cornered, that she had no options, no trump card to play. She couldn't have planned a more perfect scenario.

Chapter 11

"Did I hear you right, Mrs. Beauregard?"

The phone rang again. Katherine swallowed the food in her mouth, picked up the receiver and said, "Beauregard residence." She handed the phone to Ethel and said, "It's a man. He says he's your lawyer."

Ethel took the phone eagerly. This was the call she had been awaiting for more than a month. "I trust you and your wonderful family enjoyed the Thanksgiving holiday in Madrid. So much so, you stayed an additional thirty days. When did you get back in town?"

"Christmas Eve."

"And you didn't think to call me? I told you I wanted the reading of the Will done immediately."

"I know, but cutting a trip we've planned for over a year would have been unfair to my family, don't you think, Ethel? It was Christmas Eve, for Christ's sake. Another day or so . . . a week, for that matter, wouldn't alter the contents of the Will one bit, would it?"

"I suppose," Ethel said, her words full of derisive exasperation. "When can we get together?"

"As soon as the other beneficiary gets out of the hospital."

"Other beneficiary?" Ethel questioned, believing she was the sole heir of the Beauregard fortune.

"Yes," the lawyer said, and ruffled some papers.

While the family attorney searched for the other beneficiary, it occurred to Ethel that Gina, Beau's wife, might be entitled to something. Gina had thankfully taken all the Beauregard children to Gulfport, Mississippi, where her parents lived, and avoided the tragic events that took place that Thanksgiving Day. She also remembered that Beau had offered an excellent excuse not to go with his wife, preferring to do all that his wicked mind imagined to Piper for a few lust-filled days. He had told Gina he wanted to spend as much time as he could with his favorite grandfather before he died.

"Yes, here it is," the lawyer continued. "The other beneficiary is Johnnie Wise. Oh, and there's also a Benjamin Wise, too; her brother."

This new revelation threatened to send Ethel into another fury, but she took a deep breath like she was taught and composed herself. She knew greed was in the heart of every lawyer, and cryptically said while looking at Katherine, "Surely something can be done about this. . . ."

"About what, Mrs. Beauregard?"

"Hold on for a second, Mr. Jamieson," Ethel said, still looking at Katherine, who was heartily devouring the food she prepared. "Katherine, will you please hang this phone up when I tell you to?"

"Ethel, I can eat in the kitchen," Katherine said, eagerly using her first name for the first time. "You don't have to leave your table."

"Don't be silly. Enjoy your breakfast and I'll go inside and pick up. It's just a few feet away. It's a business call. You understand, don't you, dear?"

Katherine nodded and continued eating.

Ethel smiled sincerely, placed the receiver on the table, and excused herself. She opened one of the French doors that led to the coffee room, where Eric, her deceased husband, entertained his men friends after a fulfilling dinner to smoke cigars and talk about the politics of the day. She picked up the phone, stepped into the doorway, watching Katherine, and said, "You can hang up now." She watched her place the receiver on the phone then closed the door. "Now, Mr. Jamieson, you do know that Johnnie Wise and her brother are not blood relatives, don't you?"

"Mrs. Beauregard, I went through this whole Will with him in detail. According to Nathaniel, they are his grandchildren from a woman named Marguerite Wise, who was his daughter from Josephine Baptiste. Besides, even if they weren't blood relatives, that fact would have nothing to do with what Nathaniel put in his Will. He became belligerent when I tried to talk him out of it. She's entitled to whatever he wanted her to have. Her brother too."

And there it was; indisputable proof that Johnnie was indeed a blood relative, just as she had claimed a little more than a month ago.

"How much did he leave them?"

"A million each."

Stunned and infuriated, Ethel, still looking at Katherine through the glass doors, quietly screamed, "A million dollars?"

"That's what I said too."

Ethel breathed hard into the phone. "Mr. Jamieson, what's it going to take to draw up another Will and leave those two out of it?"

Astounded, Jamieson said, “Excuse me, Mrs. Beauregard? You want me to do what?”

“You heard me. How much money would you need to take Johnnie and her brother out of the Will and make sure it all goes to me? They’re Negroes. It’ll never even cross their minds to get a lawyer of their own to authenticate the document. I’d pay you handsomely if you did this for me. What do you say?”

A thick fog of silence lingered as attorney Jamieson considered what he was about to do, which was to illegally disinherit Johnnie and Benny.

“Ten percent oughta do it,” he said and then clarified, “seventeen point five million.”

“Done,” Ethel said without hesitation, believing ten percent was a bargain. The amount really didn’t matter. She hated Johnnie. Two cents would have been too much for her to inherit. If she thought she could get away with it, Ethel would try to kill her again, but the next time, she wouldn’t miss. “For seventeen million dollars, I expect the new Will to be verifiable and immutable. Do you understand, Mr. Jamieson?”

“Understood.”

“Good day, Mr. Jamieson.”

She hung up the phone.

The thought of disinheriting Johnnie exhilarated Ethel. Her heart pumped hard, her face flushed, and a wide smile emerged. But just before she turned the knob on the French door to return to the terrace, she heard someone say, “Did I hear you right, Mrs. Beauregard? Are you going to cheat Johnnie and her brother out of what they rightfully have coming to them?”

Chapter 12

"What are you doing down there?"

Ethel turned her head to the right and saw Morgan staring at her. He had heard every word she'd said. Nervously, she turned completely around and looked at her butler and offered him her blue-blood confidence, saying, "Why, whatever are you talking about?"

Morgan looked directly at her, his lids unblinking, his eyes burning into hers, intimidating her with the knowledge that lay behind them. He said, "I'm talking about the new Will and what it would take to keep Johnnie and her brother out of it, Mrs. Beauregard."

Upon hearing that, Ethel took a few steps backward, realizing she was caught before she even began. She thought for a moment and decided to bluff him, believing that she could persuade him to believe what she wanted him to believe. "Listen, Morgan, I know how fond of Johnnie you are, but she's not a relative, so you couldn't possibly hear what you think you heard, now could you?"

"Well, ma'am . . . you might be right. But I think a lawyer might know what to do. I know just the one, too. Robert Ryan. He's the lawyer who sued the city and won when the police didn't do their sworn duty to stop the rioters from destroying Main Street and Sable Parish. I'll tell him what I heard, and maybe he can figure out whether or not I heard it and more important, Mrs. Beauregard, what to do about it. Maybe Mr. Ryan can contact Mr. Jamieson himself, and make sure Jamieson knows that Ryan knows the first Will was destroyed. I'm sure Ryan could make *him* understand that we know the second Will is as phony as three-dollar bill. It's a fictional creation for personal gain and to appease you because of your hatred of the truth. Perhaps I'll let him know that you think it's okay to have Negroes opening your doors for you, cleaning your house for you, cooking your meals for you, and being a conduit for sexual gratification whenever one of the Beauregard men required that kind of immoral thing. But having a Negro in your lineage from the same sexual activity you sanctioned by looking the other way is where you draw the line."

Stunned by his provocative comments, Ethel backed up a few more steps and leaned against the door leading to the terrace, devastated by his ability to articulate the principles on which he, a Negro, would quite possibly demand something of value. A wicked idea came to mind, and she took a few steps toward him. She smiled and said, "What would it take to keep this between me and you? You know how fond I am of you, and now that I'm a widow, I could maybe . . . you know . . . not be so lady-like with you. Wouldn't you like that, Morgan? I hear that's what Negro men want more than gold . . . to have a pure white woman."

Morgan frowned and took a few steps backward, knowing,

or at least believing that later, whether he accepted the offer or not, she was going to say he'd raped her. He thought she was hoping he'd take the offer because then there would be physical evidence, not that she needed it. There would be semen, of course, which would have been evidence to nearly any white police officer that an assault had taken place. The fact that she bled during intercourse was a family secret that everyone in the house knew about. Blood in the vagina of a white woman who claimed she was raped would be more than enough evidence to convict him.

With Eric having been dead for over a month, Morgan couldn't acquit himself. A white jury of his "peers" wouldn't consider any explanation he offered. The word of a white aristocratic female who had already been devastated by the deaths of all the men closest to her would be impeccable. They would see Morgan as an animal who had been waiting for this opportunity to invade her—consequences be damned. They would assume that having sexual relations with Ethel was something his evil heart had always wanted. With all the men in the family in their graves, Morgan had finally lost control and showed himself to be the beast that all Negro men were—even the good ones.

He said, "To keep the same secret, you offer your lawyer money, but me, your dumb nigger butler, *me* you offer sex. Now this is a marvelous thing, Mrs. Beauregard. A fine Southern belle like you? An aristocrat? The president of the Christian Ladies Social Club and all, offering bribes? Offering sex to a nigger butler? For shame. Why, I never would have believed it if I hadn't heard it with my own ears.

"I wonder what the reporters at the *Sentinel* and the *Raven* will think when they hear this fascinating tale about you. And of course, they'll believe it. As a matter of fact, just to spice it up a bit, I'll have to embellish the story to the nth degree, and by God, those reporters'll have the story of the century." He shook his head and continued. "To think, just this morning, there was an article on the *Sentinel's* society page advocating this same story. With me as a witness, I'm sure the *Sentinel* will sell lots of newspapers. And even if they don't believe me, I know the Negro newspaper will print it. Who knows? We might have ourselves another riot. A lot more white folks'll die. Probably the rich ones this time."

"Morgan!" Ethel raised her voice a bit, but not loud enough for Katherine, who was still on the terrace, to hear. "Be reasonable. If it's money you want, just say so."

Morgan doubled over, laughing at her.

"Stop that laughing this instant!" Ethel commanded. "It's disrespectful and terribly insulting."

Still laughing a little, Morgan said, "Listen, Mrs. Beauregard, you have obviously forgotten that I'm an educated man. As a matter of fact, I'm better educated than you. Talk about insulting. For years, I've had to let you teach me how to speak English just so I could have a job that pays well enough to put food on the table and buy my wife—who's beautiful, by the way—nice things from time to time. Insulting? Your husband's father brings a child into the world and doesn't even acknowledge her for over forty years. Nothing surprising about that, since white men have been fathering Negro children for centuries. But then the good Lord up above stepped in and gave old Nathaniel some conscience in his last days, and some much needed gumption, and you take even that away? Insulting? Nathaniel, who hadn't been able stand because of the stroke he suffered, stands up in your dining room, a damn miracle if you ask me, tells all of you who Johnnie is, and you cut her out of the Will? And you talk to me about insulting *you*?"

"What's it going to take to keep this between me and you forever?"

"Well, now, this here is a powerful secret. Yes, ma'am, a powerful secret indeed. I think fifty thousand is a fair price to keep a secret like this, don't you? Twenty-five thousand to keep my mouth shut and twenty-five thousand to quiet my conscience. Johnnie doesn't deserve what I'm about to do, but this is my chance to have a good life, and I'm taking it. From what I hear tell, she'd do the same thing if she were in my position."

"If I pay you the money, how do I know you won't come back later, asking for more?"

"*If* you pay? *If*? Mrs. Beauregard, you're going to pay and you're going to pay it today, and you know it because if you don't, it's all going to come out. When it does, the revelation will make it impossible to show your face in public ever again. The façade, the mask you've been wearing all your life will be ripped off, exposing you and your family as salacious vagabonds who pretend to be of high moral character publicly, but lack the self-control necessary to authenticate the essence of it."

After hearing his truth, Ethel looked at the floor and spoke without looking at him. Their roles had reversed themselves, she now knew. Not only was her Negro butler superior to her intellectually, but by rejecting the sex she proffered, she now saw him as morally superior as well. If nothing else, he was certainly morally superior to the men in her family. Nevertheless, rather than deal with his guns of judgment, the words he used to skillfully dismantle any thought of superiority she imagined she had over him, she repeated, "How do I know you won't ask for more money later, Morgan?"

"You don't have to worry about that, Mrs. Beauregard. Fifty thousand dollars is more than enough to make a life for myself somewhere else. My wife and family will be out of New Orleans so quick, you'll wonder if I ever existed . . . that I promise you."

Ethel walked around the room, thinking about the possibilities. What was another fifty thousand, she questioned. She still would have over one hundred and fifty million of the Beauregard fortune, and it would be collecting interest. In a couple of years, she'd have every penny back on the interest alone. It would almost be like she never paid any of them off. She walked over to a desk, opened a drawer, and pulled out the checkbook. Then she began to write out a check.

"Cash, Mrs. Beauregard," Morgan called out angrily. "You must take me for a fool."

"I don't have that kind of money lying around the house. I'd have to get it from my banker."

"What about the money in the safe? How much do you have in there?"

Desperately, she said, "I don't know, Morgan. I haven't been in the safe for years."

"But you do know the combination, right?"

"I might."

"You *might*?"

"I might," she said firmly. "I'll tell you what. There should be a sizable amount of cash in the safe; Grandpa always said the stock market could crash again and we'd be in the poor house, but I honestly don't think it will come close to the sum you requested. I'll give you all the cash I have, and you leave this house immediately. Take it or leave it. Either that, or take a check."

"I'm no fool, Mrs. Beauregard."

"Why, whatever do you mean by that, Morgan?"

"I mean that I want cash. Cash is harder to trace. Besides, who's going to cash a fifty thousand dollar check for a Negro in the United States? Any bank I go to is bound to call the police, or at the very least, ask me a dozen uncomfortable questions and then call the police. No, thank you!"

"What if there's hardly any money in the safe? What then?"

"Then you're stuck with me until you can get every dollar. You'll get it little by little until I have it all," he said, bluffing.

"Fine. Come on. I'll open the safe for you." As they made their way down the stairs to the basement, she said, "When you get your money, please leave. I don't ever want to see you again."

"Don't worry, you won't, unless the cops come to my house saying I robbed or raped you. I don't have to worry about either of those scenarios, do I, Mrs. Beauregard?"

"No. I won't say a word."

"Good. Now, open that safe."

Ethel walked over to the safe and opened it.

"Ethel," Katherine called out from the top of the stairs, "are you down there?"

"Why, yes, I am. I'll be up in a second."

"What are you doing down there?" Katherine called out and descended a few steps. "Can I help you find anything?"

"Katherine, uh, no need to come down here. I'm on my way up now." She looked at Morgan and harshly whispered, "Get the money and go. Don't say good-bye, don't say anything to Katherine either. Just leave and never return—ever!"

Chapter 13

"You'll never see me again."

Morgan waited until she climbed the stairs and closed the door. He hadn't intended to collect his money without her being inside the safe with him. If he went in by himself, she could close the door, let him suffocate, rot, and then when she couldn't stand the stench any longer, open the safe, and tell everyone he had locked himself in during an attempted robbery. He wasn't about to let that happen. As a matter of fact, he was leaving New Orleans that night if there was enough money in the safe. He knew he'd startled Ethel when she hung up the phone, which was why she gave into his demands so easily.

He knew she was an inexperienced woman who didn't yet know that her riches and her white skin could buy her any brand of justice she wanted. He also knew that if she called her lawyer back, he would be in a world of trouble because no one would ever take the word of a Negro butler over a widowed, wealthy white woman. If she and her lawyer played their cards right, even the *Sentinel* would have to take her side, and then where would he be?

He walked into the safe, and to his surprise, saw stack after stack of hundred-dollar bills wrapped in strips marked TEN THOUSAND DOLLARS. He began to calculate the sum. Ten thousand, twenty thousand, thirty thousand . . . seven hundred fifty thousand . . . one million two hundred thirty thousand in U.S. currency. And there was more in gold coins. Morgan couldn't believe his luck. He had gotten nearly twenty-five times more than what he'd asked for.

On a shelf near the gold coins lay a leather-bound book. He picked it up and opened it. The first page read: The Diary of Josephine Baptiste. After reading a few pages, he knew he'd have to get the diary into Johnnie's hands. It was the least he could do after selling her out. He left the safe, ran up the stairs to the linen closet and grabbed several white pillowcases. Then he hurried back down the stairs and into the safe, where he stuffed four pillowcases with the money and the diary, and hurried to his car.

Within the hour, he and his beautiful wife and family left New Orleans without taking the time to pack even one suitcase, and moved to Quebec City, Canada. As he drove, he thought about the gold coins he'd left, and wanted to go back and get them.

He looked at his wife and said, "Honey, you know what? I forgot to drop the diary at Johnnie's place. We've gotta go back and give it to her. It's the least I can do, don't you think?"

But his wife intuitively knew his heart and said, "We've got more than enough money, Morgan. If you turn around and go back because of your greed, I swear to God, I'll get out of this car and you'll never see me again." She quietly stared at him, knowing he could sense her penetrating glare. "If you really want the girl to have her grandmother's diary, we'll send it to her in the mail, okay?"

In a voice saturated with disappointment, he said, "Okay."

Were it not for her threats, he would have gone back, and who knows what would have become of him. Morgan and his family were never seen in New Orleans again.

Chapter 14
Day 2

"Mail call!"

Lucas Matthews was sitting on his cot, reading a book titled: *The Negro in the American Rebellion: His Heroism and His Fidelity*, written by William Wells Brown. He had devoured Booker T. Washington's *Up From Slavery*, having nothing to do after they finished their daily chores. His dyslexia made it difficult to read every word, but he was able to gain a good understanding nevertheless. Fascinated by Washington's ability to make something of his life through vision, hard work, perseverance, and selflessness, Lucas began to grow. His mind began to think about things, possibilities he had never considered before, particularly since Washington overcame so much under the most difficult circumstances. And now, he was eating the work of William Wells Brown, learning about Negro men who had served in the United States military and all their accomplishments; genuine history he never learned at Abraham Lincoln High School.

Upon entering The Farm, he was surprised to learn how

well known he was by the criminals he lived with. They had a grapevine that extended all the way back to New Orleans. The prisoners generally learned what was going on in their hometowns no earlier than three weeks after something happened because they could only have visitors once a month. The first day he arrived, people he'd never met called him by name. Later, he learned that their family members knew nearly everything there was to know about him, including his football prowess on the gridiron. They even knew he was connected to Napoleon Bentley, which made his stay a whole lot easier.

He had been incarcerated for thirty-five days of a ninety-day sentence; thirty of them in Angola State Prison with some of the most hardened criminals in America. Stabbings, murder, man-on-man rape was something that shocked him at first, but after seeing this in the open bays the prisoners lived in, he was getting used to it. One day, he saw a guy he'd played football with during his freshman year. His parents named him Willie Towers, but now his name was Wilamina because he had been turned into a woman by a man twice his size.

When he saw the man mercilessly beating Willie for taking too long to bring his meal, Lucas felt compelled to intervene. As he stood, he felt the heavy hand of one of the older prisoners on his shoulder. The man's name was Clancy "One Punch" Brown. Rumor had it that he had knocked out ten men during a barroom brawl, all with one blow. He was six-foot-six and easily weighed three hundred solid pounds.

One Punch Brown said, "You got ninety days, kid, and you can leave this hellhole, hopefully forever. Them two . . . they ain't neva leavin'. Neither one of 'em. I know he used to be yo' friend on the outside, but this ain't yo' business. Don't worry, when yo' friend's had enough, he'll kill 'im. That's why he's neva goin' home again. Even if he did get outta here, he'll never be a man again after what done happened to 'im. You, on the other hand, you still got choices. He's through. Don't be no fool, son. Keep readin' them books I see ya readin'. When ya get out, remember all ya done seen in here and don't ever come back."

"But I knew him in school, man. I can't sit back and watch him lose his manhood. I can't!"

"You can and you will. And here's why. I done been at The Farm for twenty-one years. I done seen 'em come and I done seen 'em go; week after week, month after month, year after year. Ain't no end to it, son. After a while, I begin tuh realize I could help some, but not others. I ain't neva gittin' out, son. Neva! Y'all know how long neva is?"

"What did you do?" Lucas asked.

"Killed three niggas, that's what. Killed 'em dead, neva to return on this earth, ah did."

"Why? I mean, what did they do to you?"

"Let me put it this way . . . a woman was involved."

Lucas shook his head. "What happened, man?"

"It was either them, or me. You understand me, son. Them or me. But you gotta understand somethin'. When you do stupid shit, stupid shit come yo' way. That's why ah done decided long ago to save as many stupid black men as ah can, see? You, son, gots powerful promise. You be a warrior without a brain. That be what ah was too. A warrior wit' no brain. That's why ah be in her'. But you, son, you be different. You be a warrior wit' a brain, and then cain't nobody stop ya."

Lucas frowned. "You callin' me stupid?"

"Ah sho' is. And ah will beat the livin' shit outta you if ah hav'ta tuh git ya tuh listen."

Lucas laughed when heard that. "Ol' man, I can whip you. It wouldn't take very long either."

"Yeah, ah suspect you can, but not before ah put a hurtin' on ya. And my friends," he looked to the left of where Lucas was sitting, where about fifteen Negroes, the same size as One Punch or larger, were paying attention to their conversation, "they won't allow me tuh fight by m'self. If it git tuh lookin' like I'ma lose, they'll finish my fight and then you still gon' listen to what the hell I tell ya when ya git out that there infirmary."

Lucas looked at the men he'd have to fight and decided it wasn't worth it. Besides, he knew One Punch was right, and he listened. "Okay, ol' man, I'll listen to you. Say what ya gotta say."

"The second piece advice I'ma give ya is the same piece advice my pappy preacher give me. Ah didn't listen, and ya see where ah am for life. There was this her' Bible verse he'd git tuh quotin'. It goes like this her'. 'A fool despises wisdom and instruction.' Ah had tuh git locked up for life tuh learn ah was a fool. Ya her' me, son? Life in *prison* and *fool* be one and the same." He paused for emphasis. "Look at all the fools there be in the world, son. Now, that there book ya readin' . . . what that be about?"

"It's about Negro men that served in the American Revolution. It says a Negro was the first to die for the country and a lot more. It talks about their medals, their heroism, and stuff."

"Ah bet it don't talk about bein' in prison, do it?"

"Not yet."

"Why ya suppose it don't?"

Lucas thought before he opened his mouth. "Probably because this book ain't about fools."

One Punch smiled. "All right then. Now you go tuh readin' that there book and stay out thangs that's gon' git ya killed, or more *prison* time, and turn ya into what?"

"A fool," Lucas said, smiling.

* * *

Two days had passed since Johnnie visited on Christmas. She had brought him gifts and delicious food. He missed her terribly. The prisoners had discussed how beautiful she was, constantly telling Lucas how lucky he was to have a woman who bothered to come and see about him. But secretly, they were taking bets on when he would get a letter from her saying she had moved on with her life, which was something he didn't have to concern himself with because he had broken it off with her. Nevertheless, he missed seeing and talking with her more every day. He also missed the warmth of her naked body against his. Were it not for the letters he regularly received from Marla Bentley to comfort him, he would have missed her even more.

Nearly every day, he got something from Marla; a letter, delicious baked goods, books, soap, toothpaste, and towels. Her gifts kept his spirits up, and gave him something to look forward to. Marla was smart enough to use her maiden name, Fiore, on her letters and packages, so no one knew it was Napoleon's wife sending them. The return address was Chicago, Illinois. She didn't even use her first name in the return address. At first, he had no idea it was Marla. It was only after he read the first letter that he realized who M. Fiore was. He was so grateful that he wrote her back, and they began to correspond. They made plans to see one another again at a hotel they had passed on the way to and from Shreveport, where he unknowingly picked out the Chevy Napoleon would give him that evening.

"Mail call," one of the prison trustees called out.

Lucas smiled, hoping he'd gotten another letter or package from Marla.

"Bauman, Griffin, Rhoades, Schneider, Peterson, Knox," the trustee rattled off name after name. Finally, he said, "Matthews!"

Lucas had gotten a letter from the United States Army. He tore open the letter, hoping he'd gotten a reprieve and wouldn't have to serve the three years he'd agreed to. If it was a reprieve, he would tell Marla he changed his mind about meeting her. He would then write Johnnie and ask her to be his girl again. If she forgave him for being so cold to her, they would leave New Orleans immediately, never to return.

Dear Mr. Matthews,

I received a package from Coach Mitchell, requesting my assistance to get you out of the "circumstances" you're in and into the U.S. Army as soon as possible. Coach Mitchell and I go way back. I played quarterback for him when I was a kid, and became the first student from Abraham Lincoln to earn a scholarship at West Point. If you take the opportunity I'm offering you seriously, I'm confident you'll have an excellent career in the Army. If you work hard and keep your nose clean, I promise you I'll recommend you for Officer's Training School.

I have diligently studied your game films over the past two weeks. I loved what I saw. I'm currently in Germany as part of a Detachment Unit, assigned to the Air Base at Rhein Main. We are a supplies unit, but we're also a football team. We travel all over Europe to play the Army and Air Force teams stationed in England, Spain, and Italy, to name a few. American football is big here, and we play in front of thousands. If you agree to play for me, you'll get to see parts of the world you otherwise wouldn't see.

I have taken the necessary steps to get you out of

prison and in to boot camp at Fort Jackson in South Carolina. In about two weeks, I don't have the exact date in front of me, but you'll have a little free time to see your girl, if you have one, and then you'll take a train, or drive, whichever you prefer, to Fort Jackson, where you'll spend twelve weeks getting in shape and learning how to do things the Army way! I look forward to meeting you, Mr. Matthews.

Sincerely,
Colonel Hannibal Strong
U.S. Army

By the time he finished the letter, Lucas' face was lit up like a Christmas tree. The letter was totally unexpected. Suddenly, he was glad he hadn't gotten involved with Willie Towers and the "situation" he found himself in. If he had he might have ended up killing the man and gotten more time, nullifying the great news he'd received. In short, he would have become the fool One Punch had warned him about. Immediately, he found the older prisoner and showed him the letter, thanking him profusely for his wisdom and sound advice.

Afterwards, Lucas returned to his cot. He was thinking of writing Johnnie a letter, letting her know he'd be home in two weeks. Then it occurred to him that he'd be leaving her again; this time permanently. He decided to write Marla instead. If she was agreeable and could leave two weeks sooner than planned, he would spend some time with her before going back to New Orleans to get his car from Johnnie and driving to Fort Jackson. When he finished the letter to Marla, he wrote Colonel Strong and thanked him for getting him out of prison early and for the opportunity to play football again.

Part 2

House of Tears

Chapter 15
Day 3

"Just think about it, okay?"

Johnnie could hear the doctors and nurses, but she couldn't fully understand what they were saying. Their conversation, the surgical vernacular they used, might as well have been thirty bumblebees flapping their wings nonstop because it sounded like perpetual buzzing. She did, however, meet her surgeon, Dr. Shore, a specialist who had been flown in from Chicago to perform the radical surgery required to repair her partially detached clitoris.

Dr. Shore was an exceptionally attractive Negro woman in her early forties, brilliant by any standards, Colored or White. Prior to performing the surgery, she had told Johnnie she was about to have an operation and if successful, she would be able to experience a normal sex life again. But because of the drugs they had pumped into her system, Johnnie didn't know now that the surgery had already taken place and was a complete success.

Nevertheless, Johnnie tossed and turned all night long,

spontaneously reliving every detail of the previous night when Billy Logan broke into her home and raped and brutalized her private place. Images of him thrusting his javelin inside her filled her drug-induced mind. She dreamed about the day he had followed her from school. Unlike the reality of that day, in her dreams, no one rescued her from Billy's verbal assault. She was all alone, dropping tears that wouldn't cease as each word he spoke pierced her heart like arrows shot by an expert archer.

She opened her eyes, no longer in the dream world where she was powerless to stop the onslaught of unwanted images, and realized she was in her hospital room. It was dark, but not completely. In the near distance, she could hear lots of movement outside her door; nurses plying their trade, she assumed. She cut her eyes to the right, looking out the window, seeing only the darkness. She had no idea how long she'd been in her room, how long ago the surgery was. Placing her hand between her legs, she felt the gauze that covered the repair, and then cringed as the rape episode threatened to fill her mind again.

She turned her head to the left. The door was cracked a bit, allowing a ray of light in, and she saw Napoleon Bentley. He was sitting a few feet from her bed, his head resting on the palm of his hand, nodding as he fought the eventual onset of sleep.

She smiled.

Napoleon was the last person she expected to see when she woke up; especially since it was probably way past visiting hours. She stared at him for a few moments, watching him nod, watching his head fall off his palm, watching the process repeat itself again and again. There was something sweet about him being there when no one else was, not even Sadie Lane, whom she almost expected to see. She inhaled deeply, romanticizing the moment, knowing that if he'd stayed the whole night, he had feelings for her—deep feelings. She realized that what was once a romp spawned by blackmail was now something altogether different for the gangster who slept a few feet from her hospital bed.

A familiar scent alerted her to the fresh flowers in her room. She reached for the light switch next to her bed and flicked it on, casting a ray of light on the right side of the room, leaving Napoleon in darkness. She saw flowers, dozens of them, everywhere she looked; lavender and China red roses, yellow acacias, red chrysanthemums, white clovers, purple lilac, an assortment of lilies and orchids, one potted lotus flower, and one potted tulip—red. She looked at Napoleon again. He was still fighting the sleep his body demanded.

Overwhelmed by the gesture, she summoned him, whispering quietly, almost as if she didn't want to wake him, yet wanting to.

"Napoleon," she called out.

His eyes blinked repeatedly as he opened them, straining to see if Johnnie was still asleep, and whether or not he was imagining her calling his name. He yawned, stretched his long arms above his head, kicked his legs out, tightened his muscles, awakening nearly every part of his pooped anatomy. Unable to see her face through the darkness, he assumed she was still asleep. He looked at his watch through the ray of light the cracked door offered—four in the morning. He figured he'd stay another hour, and then he had to get back to the mansion before anyone in his organization realized he was gone. He had told the nurse to wake him at five. Positioning his head on his palm, he nodded again.

"Napoleon," Johnnie whispered again.

He opened his eyes and whispered, "You awake?"

"Yep. What are you doing here?"

"Just making sure you're all right."

"You been here all night?"

"The last two nights, actually. You were in and out. Sadie's here during the day, and I come at night."

"Two nights? I've been here for two days?"

"Yeah. Two days. You were in a lot of pain. When they told me you needed a specialist, I had the best one they could find flown in to make sure the surgery went well. You're gonna be as good as new in a few months, maybe six. With you being young, they expect the healing process to go much quicker."

"I know you're disappointed, huh?"

"Disappointed?"

"Yeah. You know what we were going to do."

"Oh that. Yeah, I was. But then I thought you musta had a good reason for not meeting me at the Bel Glades, so I swung by your place and found you on the floor. Do you remember what happened? Do you remember who did this to you?"

Johnnie looked away, saying nothing.

"You do know, don't you? And so do we. Don't worry. We'll take care of him when you're better."

"Take care of who?"

"Billy Logan, that's who!"

Johnnie looked away again, wanting revenge, yet not wanting to get involved. Too many people had been killed already, and she knew that's what Napoleon meant when he said, "We'll take care of him."

"How much is all this going to cost?" she asked, changing the subject.

"I've taken care of everything. Don't worry. You just get better."

"When can I go home?"

"Not for another three days."

"I wanna go home today. Can you get them to let me go?"

"If that's what you want, sure. They can't make you stay if you don't want to."

"Thanks," she said absently, like her mind was on other matters.

"What's wrong? You sure you don't want to stay another day or so?"

"No. I wanna go home, Napoleon."

"Okay. When Sadie comes, you tell her I arranged everything. Now back to Billy Logan. You don't want to—"

"Why so many flowers, Napoleon? What do they mean?"

You may not want to talk about the rape or Billy Logan, but I'm going to talk to Billy Logan about the rape.

"Flowers have their own language," Napoleon began, smiling. "It all began with the Turks in the 1700s. They developed a secret language with flowers, which communicated how one felt. Pick one and I'll tell you what it means. The rest . . . I want you to look up when you have the time."

"Okay, hmm, let's see. How about those white ones next to the purple ones? What do they mean?"

Napoleon stood and walked over to the other side of the room to make sure they were talking about the same flowers. "These?" he said, pointing at the white clovers.

"Yeah, those."

"What do you think they mean?"

"Well . . . they're white, so I assume they mean purity. But it couldn't be that easy, could it?"

Napoleon looked her in the eyes and said, "No, not that easy. The white clover means . . . think of me."

After he answered, they stared at each other for an uncomfortable moment, neither of them saying anything, both of them realizing the relationship was moving to another level. She liked Napoleon, but she was far from loving him.

After everything he'd done to purchase her love, all he was able to procure was her body because her mind, her heart, and her very soul still belonged to Lucas Matthews, and they always would. Even the sex they were going to have prior to the rape was because Lucas had rejected her. During the silence between them, as she and Napoleon stared into each other's eyes, she wondered if Lucas would change his mind. She wondered if they would ever get back together. Nothing bad ever happened to her when he was around.

Napoleon's new status as the Boss of New Orleans hadn't kept her from being violated in her own home, in her own kitchen. Besides, Johnnie believed that she'd gotten what she deserved. She had slept with Napoleon before Lucas had broken the relationship off, and she was tormented by the knowledge of it. She blamed herself for Billy Logan's lack of self-control.

"Well, I better go," Napoleon said, looking at his watch. He walked over to her bed and kissed her forehead. "If you need anything, let Bubbles know, and I'll make sure you get it. But whatever you do, don't tell him I've been coming to see you at night."

"Why not?"

"It's an Italian thing. And it's dangerous. The fewer people that know, the better."

"What about the people who know you come at night?"

"They won't say anything. They know who I am and what I

can either do *for* them or *to* them." He kissed her lips and she kissed back. "Now, do you need anything before I go?"

She shook her head.

"I probably won't be back since you're leaving today, but I'll be checking on you by phone. How would you like to go to Paris together? You don't have to answer now. Just think about it, okay?"

"Okay."

"Promise?"

"Promise."

Chapter 16
Day 3

"I've done an incredibly foolish thing."

Ethel Beauregard nervously sat in Parker Jamieson's outer office. She was waiting to be called in for the urgent meeting they needed to have. A few hours after Morgan left the mansion, she'd had time to think, and she didn't like the conclusions she'd drawn. She was in real trouble, and she hoped Jamieson, the family lawyer, could get her out of the mess she'd made. Demanding the Will be changed was the first mistake, and it was huge. She compounded the first mistake by allowing herself to be blackmailed by a Negro who was still in a position to extort money from her, and could quite possibly put her in prison for a very long time.

Full of regret now, she wished Katherine hadn't called out to her from the top of the basement stairs. She wished she hadn't hastily left Morgan all alone before she had a chance to see how much cash was actually in the safe. For forty-two years, someone other than her had been in charge of her life. When she lived with her parents, they made all her decisions for her; who her friends were, where she went to college, and who she'd marry. Her mother even chose her wedding date, her wedding dress, and arranged everything. Eric began making decisions for her the day after she recited her vows.

She had patiently waited until Katherine went to the store to get groceries before going back into the basement and re-opening the safe. Morgan had taken all the cash it contained; only the gold coins remained. She assumed he was in too much of a hurry to take them. She'd phoned Morgan a hundred times it seemed, once an hour, beginning at eight that evening, but he never answered. She called at twelve midnight, and again at six that morning. She called one last time before leaving for Jamieson's office, hoping she could talk some sense into Morgan and get him to give back the money she'd allowed him to take.

On her way to Jamieson's office, she even stopped by Morgan's house in Ashland Estates, something a woman in her position would never do, but no one answered the door. Eventually she left, believing Morgan and his wife had left New Orleans, perhaps even the state of Louisiana, which left her feeling completely vulnerable.

As she waited to be called into Jamieson's office, she sat there, scared to death that the first two decisions she'd ever made on her own were going to land her in prison. She wished she'd been more proactive in her husband's business affairs while he was alive. That way she'd know, or at least have some idea how much money Morgan took.

Her pride had been shaken to its core by the article in the *Sentinel*, but she still had a healthy amount left, even though her life was unraveling. If it ever got out that Nathaniel had actually left money, even a negligible amount, to his Negro grandchildren, the Beauregard name would lose much of the influence it wielded over the other blue-blood families. And of course, Charlene, the vice president of her social club would pounce on the opening like a fox in a henhouse. She had a plan, but she didn't know if it would work well enough to silence her critics. *Can Morgan be trusted to keep his word?*

Even if Morgan could be trusted, her Negro niece was in the perfect position to have her credibility called into question if she was so inclined. Though Johnnie never threatened to tell the police what really happened on Thanksgiving Day, if she ever found out she was entitled to an inheritance and Ethel had tried to cheat her out of it, that bit of information would certainly motivate her to tell the police what really happened and why. If she told all, the jury might believe that Ethel planned to kill Eric all along, hoping to secure the entire Beauregard fortune for herself.

These were but a few problems on the horizon that Ethel didn't want to contemplate, but her mind continued to conjure up scenario after scenario of what could befall her. She tried telling herself no jury in the country would believe the word of a Negro over hers; particularly one that should be grateful to be alive in the first place, but she found no lasting comfort in that line of thinking.

The secretary's phone buzzed. She picked up the receiver, listened, and said, "Right away, Mr. Jamieson." She looked at Ethel. "Mr. Jamieson will see you now, Mrs. Beauregard."

The secretary opened the door for her and she walked in.

"Hello, Ethel," Jamieson said, standing behind his desk, his right arm extended. After taking her hand into his, he said, "Have a seat," and gestured to one of the two chairs in front of his large desk. "Now, what was so urgent?"

"Mr. Jamieson," Ethel began as tears formed and dropped. "I've done an incredibly foolish thing."

Chapter 17

Jamieson stood up and walked around the desk and offered her his white cotton handkerchief. Ethel took it, dabbed her eyes, and fought the onslaught of an emotional release she hadn't had. Even at the funeral of four dead Beauregard men, she maintained her dignity and never shed a tear. Seeing the distress that threatened to consume her, Jamieson sat in the chair next to her and said, "I'm here to help, Ethel. What happened?"

"My butler overheard our conversation yesterday, Parker."

Incredulous, Jamieson said, "That's what's bothering you?"

Ethel stopped crying suddenly, perplexed by his incredulity, stunned that he didn't see the seriousness of the problem immediately.

"You act as if I have nothing to worry about. Did you hear me when I said he heard our conversation?"

"Yes. What's the problem?"

Astonished, she said, "He blackmailed me."

"What?"

She looked him in the eyes. "You heard me right."

As if he knew the answer, he said, "Please tell me you didn't pay him."

Ethel diverted her eyes from his to the floor.

Jamieson exhaled hard. "Where is he? Maybe I can scare him into giving you your money back. But for the life of me, I don't understand why you didn't call me back immediately and let me deal with him personally."

"It all happened so fast. When I hung up the phone, there he was, standing there, listening. He told me he heard it all."

"Are you sure he knew what we were planning to do?"

"Quite sure. He even told me he knew about the creation of a second Will to cut Johnnie out of the first one. He threatened to get an attorney to sort the whole mess out when I tried to tell him he didn't hear what he thought he'd heard."

"Is that all?"

"Is that all? That's enough, isn't it? Am I going to jail for this?"

Jamieson laughed heartily. "Rich people rarely, if ever, go to jail in this country. For something like this, you won't do a day of jail time." He reached out for her hand and cradled it to comfort her. "But don't worry, it won't even come to that."

"Why not? He knows everything, Parker."

"He knows nothing . . . next to nothing anyway."

Confused, Ethel said, "But he heard the conversation."

"No, he didn't. He heard part of the conversation, and that works to our advantage."

"How?" Ethel asked, no longer in tears.

"This'll be handled easily by putting something of value in the new Will for Johnnie and her brother."

"But I don't want her to have anything, Parker. Nothing! Not a dime! Not even a penny! I hate that girl. Don't you understand?"

"If you want to get away with changing the Will and silence any charges your butler can ever bring against you, it's smart to give her something. That way, she can't say her mother or her grandmother told her he promised to leave her something in his Will, but didn't fulfill his promise. If she gets a good attorney and he's lucky enough to find a judge to hear any charges she might bring, her attorney could tie us up in a long court battle."

"It was outrageous for Grandpa to leave her that much money! Didn't he know this could get out?"

"I thought it was outrageous too. I did my best to talk him out of it, but he wouldn't hear a word of it. I told him the same things I'm telling you. Nathaniel found God a few days before the stroke ravaged him. That's when he included the girl and her brother in the Will. He kept talking about being responsible and how he owed them both. He said he couldn't acknowledge them while he was alive, but he could acknowledge them after his death."

"Are you certain he didn't have the stroke before he included them in the Will?"

"I know it's hard to believe, but I'm quite sure."

"Well, if Morgan ever accused me of changing the Will, couldn't we say he was sick when he included them?"

"We could, but it would be so much simpler to give them something of value and send them on their way. They'll be happy with whatever you give them, and they won't question a thing because they never expected to get anything anyway. But if you cut them out completely and they get an attorney, we might have to go to court. Birth certificates and lots of other history are going to come into play. And we want to keep this thing as quiet as possible. We've both got a lot riding on this and if it falls through, I could be disbarred, and they'd still get the million, perhaps more. On top of that, you don't want any more publicity. So give them . . . let's say . . . college educations at one of the Negro colleges—perhaps Grambling, Howard, or perhaps Hampton. It would be up to them. We can even offer them the money in lieu of college and allow them to choose. I think about five thousand each should cover tuition, room, board, book fees, travel, and a little spending money. What do you think?"

Ethel smiled. "Ten thousand sounds a whole lot better than two million dollars." She reveled in the idea of it and then said, "Now, are you sure this will take care of Morgan and any charges he could bring in the future?"

"I'm sure. This kinda thing happens more often than you know. When someone dies and money's involved, there's always a sibling or relative who thought the deceased forgot them unintentionally. That's why you give them next to nothing and the judge rarely disputes the Will. Now, as for your butler, I'm certain I can persuade him to give back all your money. Just tell me where he lives and I'll take care of that too."

Ethel sighed deeply before saying, "I think Morgan has flown the proverbial coop, Parker."

"What do you mean? You think he's left New Orleans?"

"Yes. I tried calling all day yesterday and half the night. I went over to his house, I'm ashamed to say, but neither he nor his wife answered the door. I think they left yesterday afternoon after he collected his booty."

"Well, that's good! He won't be back. How much did you give him? A few thousand?"

"I have no idea what he took out of the safe, Parker. I only know that he took it all. The only thing left are the gold coins."

"If you had to guess, how much would you say he got?"

"Quite a tidy sum, I'm sure of it. He asked for fifty thousand and told me that if I didn't have that much cash in the safe, he'd wait until I could get it little by little. So whatever he got, it was enough to make him flee New Orleans that very day."

"Well, the good thing is, we know he won't ever risk coming back. Now all I have to do is contact Johnnie and her brother, and this whole thing goes away."

"You know, Parker, I read an article in the *Sentinel*, and it said she had been raped. I hadn't given that a second thought until now. I suppose she's all right by now. Negro women are accustomed to that sort of thing, I hear. Here's her phone number, but if you don't catch her there, you should try the Negro hospital. They'll know something, I'm sure. I want this wrapped up today, Parker. See to it."

Chapter 18
Day 3

"So you did see who raped you?"

"Johnnie Wise?" a white man dressed in a suit and tie called out as he walked through the open door. He was medium height and build, with red hair and freckles.

Johnnie, who was being assisted by Sadie and a nurse into a wheelchair, looked at the man. She had received a call from Parker Jamieson, telling her about her inheritance check. She smiled. "Yes, I'm Johnnie Wise. You must be Mr. Jamieson."

"I'm Detective Meade of the New Orleans Police Department," he said politely. "I've been here a couple times, but you were asleep. I have a few questions, if you're up to them."

Sadie looked at Johnnie, wondering if she should tell the detective about the rape or if she would let Napoleon and Bubbles handle Billy Logan.

"I don't know who raped me, sir," Johnnie said, looking at the floor.

"Well, did you see his face? Can you describe him?"

"No, sir."

"I find it strange that of all the houses and all the women in the parish, he picked your house to break into, don't you?"

Still looking at the floor, Johnnie said, "I guess it's a burden we Negro women have to bear. It's been going on for so long, sir."

Detective Meade stooped low enough to look into her face and asked, "What do you mean by that? Are you saying it was a white man that did this to you?"

Without thinking, she said, "No, sir."

"So then he was Colored?"

Realizing she'd made huge mistake, she said, "Sir, I never saw him."

Detective Meade exhaled like he knew she was lying and said, "If you never saw him, how do you know he wasn't a white man?"

Johnnie thought for a second as it occurred to her that she was getting in deeper and deeper, knowing that Napoleon and Bubbles were going to kill Billy Logan. If it ever got out that he was her rapist, it would all come back on her. She said, "Sir, I don't want no trouble. God will give me justice."

Detective Meade wrote down everything she said and continued to press her. "Tell me what happened the night you were raped."

"I was about to leave the house when I heard someone moving around outside my kitchen window, I went to look out the window and he kicked the door in and raped me."

He flipped the pages of his notepad and said, "Is that when your neighbor . . . a Sadie Lane, found you?"

"Yes, I found her," Sadie said. "How did you know that?"

"As I said, I've been here a number of times, and I talked to the nurses. They filled me in. So, tell me, Sadie, did you hear anything that night?"

"Yes, I heard the man kick in her door."

"And what did you do?"

"I ran over to help her."

"You didn't look out the window to see what was going on? You just ran over to help her?"

"Well, yes, sir, I did look out the window first, and then I went over to help her."

"So you saw the guy breaking in?"

"Not exactly."

Growing more frustrated, the detective exhaled. "What exactly did you see then?"

"A man breaking in, but I didn't see his face or anything."

"So how long did it take you to get over to her house?"

"About three minutes."

"Three minutes! You saw someone breaking into your friend's house and it took you three minutes to help her."

"Well, I had to put on some clothes, detective."

Meade stared at her for a long time, studying her, discounting everything she'd said. Then he said, "Did you call the cops first? Is that what took so long?"

"Uh, yeah," Sadie said, knowing that if she answered any other way, the detective would then ask her why she didn't call the police first.

"Why didn't you say that?"

"I guess it slipped my mind."

"It slipped your mind, huh?"

"Yes, sir."

"I supposed it slipped the operator's mind too, huh? Because there's no record of a call about a rape in Ashland Estates that night."

When caught in her bold-faced lie, Sadie didn't miss a beat. "Detective, you know how it is. When the Coloreds call the police, it's going to take two hours to get a response—even in Ashland Estates."

"So the operator that took the call decided on her own not to document that call because you're a Negro?"

"Yes, sir. You make it sound as if that's so impossible to believe."

Meade took a deep breath and exhaled hard again. He was growing weary of the game both women were playing with him. All he wanted to do was solve a vicious crime against one of their people, and they were doing everything they could to derail his investigation, which made no sense to him. Irritated, he said, "How is it that this same operator took several calls that night from Negroes in Sable Parish, where the crime is three times worse? Why would she document those calls and not the one call that came from Baroque Parish, where the well-to-do Negroes live?"

"Jealousy, maybe, who knows? Honestly, detective, I have no idea. All I know is that I made the call."

"Uh-huh . . . right." He looked at his notes again. "And you say it took about three minutes to get over to your friend's house to help her?"

"Something like that, yes. I didn't look at the clock and I didn't time myself. I just hurried out of the house."

"Was the man still there when you arrived?"

"No."

"What about your husband, Sadie? Did he go with you?"

"I'm not married, detective."

Meade shot a hot glare at her again. None of what they were saying made much sense. *Why don't they want to catch the rapist?*

"Didn't you tell the nurse you had to get home to your three children when you left the hospital that night?"

"Yes."

Meade thought for a second. "Is there a man living with you?"

"No, sir."

"Hmm. And what do you do for a living?"

"I work for the Mancinis in the Garden District."

"Uh-huh. I see . . . so you're a maid?"

"Yes."

"And the job pays well enough for you to live in Baroque Parish?"

Sadie quieted herself and gathered her thoughts, watching the detective as he watched her collect herself. "Detective, my friend was raped. May I ask why you're prying into my personal life?"

"Why I'm prying into your *personal* life?" Meade shook his head. "Because your friend, as you call her, has been raped and you're lying about what happened that night." He looked at Johnnie. "Both of you are lying and I wanna know why."

Johnnie and Sadie looked at each other, saying nothing.

"Johnnie, did her boyfriend rape you? Is that what happened?"

Sadie said, "My boyfriend wouldn't rape my friend, detective!"

"Shut up!" Meade said to Sadie. He looked at Johnnie again. "Did her boyfriend rape you? Is that what happened?"

"No, sir," Johnnie said.

"How would you know, Johnnie, if you didn't see him?"

Johnnie's eyes offered a look of vacancy. The more she said, the worse it got.

"Now . . . who raped you? I know you know, don't you? It was her boyfriend, wasn't it?"

"No, sir!"

"You're sure!"

"Yes, sir!"

"So you did see who raped you?"

Johnnie looked at Sadie and said, "I wanna go home."

"Not so fast," Meade said. "You can go when I say you can go. There's something really wrong here, and I aim to find out what it is." He looked at Sadie again. "What's your boyfriend's name and address? I wanna talk to him."

"Uh . . . his name?" Sadie stammered a bit, knowing she couldn't divulge the information requested.

"It's a simple question, lady," Meade growled. "And don't tell me you don't have a boyfriend. It's too late for that."

The pressure had gotten to Sadie, but she wasn't about to tell Meade that Santino Mancini, her employer, was the father of her children. She thought for a second, and the only man she could think of was George Grant—affectionately known as Bubbles. If Meade kept pressuring her, she planned to use Bubbles' name as cover, and then tell him about it later, just in case Meade questioned him.

Just as Detective Meade was about to apply more pressure and ask more invasive questions, he heard someone knock on the door. He whirled around to see who was interrupting his not so subtle interrogation.

"Excuse me," another white man wearing an expensive-looking blue suit said. "I'm Parker Jamieson, and I'm looking for Johnnie Wise."

Chapter 19

"I'll make sure Ethel gets the message."

"And who might you be?" Detective Meade asked Jamieson.

Jamieson reached into his inside breast pocket and pulled out a business card that read: PARKER S. JAMIESON, ESQUIRE, and handed it to the detective.

Meade took the card out of his hand and read it out loud. "Parker S. Jamieson, huh? Esquire, huh?" He looked him up and down. "So . . . you're some kinda lawyer, huh?"

"I am, sir," Jamieson said.

"Well, she's gonna need a real good one," Meade said.

Johnnie frowned, having no idea why she would need a lawyer when she was the one who'd been raped. She was about to respond when Sadie spoke on her behalf.

"Why does she need a lawyer, detective? She's the victim."

Seeing an opportunity to win favor with Johnnie, Jamieson said, "I couldn't help but overhear you grilling her about the rape, detective. I, too, am curious as to what your motivation is."

Meade sucked his teeth and said, "Are you here representing her, Mr. Esquire Lawyer?"

"No, actually I'm here representing the late Nathaniel Beauregard. I'm the executor of his Will."

"Ahh, so there *is* some truth to the article in the *Sentinel*, huh? Well, that makes me wonder if the rest of it's true too."

"What article?" Johnnie asked forcefully.

"The article about you being Nathaniel Beauregard's granddaughter. Is that true?"

Johnnie looked at the floor.

"Ahh, so then the Beauregards were paying you off to keep Grandpa's dirty little secret, huh?"

"Don't answer that, Johnnie," Jamieson said.

"She don't have to answer, Mr. Esquire Lawyer," Meade said. "The fact that you're here representing the Beauregard clan is more than enough for me." He turned to Johnnie and said, "And you're lying. You're protecting the identity of the man who raped you. That's up to you, and that's fine with me. But this business about Sharon Trudeau stealing from you . . . then her and that bellhop ending up dead in her hotel room . . . that's something you're going to have to answer for eventually. And I'll tell ya another thing that sticks in my craw—the death of Eric Beauregard. I get why Blue Beauregard would murder his twin brother and his wife Piper since they were having an affair. I even get the death of Nathaniel. The poor guy just keels over. But why Ethel Beauregard would kill her own husband to save the life of a Negro woman who turns out to be her husband's niece . . . makes no sense." He looked at Jamieson again. "You say you're the executor of Nathaniel Beauregard's Will, right, Mr. Esquire Lawyer?"

"Yes," Jamieson said.

"Then that means Miss Wise here has something coming her way, right? Why else would you be here?"

"The Beauregard estate is a private matter, detective. You have no idea if any of it's true. You're fishing."

"Uh-huh. I see. Perhaps the inheritance money is just another payoff to keep her quiet." He looked at Johnnie again. "Maybe you both killed Eric and neither of you can tell the truth on why you did it."

"I didn't kill nobody, sir," Johnnie said desperately.

"Maybe you did, maybe you didn't, but I'm sure as hell gonna find out what really went on in that dining room, one way or another. Cooperate and I'll make sure they take it easy on you."

Jamieson said, "Don't say anything, Johnnie."

"I didn't do nothing, Mr. Meade. I didn't kill nobody, honest."

"But you did know Sharon Trudeau, didn't you?"

"Yes," Johnnie said reluctantly, ignoring Jamieson's advice.

"How did you know her?"

"She was my stockbroker."

"Now, don't that beat all," Meade said, shaking his head. "A Negro with a stockbroker. I don't have a stockbroker, do you, Mr. Esquire Lawyer?"

"As a matter of fact, I do," Jamieson said. "But having a stockbroker is insufficient grounds for accusing someone of murder, *detective*."

"How much money did she steal from you?" Meade said, looking at Johnnie.

"Don't answer that," Jamieson said.

"I hear it was two-hundred and fifty thousand and change. Is that right?"

"Don't' answer that," Jamieson said again.

Meade laughed a little. "This sure is interesting. Sharon Trudeau steals your money and ends up dead. People seem to die when you're around, Miss Wise. Richard Goode, Sharon Trudeau, Eric Beauregard. And let's not forget the bellhop . . . your own mother, for God's sake. I suspect that the man who raped you will end up dead too."

Hearing the names of all the murder victims, particularly the mentioning of her mother's murder, pricked Johnnie's conscience. She'd taken an active role in the murder of Richard Goode. While she didn't participate in the murder of Sharon Trudeau and the unsuspecting bellhop, she knew she was partially responsible for their deaths. It was quite unsettling to hear detective Meade's rendition of a truth he was so close to, yet a million miles away from. Feeling the need to defend herself, she repeated, "I didn't kill nobody, sir. I swear to God, I didn't."

"I'll just bet you didn't, Miss Wise. I'm gonna check and see if the amount you lost was two hundred and fifty thousand. If so, you're going to be arrested for a double murder. You'll be going to jail for a very long time. Unless, of course, you wanna help yourself out now and tell the whole truth."

"Which is what?" Jamieson asked. "Let's hear your theory."

"I don't have to answer you, Mr. Esquire Lawyer. But I will say this: It don't look good that a Colored teenager is even mixed up in this. And if we find out you did have two hundred and fifty thousand invested with Sharon, you're going to have to explain how you acquired so much money so quickly. What are you, eighteen years old?"

"Seventeen."

"Seventeen? A seventeen-year-old Negro with a quarter of a million bucks? Why, that's more money than I'd make in three lifetimes." He shook his head. "Colored . . . beautiful . . . seventeen. And rich beyond your imagination. That just ain't right. If it's true, of course." He continued shaking his head and looked at Jamieson. "Frankly, I think the reporter over at the *Sentinel* had it right. The Beauregards are paying this girl off to keep her mouth shut about what really happened that day. But I'll tell you what, the law won't stand by and let her get away with killing not one, but two white people. Four, if we count Richard Goode and Eric Beauregard. The country just won't stand for it. I'll say this, though." He turned back to Johnnie. "If the Beauregards have been paying you off, maybe they'll do what they can to keep you outta jail too."

Jamieson looked at Johnnie. He could see the fear in her eyes, and that made the whole situation even more volatile because once she was arrested for murder, nothing was going to keep her from talking about it all. If Meade ever got her alone and pressured her, she would tell whatever she knew about Sharon Trudeau, how she acquired her money, her relationship to Nathaniel Beauregard, the Will, the education stipend, all of it would become fodder for an experienced district attorney to wade through. Jamieson knew he had to protect Johnnie and in so doing, protect Ethel, himself, and his newly acquired seventeen million. It was getting complicated. While the death of Sharon Trudeau had nothing to do with the Beauregards,

Meade could use it to pressure Johnnie into talking about what really happened to Eric. He decided to shut down any further questions.

"Okay, detective, that's it. I'll be representing this woman. This is one Negro the law won't be able to coerce a confession out of. I won't allow the state to railroad her either."

When Johnnie heard that, a sense of relief sprung up like a flower in springtime. She believed Jamieson had to be the best lawyer in New Orleans if he represented the Beauregards.

Meade cut into Johnnie's thoughts. "Sure you don't wanna tell me about the money? I promise to speak on your behalf if you do."

"Don't answer that, Johnnie," Jamieson said. He looked at Meade. "If you want to talk to my client again, get a warrant and I'll make sure she comes in, but she won't be saying one word. Not one, do you hear?"

"I hear you, Mr. Esquire Lawyer. But I'll tell ya, it looks bad for her and Ethel. They're the only ones who know what really happened in that house, unless of course the cook or the butler killed Eric. However, we know neither of them did it, because if either of those two killed the husband, why would Ethel say she killed him? She wouldn't, I don't believe. If the closet relative killed Eric, Ethel might be persuaded to say she killed her husband to keep the family secret from getting out, which explains your presence here, Mr. Esquire Lawyer." He shook his head. "Puzzling case."

And with that, Meade left Johnnie's hospital room.

Jamieson handed Johnnie her check and his card. "This money is for college, if you choose to go. Call me if the police trouble you again."

"Why are you defending me, Mr. Jamieson? Did Ethel tell you to or what?"

"No, she didn't. I just think you need a good lawyer any-time the cops start asking questions."

"Hmm," Johnnie breathed. "Nurse, could you wait outside for a few minutes? I need to speak to Mr. Jamieson."

The nurse left quietly and closed the door.

Johnnie said, "What's Ethel afraid of, Mr. Jamieson?"

"Afraid of?"

"Yeah. I mean you're protecting me like I'm a member of the family."

"She's not afraid of anything, Johnnie."

"Really," Johnnie said sarcastically. "I think she's afraid of what I might say, Mr. Jamieson."

"And what would that be?"

"She knows what happened and I know what happened. I hope you're a really good lawyer, Mr. Jamieson; otherwise, I might have to tell everything I know. If the police leave me alone, I say nothing. If they put me in jail . . ."

"I'll make sure Ethel gets the message."

With that, Jamieson left.

"Sadie, let's go see Ethel."

"You sure you don't want to go home and rest?"

"I can't afford to rest right now. They're coming after me. They want to pin all those murders on me. I'm telling you right now, if it comes down to it, if it's me or Ethel, who do you think Jamieson is going to protect?"

"Ethel."

"Absolutely. Who do you think he was protecting by telling me not to talk?"

"Ethel."

"Now, do you really think I have time to rest? I gotta get over to the Beauregard mansion and make sure Ethel understands how important it is to keep me out of jail."

"Okay, I'll drive you over."

Chapter 20

"Excuse me? Who did you say, sir?"

Santino Mancini was in his study, tallying the monthly bills in a vain attempt to stay busy and mentally extricate himself from the brutal rape that took place near his second home in Ashland Estates, where his long-time lover and mother of his illegitimate children lived. Two days had passed and he couldn't get the image of the Negro woman who was on the floor, nude, bleeding, and in need of emergency medical attention, out of his mind. He had never met Johnnie, but he'd listened to Sadie talk about her endlessly whenever he visited her and his children.

Since that night, his relationship with Sadie had been strained. She'd taken a few days off, which he approved, being her boss, and understanding how grave the situation was. But he could tell she was angry with him for not only running away when she needed him to take charge, but for being callous and emotionally vacuous. Santino couldn't understand why she didn't understand the position he was in just by being in a house where a Negro woman was raped. The scandal would prove to be overwhelming if what people knew, but pretended they didn't, was ever made public.

The scathing article in the *Sentinel* was a clear example of what would have happened to him if he had done the right thing that night. Even though his wife knew about the relationship, it wasn't talked about publicly and could be easily disregarded as malicious gossip. To get involved in Johnnie's troubles would have brought trouble to his own house in the form of public humiliation for his wife. The last thing Santino needed was to answer uncomfortable questions the police might ask.

"A Detective Meade is here to see you," Mrs. Mancini said after knocking.

Santino opened the door. "I'm sorry, dear, but did you say a detective was here to see me?"

"Yes."

He had heard her the first time, but he didn't want to believe the thoughts that were suddenly ricocheting in his mind now. "For what reason?" he asked rhetorically, knowing, or at least believing he knew why the detective was there. What he couldn't believe was that Sadie was so upset with him that she would tell the police he was with her that night, or even that they were "secretly" seeing each other. Anger began to mount as his fears surfaced.

"He said it was a personal matter. Will you see him?"

Santino breathed an undetectable sigh of relief. He still believed the detective was there about the rape, but he was prudent enough not to tell his wife.

"Bring him to me in about five minutes. I'm finishing up the bills. And could you make us some coffee?"

"I put some on when he told me who he was. I'll bring it to you shortly."

Immediately after his wife left him, Santino went back to his desk, cleared off the bills and thought about how he would handle the detective. He picked up the phone and called Sadie. He wanted to find out what she said to him. That way he could tailor his answers to coincide with hers. The phone must have rung thirty times. He would probably still be holding the phone if he hadn't heard the knock on his study door. He put the receiver back in its cradle.

After opening the door, he said, "Detective Meade, I'm Santino Mancini. What can I do for you?"

He extended his hand.

Detective Meade reached out and shook it firmly, looking Mancini over, sizing him up. As he entered the study, he couldn't help noticing the décor of the room. Expensive-looking cherry oak built-in bookshelves covered every wall, making the room seem smaller than it was. A crystal chandelier hung over a desk made of wood that matched the bookshelves. Meade figured the desk weighed somewhere in the neighborhood of five hundred pounds.

"I know you're a busy man, Mr. Mancini, so I won't take up too much of your time."

"Please . . . have a seat," Santino said.

Meade sat on the sofa. Santino sat in one of two red velvet spoonback chairs and repeated, "What can I do for you, detective?"

Meade leaned forward and fingered the cigar box that sat on the coffee table positioned between them.

"Would you like a cigar, detective?"

"If you don't mind."

"I don't mind. Take a few, if you like. Ever had a Havana Montecristo, detective?"

"No, sir," Meade said and scooped up a handful. He put the cigars in his breast pockets and said, "Are you Sadie Lane's lover, Mr. Mancini?"

Agitated, he said, "Excuse me, sir?"

"Come on now, Mr. Mancini, let's not play games here. I didn't tell your wife why I wanted to see you for a real good reason."

"For what ungodly reason could you possibly ask me that question, detective?"

"Mr. Mancini, we can do this the easy way, or we can do it the hard way. It's up to you."

"Are you two ready for your coffee?" Mrs. Mancini called out after knocking on the door.

Santino went to the door and opened it.

His wife rolled in a tin cart carrying a silver coffee tray and set it on the table. She poured them each a cup and said, "Help yourselves to the cream and sugar." Then she left the two men alone again.

"Are you having an affair with your maid?" Meade repeated as he put two teaspoons of sugar in his coffee.

"This is not an admission, but what if I were having an affair with her? What then?"

Meade tapped his spoon on the side of the cup, placed it on the saucer, and then sipped his coffee. "What are you afraid of? Me telling your wife? No chance of that if you cooperate. But if you keep playing this cat and mouse game, you're going to force me to call Mrs. Mancini in here and ask her some questions too. It's up to you, sir."

"Okay, detective. Yes."

Meade smiled wickedly, believing the rest would be easy now. "So what happened the night Johnnie Wise was raped?"

"Excuse me? Who did you say, sir?"

Meade pulled his notebook from his pants pocket and flipped a few pages. "Johnnie Wise. Sadie's next-door neighbor. Sadie was in the hospital room when I questioned the victim about the rape this morning."

Deflated, Santino looked at the floor and ran his hand down his face. "Listen, detective, I can't get mixed up in that."

Meade pretended to be reading from his notes when he said, "So you were there the night of the rape, right?"

"Right, but I left as soon as I saw the girl."

"Tell me what happened."

"Didn't Sadie and Johnnie tell you?"

Meade knew Santino was scared, which was the point of paying him a surprise visit. Now it was time to bluff him into spilling his guts. "I wanna hear your side of it. I think they're covering for you, Mr. Mancini. I think you raped the girl. I think the two Colored women are afraid to say you did it. But I know you did, and you're gonna have to answer for what you did to her."

"Me? Rape Johnnie? I would never do such a thing, sir. And I certainly wouldn't do it to Sadie's best friend."

"If you didn't, who did?"

"I don't know."

"Tell me everything that happened that night."

"Do you promise to keep my name out of this if I tell you? Or do I have to call my attorney?"

"If you didn't rape her, yes. I'll keep you out of it."

"Okay, then. It all started when Napoleon Bentley began banging on Sadie's back door. . . ."

Chapter 21

"He was loud. I know that."

"So do you know who raped you, Johnnie?" Sadie asked as she drove to the Garden District. "I tried asking you when the doctors first let me visit you, but you were out of it."

"Yes."

"Who?"

"Billy Logan."

Sadie shook her head like she couldn't believe Billy would do something that awful. "What did Napoleon say about it?"

"He doesn't know for sure that Billy did it, but he—"

"You didn't tell him?"

"No."

"Why not?"

"That's what I was about to tell you. He already *believes* Billy was the one who raped me, Sadie. I can't get involved. Too many people have been killed already."

"Why not tell the police then? Let them handle it."

"Because Billy might be dead already. Eventually the cops

are going to find the body somewhere. And if I told them it was Billy who did this to me, they would know I had gotten him killed. If I tell them who did it and they find Billy dead, they'll put me in jail, believing I had something to do with it because he raped me. They already think I had something to do with Sharon's murder, and they're going to find out about the two hundred and fifty thousand sooner or later. I'm in a lot of trouble already."

"What are you going to do?"

"I'm going to talk to Ethel. It's time to ask my aunt for a big favor. Maybe Mr. Jamieson can get me out of trouble."

"If you ask me, none of this would have even started if it weren't for the article in the society section of the *Sentinel*."

"I wonder how they found out about it, Sadie."

"I have no idea, but it has caused an uproar like you wouldn't believe."

Johnnie shook her head as she listened.

"White folks are angry and they're talking about it. You know what that means, don't you?"

"You think they're going to come after me, Sadie?"

"Not at first. When they tried that shit before, they got a taste of their own medicine. To tell you the truth, though, it wouldn't surprise me if they tried again, but this time, they'll be far more organized."

"I think I better get outta town while I can. I have more than enough money. Lucas isn't here anymore. My grandfather's dead. And I have my inheritance money. The only thing left for me is you, and I'd hate myself if something happened to you because of me."

"Nothing's going to happen to either of us, Johnnie. Santino won't let anything happen to me, and Napoleon won't let anything happen to you. You know he's in love with you, don't you?"

"Who?"

Sadie laughed. "Don't be coy, girl. You know Napoleon has deep feelings for you. Otherwise, why would he risk sneaking out of his mansion night after night to see you in a Negro hospital, and staying there until just before the sun came up, if he didn't? The man is divorcing his wife and you know he's gotta be lonely."

"Well, he can't get any for a while now."

Sadie frowned, remembering what she had wanted to ask her. "By the way, were you planning to see Napoleon that night or what?"

Johnnie looked out of the window and remained quiet.

"Okay," Sadie said, smiling. "So tell me this . . . when we were in Las Vegas, I spent the night with Benny. Did you spend the night with Napoleon?"

"I didn't spend the night, no."

"But you did get a little, didn't you?"

"I got a little for myself, but I made sure he understood that I know my way around a bed and that I wasn't a little girl anymore. He was in a very deep sleep by the time I left."

"And that's why he came by your house that night, huh? He wanted you to put him to sleep again, didn't he?"

"I suppose."

"You suppose? Girl, please. You should've seen how worried he was about you. I think it's going to be hard to get away from him now. From what I hear about him, *he* puts women to sleep. But you put him to sleep? What did you do to him?"

"A little of this and a little of that."

Sadie laughed.

"He was loud. I know that. And when I made it come out, he started babbling words I couldn't understand, like an infant."

"Yeah, you're going to have to leave New Orleans. He's not going to give you up. Either that, or the Mafia will end up killing him."

"You think so?"

"Shit, yeah. They don't play. How do you think he got to be the Boss of New Orleans?"

"How?"

"He had a Japanese husband and wife team, the Nimburus, or something like that, kill John Stefano while we were in Vegas. I overheard Bubbles and Napoleon talking about it. They were talking about how things were going to be different now that Napoleon was running the Crescent City."

"Hmm, so that's what the phone call was all about?"

"What phone call?"

"In the middle of doing it, the phone rang and he told Bubbles that Tia and Khiro would meet him at the Moulin Rouge. It didn't make any sense at the time, but now it does."

Cars lined both sides of the street in front of the Beauregard mansion. It looked like a funeral procession. Sadie drove around the block, looking for a place to park. By the time they circled the block a second time, they saw Parker Jamieson coming out of the front door of the mansion. He got into his car, and drove off. Sadie parked in the vacant spot. She got out of the car, and walked around to the passenger side to help Johnnie. As they slowly walked to the iron gate, detective Meade came out of the Mancini mansion.

"Sadie Lane and Johnnie Wise," Meade called out. "I was just about to head over to your houses to speak to you."

Chapter 22

"I expect you'll be ready by about ten."

"You lied to me . . . both of you!" Meade said, almost shouting. He looked at Johnnie. "What was a mobster, Napoleon Bentley, doing at your house at that hour of the morning? And don't tell me he was just passing by."

"Detective Meade," Johnnie began, looking at the ground. "Anything you have to say to me, say it to my lawyer, Parker Jamieson. Now, if you'll excuse me, I have to speak to Mrs. Beauregard."

"You mean Aunt Ethel, don't you?"

Johnnie didn't bother answering Meade. She turned away and gingerly walked through the open gate.

"Where do you think you're going, Sadie?" Meade said when she followed Johnnie.

"I'm helping my friend into the house," Sadie said, defiantly looking him right in the eyes. Negroes were never supposed to look Whites in the eyes.

Meade stared back, and then looked her up and down. "Just who in the hell do you think you are, talkin' to me like that?"

"Like what, *detective*?"

"Like you're talkin' to a nigger. Am I going to have to haul your black ass in?"

Sadie exhaled hard. "No, detective."

"Good, because I think a fine nigger wench like you oughta be grateful." He licked his lips as debauchery filled his mind. "In fact, I'm plannin' to come by your place later so you can show me just how grateful you can be."

Sadie laughed. "Detective, you have to be joking."

"Joking is the furthest thing from my mind. Bedding you is gonna be pure pleasure, missy."

"If you think I'm going to lay down with you, you need to wake up, because you're dreaming, *detective*. You might as well get that out of your mind."

"I know what you're thinkin', missy."

Mocking him, Sadie said, "What am I thinkin', *detective*?"

"You're thinkin' you don't have to do nothin' 'cause Santino Mancini's gonna protect you, but he can't. I just talked to him and he spilled it all. He was there the night your friend Johnnie got raped. Napoleon was there too." He paused briefly and stared at her, enjoying the moment of unexpected revelation. "You gotta know that no white man, when cornered, is ever gonna choose a nigger wench over his white wife and respectability. Don't you know that, Sadie?"

As much as she didn't want to believe Meade, his words were a sobering reality. "I don't care what he told you, detective. My story is the same as it was this morning. If you expect some kind of intimacy from a woman of color, I suggest you go to the quarter and seek her out there."

A wide, salacious smile slowly crept across Meade's face. "You just don't understand, do you, missy? I've talked to Mancini and he expects you to cover his ass on this one. The way he tells it, he's been taking care of you and his pickaninnies for years. It's time you returned the favor." He laughed from his belly.

Enraged, Sadie stormed off and opened the gate leading to the Mancini mansion.

Meade yelled out, "I expect you'll be ready by about ten." He laughed again. "I wouldn't want anybody seein' me gettin' a rich man's poon tang."

Chapter 23

"Relax. I own the place."

As she limped away from Detective Meade and Sadie, Johnnie heard bits and pieces of their conversation, but not enough to understand much of what was said. Over the course of a year and a half, she and Sadie had become close. For that reason, she knew Sadie wouldn't tell Meade anything that would lead the detective to Billy Logan's doorstep. Sadie wouldn't let her down. Sadie would tell her everything each of them said on the way home. Having to walk cautiously, it took her a while, but she had made it to the side of the Beauregard mansion, and was nearing the back.

As she struggled to reach her destination, she remembered the brief conversation with Detective Meade at the Beauregard gate and how he reacted when she told him he'd have to speak with her attorney if he wanted to speak to her about the rape. She found his reaction interesting because as soon as she uttered the words, Meade backed off. She began to realize that even with black skin, just mentioning a lawyer got the attention of a police officer and shut him up. She realized that lawyers would be a permanent part of her future. She also remembered that Robert Ryan, the leading black attorney in the parish, had slapped the city of New Orleans with a multimillion-dollar lawsuit and won. After the *Sentinel* and *Raven* newspapers had published inflammatory articles about the death of Richard Goode, a race riot ensued. The police hadn't shown up to stop the riot. She concluded that money and lawyers kept white folk from running roughshod over the Negroes who lived in Ashland Estates—that and the white men who had Colored families living there.

She stopped when she heard voices coming from a cracked window in the library. It was warmer than usual that day, about eighty degrees. Walking so soon after the surgery was stressful, and she was beginning to perspire and needed to catch her breath. Peeking through the window, she saw about twenty to thirty white women chatting. It occurred to her that the women she was spying on were responsible for all the cars in front of the mansion. She knew she shouldn't eavesdrop and move on, but she couldn't help herself.

It's not going to hurt to listen to a little bit of what's going on in there.

Like magic, Ethel Beauregard and another woman entered the room and began to address the ladies. The women were on the edge of their seats with anticipation, sitting like little schoolgirls at their desks, waiting for the teacher to enter and pass out certificates for being good citizens, which piqued Johnnie's curiosity even more. They looked like this was the moment they had all been anticipating for a long time. So as not to be seen staring into the room, she positioned her back against the wall and listened attentively.

"Women of the Southern Christian Ladies Social Club," Ethel began with refined, aristocratic poise, "thank you all for coming to this impromptu gathering. Let's give Charlene a big hand for being able to get everyone together on such short notice."

The women stood and applauded enthusiastically like they were at a rock and roll concert.

Johnnie peeked inside when she heard one woman say to another, "Ethel is holding up well considering the pressure Charlene applied to get this emergency meeting."

The other woman said, "Do you think she'll resign as president?"

The two women laughed and continued applauding.

Ethel continued, "As you all know, a little over a month ago, the Beauregard family experienced an enormous tragedy during the Thanksgiving Day weekend. I lost my beloved husband, Eric. My two sons, Blue and Beau. I also lost my father-in-law, Nathaniel. And now the *Sentinel* has acted irresponsibly by printing a story depicting my father—"

"What about Piper?" Charlene interrupted, knowing how much Ethel disliked the tart who swept her favorite son, Blue, off his feet. "We don't want to forget her, do we, dear?"

"Did I not mention Blue's dearly departed wife?" Ethel said with pseudo contrition, knowing she hadn't mentioned Piper deliberately. From her perspective, with the exception of Nathaniel's death, Piper was responsible for the other three. But Johnnie Wise was more culpable than Piper, which was why she was the next target on Ethel's retribution list. As far as she was concerned, if Nathaniel hadn't struggled to stand and speak out on her behalf, he too would be alive. Therefore, Johnnie had the greater condemnation. "I'm sorry about that.

But ladies, I'm so upset about the article that it clings to my waking hours."

"We truly understand, don't we, ladies?" Charlene said and embraced her.

One by one, all the women followed Charlene's lead, offering toxic hugs. Charlene had convinced them it was time someone other than a Beauregard held the presidential reigns of the social club. A Beauregard by blood or by marriage had been the president of the club they started for more than one hundred years. Charlene had led the members to believe that if they didn't get a new president now, under the current circumstances, it might be impossible for any family to get the coveted position and thus lead the organization in a much needed new direction.

The women returned to their seats again, some of them wiping their eyes as deceitful tears slid down their counterfeit faces.

"As I was saying," Ethel began again, "the *Sentinel* printed that horrible article about my father-in-law, purporting to know things they have no way of knowing. My first thought after reading the article was, this is such rubbish. Then I thought . . . what if it's true?"

The women were still, the room deathly quiet, and the anticipation was edge-of-the-seat.

"I tried to ignore the article. I even tried to ignore what I was feeling, and my natural inclination to find out if what I'd read was true. But I confess before you all that my curiosity got the better of me. I had heard about this sort of thing all my life. From childhood to adulthood, rumors swirled. My mother and the other women in our family mentioned these things. They often spoke in hushed tones when they thought their little girls weren't near. I remember mentioning what I heard to my mother. I was told never to believe a word of it. I was sworn to secrecy. My mother and her sisters made me promise to never speak of these things again. In fact, I was told not to even give ear to it because it could only cause unnecessary problems in the family. As I said, dear friends, curiosity got the better, and I discovered that the *Sentinel* was correct."

She hung her head low when she finished her confession.

A synchronized gasp saturated the room when Ethel confessed to what the women had believed all along. What they couldn't believe was that she had actually acknowledged the truth publicly. They thought she would resign as president as soon as Charlene told her abdication of the position was the only viable way to avoid the humiliation of having to acknowledge the article at all. Everyone would know the truth as to why she stepped down, but the women were led to believe that Ethel would gracefully vacate the presidency, citing undue family stress, due to the surprising deaths of the Beauregard men.

Charlene could barely contain herself when she heard Ethel's humiliating confession. She stood up and nearly ran over to embrace Ethel, making a mockery out of compassion, voiding friendship, embracing mendacity. Again, one by one, all the women followed Charlene's lead. They had planned the whole charade, and it was working perfectly. They had came over unannounced, hoping to catch her off guard and completely vulnerable to Charlene's manipulative persuasion.

"I suppose you'll step down from your office as president of the social club." Charlene sighed, leading her unsuspecting stooge to unconditional surrender, wiping her wet eyes as the tears of joy flowed freely. "I know I speak for the entire club when I say I don't know how we'll ever replace you. We only hope we can do as good a job as the long line of Beauregard women who came before you and started this illustrious organization."

"Resigning was my first thought, too, Charlene, dear. And I couldn't think of a better person to take my place as president of this prestigious club."

Thunderous applause rang out.

Charlene's smile lit up the entire room. This was her moment of triumph, her moment of grand glory, and she bathed herself in the bright glow of it.

Ethel loved every moment of the farce too, but for different reasons. She watched Charlene as the reality of being president, a position she'd coveted for so long, washed over her. Ethel waited until just the right moment to drop the other shoe. When the women of the club offered congratulatory hugs and jubilant smiles, Ethel thrust her double-edged blade into their unsuspecting hearts.

It took an enormous amount of strength to contain the incredible glee that threatened to burst forth when she said, "But, ladies . . . it turns out that there isn't a member of the club who doesn't have Negroes in her family tree."

Every mouth fell open, horrified by her statement.

If a mouse peed on cotton, it would have been heard in that room.

Starting with Charlene's father, Ethel read from a piece of paper she was holding, listing every member's Negro family name, where they lived, children's names, and who the Negro mistress was. After that stick of TNT blew their plans to smithereens, real sorrow, real weeping began.

Katherine knew all this information and had known it for

some time. She told Ethel a few days after they buried Piper and the Beauregard men. So there Ethel stood, looking at each woman, offering them all the same phony hugs and encouragement they had previously offered her. But the look on Charlene's face was the most delicious dessert she could have ever ingested. Ethel knew she had shattered all of Charlene's dreams in front of the very crowd she'd brazenly brought to her home. Ethel had skillfully taken her head off at the shoulders as if by guillotine, vicious and bloody. The meal she'd served them all was luscious, perfectly timed, and colder than the howling winter wind in Chicago.

Ethel continued, "But, ladies, we truly have nothing to fear. We can overcome this quite easily."

The women quieted themselves and listened intensely.

"First, we deny the truth about our families. Second, we never, ever discuss this again in public or in private. Our mothers in their wisdom have shown us the way. All we have to do is continue what they started, and all of this goes away with no one to substantiate or discuss it. We can turn this thing around if we stick together and call the *Sentinel* article malicious gossip; it will cease to be news."

Johnnie, who had seen and heard it all, put her hand over her mouth and laughed uproariously. For the first time, she began to like Ethel. She was almost proud of her. Having been thoroughly entertained, she made her way to the back door and entered Katherine's kitchen.

"You done forgot how to knock on people's doors before you enter, I see," Katherine said loudly.

"Relax. I own the place," Johnnie said and smiled.

Chapter 24

"Y'all take as much time as y'all need to recover."

"Sadie . . . what a surprise," Mrs. Mancini said, holding the screen door open, allowing her maid to enter. "What brings you by today? We thought y'all was takin' a few days off to help your friend, Johnnie. We heard she was raped the other night. How is she?"

"She's doing better, Mrs. Mancini," Sadie said forcefully—her anger visible.

"Why, y'all look angrier than a yellow jacket whose hive has been disturbed. What on earth is the matter?"

She stepped into the kitchen. "Ma'am, I just need to speak to San—I just need to speak to Mr. Mancini. It's really important. Is he here?"

"Y'all wait right there and I'll check and see if he can see you."

A few minutes later, Mrs. Mancini came back into the kitchen. "He'll see you now. He's in the study. Make sure y'all knock before entering, ya hear?"

"Yes, ma'am," Sadie said and fast-walked to the study. Instead of knocking, fueled by rage, she barged in. "Where the fuck do you get off telling Detective Meade he can fuck me tonight?"

Santino stood up and walked up to Sadie. Through clenched teeth, he said, "Will you lower your voice? My wife might hear you."

"Why the fuck should I care?"

"You should care because if she finds out what's going on, she'll divorce me."

"That's a bunch of bullshit! She already knows, Santino. She's a woman. We always know when our man is fucking somebody other than us. She just isn't acknowledging it."

"Sadie, lower your fucking voice," he whispered, still clenching teeth.

"Well, explain yourself," Sadie quietly demanded.

"What the hell could I do? He knew I was with you that night, and he knew I knew something about the rape."

Incredulous, she said, "So you confirmed his suspicions, Santino?"

"He already knew everything."

"If he knew, why did he come here? Did you ever think about that?"

Santino thought for a brief moment and said, "What are you saying? He didn't know and I told him everything?"

"You told him everything?" Sadie said, shaking her head.

Dejected and feeling like a total imbecile, Santino slowly walked back to his desk and plopped down in his chair like he had just learned that his dog had been run over. He looked at his dark-skinned mistress and with a shaky voice said, "I still need you to give him what he wants."

"Why on earth would I ever consider doing that, Santino?"

"Because if you don't, he's going to arrest me for raping your friend. And it will stick too. I'll be ruined socially, and so will my wife. The stigma will linger for decades. When people see me or my wife, they'll say or think, 'There he goes, the man who rapes little girls.'"

"So you're worried about what people are going to say about you and your precious wife's reputation? What about me? What about my dignity, Santino? Did you ever think about that when you sold me?"

"Come on, Sadie. You're being melodramatic. No one has sold you."

"Oh, really? Do you really believe that, Santino? Do you really believe that you haven't sold me because currency hasn't changed hands?"

"It's just one time. I wouldn't dare ask this of you if it weren't absolutely necessary."

Wounded by his severe apathy, Sadie said, "Do me and the three children I had for you really mean that little to you?"

"What can I do? The man has me over a barrel. Help me out, please, Sadie. Just this one time. I swear to God I'll never ask anything like this of you again as long as I live."

A short, sardonic laugh within Sadie erupted as the epiphany manifested itself suddenly. "All this time . . . I thought you loved me, but all I've ever been is your propped up courtesan. It might have been better to be an ordinary streetwalker, a strumpet, a simple-minded tramp. That's what I've allowed myself to become." She paused for a brief moment of reflection. "You know what's worse? I don't have anything to show for what I've given you, Santino. All I have is three wonderful children, two of which you wanted, and the clothes on my back." She laughed a little again. "I guess this is what I get for settling for a life of leisure instead of going after my *own* dreams, *my* wants, and *my* desires. I could've had a life, Santino. I could've had a man, a *real* man; one that I didn't have to share, one who didn't sneak into my house at night and made sure he was gone before the sun rose in the morning. I could've had a man to share a house we owned, with a bank account I had access to. But I tossed it all away. And for what?" She looked him up and down. "Not much." She laughed again. "They say experience is the best teacher. Well, I've learned a magnificent lesson. Truth prevails and reveals itself in all who attempt to hide it."

She turned around and walked out of his study and gently closed the door. When she saw Mrs. Mancini bubbling over with what must have been sheer joy, having overheard the entire conversation, the humiliation Sadie had just suffered at the hands of her benefactor was now complete. She realized that not only did Mrs. Mancini know about the affair, she was and always would be number one in Santino's life. The two women stared at each other, looking each other directly in the eyes. Mrs. Mancini quietly laughed uncontrollably so Santino couldn't hear, maintaining the ignorant façade. Sadie quietly wept, tears falling, nose running, having had what little dignity she'd built over the years yanked away like it was a rotten tooth—brutally, and without compassion.

As she walked down the hall, Mrs. Mancini followed, laughing hilariously the entire time. When Sadie opened the back door, Mrs. Mancini said, "Y'all take as much time as y'all need to recover, ya hear? You'll always be our welcomed maid, you black bitch—I mean whore. Bitch is too good for you. Y'all think long and hard about that, ya hear?" She laughed again, this time unceasingly as Sadie walked down the stairs, humbled and devoid of dignity.

Chapter 25

"It worked, Katherine!"

"What are you doing here anyway, Johnnie?" Katherine said. "You don't work here no more. Don't you know that?"

Katherine was a thick woman, big-boned, tall, but not fat.

"That's *anymore*," Johnnie said sarcastically as she eased into a chair at the table.

"Who the hell are you to correct me?"

"You know who I am, Katherine. You know very well who the hell I am. I'm Johnnie Wise, BITCH! Heir to the Beauregard fortune, and don't you forget that shit again."

"Hmpf, well, what do you want?"

Johnnie studied Katherine, knowing she not only wanted to be a Beauregard, but wanted to be white too. She calculated the damage her response was about to do to her rival's inquiry. "I want to see *my* aunt."

When Katherine heard that, she rushed over to her and said,

"Listen, you little slut, you're not a part of this family and you never will be."

Johnnie smiled. "And you are? It kills you that I'm actually blood, doesn't it?"

Frustrated, she yelled, "What the hell do you want, Johnnie?"

"And that's another thing. I'm a Beauregard, so from now on, when you address me, I expect you to call me Miss Wise, or ma'am. And when I ask you a question, say, 'Yes'm,' like the good Jemima you are. Okay, Katherine?"

That was it. Katherine had heard enough, and raised her hand with every intention of slapping the taste out of Johnnie's mouth.

"Do it! And I'll tell the police everything I know! When Ethel's in jail, what will become of you?"

That last barb ended the joust and Katherine wept, unable to respond to her sharp words, unable to overpower the young woman with her size and strength.

"It must be the day for weeping women," Johnnie said, laughing loudly, insensitive and callous. "Maybe we should change the name of the mansion to House of Tears with all the crying going on today. You'd think somebody people loved died. Instead, we've got wicked women who've been caught in their own bullshit, crying like two-year-olds. Don't expect me to feel sorry for you, because I don't. You haven't been through half the shit I've been through, and I'm not crying."

She waited for Katherine to respond, but she just cried even more, which didn't solicit an ounce of remorse from Johnnie.

"So where's my good friend Morgan?"

Katherine sniffed and wiped her eyes. "He quit."

"What? When?"

"Two days ago."

"Do you have his phone number? I'd like to talk to him. He's a good man."

"We think he left town . . . moved away. Him and his family."

"Why would he do that?"

"I don't know."

"Does Ethel know?"

"If she do, she hasn't said."

They heard a commotion down the hall, coming from the library where the social club meeting was being held. They could see women were leaving, saying their heartfelt goodbyes.

When the last woman left, Ethel closed the front door and hurried toward the kitchen. The corners of her mouth rose as her wide smile broadened. "It worked, Katherine! I'm still president!" she screamed, entering the kitchen. But when she saw Johnnie, she said, "What the hell are you doing in my house?"

Chapter 26

"No you're not, Johnnie."

"My house? You mean our house, don't you, Auntie Ethel? Isn't that what you mean?"

"Just who in the hell do you think you are?" Ethel blurted out.

Johnnie looked at Katherine and said, "Tell her, Kathy. I just explained it all to you, and I'm not in the mood to explain it again. I had surgery down there,"—She looked between her legs—"and I'm tired. I need to get home and rest up a bit."

"So who's stopping you?" Ethel shouted, "Get the hell out!"

"Such language. And from the president of the Christian Ladies Social Club no less."

"How do you know about that?"

"I know plenty. Now, where's my good friend Morgan? When did he quit? What did you do to him?"

Ethel silenced herself, thinking about the question, realizing Morgan had at least kept his word so far if Johnnie didn't know where he was either. It became clear suddenly that she needed her niece to like her, at least until everything was settled by Parker Jamieson. "Maybe we should talk in the library. This is a delicate matter."

"You mean alone, like we's family," Johnnie said sarcastically, purposely speaking like an unschooled Negro, just to get under her skin. She knew improperly spoken English irritated her. "Is that what you mean, Auntie Ethel?"

Ethel remained remarkably cool in the face of incredible hubris from the young upstart who sat in her kitchen, talking roughly to her. She acted like she was a police officer who didn't like rich people and gave them a hard time because they had a measure of power to wield. She said, "Would you like something cool to drink and some of Katherine's delicious oatmeal raisin cookies?"

Looking at Katherine, she said, "I sure would. You don't mind, do you, Kathy?" Feeling like she was in complete control of the Beauregard house and everyone in it, Johnnie plunged another dagger into Katherine's heart. "We're going to have it in the library. Just bring it to us in there like the well-trained cook your dear mother raised you to be."

"I heard about what happened to you the other night," Ethel said in a voice full of manufactured compassion. "I'm so sorry for you, dear. Here . . . let me help you to the library." She extended her hand and helped her stand.

Johnnie took her hand and stood up slowly. As they walked toward the hallway leading to the library, they heard a knock on the screen door. They turned to see who it was. It was Sadie.

"Come on in, Sadie," Ethel said. "Have a seat. Johnnie will be ready to go in just a little while. In the meantime, have something to eat while you wait. Katherine will fix you something. Just tell her what you want."

Sadie frowned. *What the hell is going on? She's never been that accommodating.* "Yes, Mrs. Beauregard," she said.

Five minutes later, Johnnie and Ethel entered the library. Ethel helped her ease into a chair at a table. Johnnie remembered seeing Beau and Piper on that table, going at it like two furry carnivores from the weasel family in heat.

"Parker tells me he's spoken to you," Ethel said, awakening Johnnie from the brief interlude her mind had taken her on.

"Yes. He brought me my check. The one my grandfather left me."

"That's what you wanted to talk to me about, I assume. I assure you, dear girl, the check is genuine. You may cash it anytime you like, but it was his hope . . . your Grandpa Nathaniel," Ethel paused briefly to make sure Johnnie heard the acknowledgment of her Beauregard lineage before continuing, "that you'd use the money to go to college. It's entirely up to you, though."

Is she being for real? Why the sudden shift? A month ago, you tried to shoot me in the face, bitch! "Actually, Mrs. Beauregard, it's about the police," she replied, suddenly all business, since her life and livelihood were on the line.

"Oh, yes, I know about that awful Detective Meade and his disgusting insinuations about you murdering Sharon Trudeau and that innocent bellhop in Fort Lauderdale a month or so ago. Parker told me all about it."

"I didn't kill anybody, but the detective thinks I did. If they arrest me, I'll have to tell everything I know, including what *really* happened here on Thanksgiving. I'm not going to jail for something I didn't do."

"Of course you didn't kill anyone, dear. And I'm sure

Parker will do a yeoman's job for you, Johnnie. I'll see to it. After all, we're family."

Johnnie pulled her head back, frowning, unable to believe what she'd just heard, even though she'd heard Ethel's confession to the women of her social club and the reference to Nathaniel as her paternal grandfather. She considered blackmailing Ethel for some more of the Beauregard money she believed she was entitled to, but decided to hold that trump card until later, if she needed it. She didn't trust Ethel's sudden "we are family" attitude. After all, Ethel had tried to kill her. She had pointed a gun at her and fired it, saying, 'You ruined the Beauregard reputation. For that, I'm going to kill you where you stand.'"

"Come in, Katherine," Ethel said after hearing a knock at the door.

Katherine entered the library carrying a silver tray with a pitcher of tea, two glasses filled to the brim with large ice cubes, and oatmeal raisin cookies on it.

"Thank you, Katherine," Ethel said and poured tea over the crackling ice.

When she left, Johnnie picked up her glass, sipped her tea, and said, "Just so there's no misunderstanding between us, if they arrest me, I'm going to tell them why you killed Eric and that you had planned to kill me too."

"No, you're not, Johnnie," Ethel said firmly, realizing she had to put a stop to that kind of thinking instantly. She didn't want Johnnie to even consider that there was a chance she would have to go to jail, let alone be tried and convicted of murdering two white people in a Hilton hotel. "You'll keep your mouth shut until Parker comes and speaks with you. He'll get those ridiculous charges dropped in no time flat. Don't do something we'll both regret. Once you ring the bell of murder, you can't unring it."

Johnnie raised an eyebrow. "I'm supposed to trust *your* lawyer to get *me* out of trouble?"

"He's going to defend you as if he were defending me." Ethel sipped her tea then bit into a cookie. "It's in all our best interests, believe me. According to Parker, they have no case against you. Even if they did arrest you, he says the thing shouldn't even go to trial. But even if it did, he's sure he can win you an acquittal. Can you account for your whereabouts when Sharon was killed if you have to?"

Johnnie thought for a second and said, "Sadie will tell the police we were together?"

Skeptical, Ethel said, "Are you absolutely sure Sadie will *say* you two were together."

Johnnie almost choked on her tea when she heard the hint of mistrust in Ethel's voice. "Why wouldn't she? It's the truth." *I'm not about to tell you we were with Madame DeMille the night Sharon got what was coming to her. I'm not going to jail for getting an abortion either! Do you really think I'd trust you with that kind of information, Auntie Ethel?*

"Okay, then," Ethel said. "If there's nothing further, I've said all I need to say on the matter for now."

"Me too."

Chapter 27

"What is wrong with you?"

Later that night, at exactly ten minutes to ten, Johnnie heard a knock at the back door. Seconds later, she heard the door open and several people come in. It was Sadie and her kids, she knew, because her friend had asked her to keep her children for an hour or so—the first time ever. When she asked Sadie why she needed her to keep her children, she wouldn't tell her, which wounded her since they told each other everything, or so Johnnie thought. She could hear the children talking as they came through the kitchen door and into her living room, where she planned to sleep until her pain from the surgery subsided enough to climb and descend the stairs regularly.

"I'll be back to get them in an hour or two," Sadie said through the open doorway then turned to leave.

"Wait a minute," Johnnie called out. "I wanna talk to you for a second."

"I'm in a hurry, Johnnie. I'll be back soon."

"Sadie, please, come and help me for a second."

By the time Sadie made it to the living room, Johnnie was on her feet, struggling, yet determined to catch her before Sadie left.

"The doctor said you have to take it easy. You don't want to bust your stitches, do you?"

"Can I see your stitches, Aunt Johnnie?" seven-year-old Simone said.

"No, Simone," Sadie answered sternly. "Make sure your brother and sister behave until I come and get you. And don't get on Johnnie's nerves, ya hear?"

"Okay, Mama," Simone said. "Auntie Johnnie, can we watch your new color TV?"

"Sure, go ahead," Johnnie said, smiling.

"Yehhhhh!" Simone chirped and skipped over to the television and turned it on.

Johnnie looked at Sadie. Instead of looking into her eyes, Sadie was looking at the floor.

"What is wrong with you?" Johnnie asked.

"You don't want to know," Sadie said, still looking at the floor.

"Did you and Santino break up or what?"

Full of fiery rage, she said, "If I could, I'd take my children and leave New Orleans tonight. He would never see me again after what he's making me do."

"Help me sit down. I'm tired." Sadie helped her ease in a chair at the table. "Now, help me understand what's going on. If it's money you need, I've got plenty. If Billy Logan hadn't done to me what he did, I might leave with you. Please . . . tell me . . . what's going on? At least tell me how much you need to get out of town."

"Would you really help me leave, Johnnie? I would never

want to take your money. I know what you had to go through to get it, and I know how you made it grow."

"It's no problem. We're practically family. Now, what's going on? What's got you so ashamed you can't even look me in the face?"

Sadie sat down and remained silent for nearly five minutes. She kept shaking her head; tears formed, and she fought them off. She stood up, paced the floor, and eventually closed the door that led to the living room, protecting her children from the wicked truth she was about to divulge. She sat down and looked at her friend again, then looked away before speaking.

"I can't believe I've allowed myself to sink so low that I'm willing to do just about anything Santino wants me to do just to keep a roof over my children's head and food on the table."

"What do you have to do?" Johnnie asked, completely absorbed by what little information she'd received so far.

Still looking at the floor, still hesitating, Sadie said, "Sleep with Detective Meade."

"What?" Johnnie shouted.

At that moment, the Savoy hotel entered Johnnie's mind again. The Savoy was where her mother, Marguerite, was meeting infamous Klan leader, Richard Goode, for kinky sex of the sadomasochistic variety before he killed her.

Johnnie continued, "What does he want you to do to him? I bet it's something really dirty, too, isn't it?"

"I honestly don't know what he wants. What difference does it make? The fact that I've put myself in the position in the first fucking place bothers the hell out of me, Johnnie. If I hadn't settled for the easy life, I wouldn't even be in the shit. Now, I've got three goddamn mouths to feed. I'm totally dependent on him."

"What I don't get is why he's making you do this."

"Because Meade will arrest him for raping you if I don't."

"What?"

"Yes. It's out-fucking-rageous, isn't it? Meade doesn't care who raped you, as long as he gets his piece of brown sugar out of the deal."

"Don't do it, Sadie. I'll take care of you. You're my only friend now with Lucas gone. I don't know if we'll ever get back together either."

"I wish I could say no, but it's bigger than that."

"What do you mean?"

"His family is on the line, Johnnie. If I force the issue, where would that leave me and my children?"

"But I told you I would take care of you."

Desperate, and deeply irritated, Sadie said, "For how long? I'd be switching from one form of dependency to another. What am I going to do if something happens to you or the money you have? What then? I mean, Sharon already stole your money once. I can't depend on that. I'm trapped, Johnnie. Trapped! Don't you see?"

"Maybe you need to do for yourself. I'm not trying to be insensitive, okay? But you once told me I could do something with my life. I think it's time you did something with yours. I think it's time I did something with mine too. I think we both ought to pack our things and move out to San Francisco where Benny is and start all over. You can find a job and a man out there. I say we leave as soon as I'm able to travel, okay? Maybe another month or so? What do you say? Please say yes, okay? Please?"

Sadie quieted herself, thinking very deeply about the matter for a minute or so, and finally said, "Okay. Let's do it."

Bubbling over with joy, Johnnie said, "Good! It's all settled then."

"Not so fast. We have to plan this thing carefully. We know what we're going to do so we tell nobody, Johnnie. I mean no one at all, not even my children, and definitely not Napoleon."

"Why?"

"Johnnie, come on now. Surely you know men don't just let women they love leave them. Please. If they even suspect we're leaving, they'll try and talk us out of it, and you know how persuasive a desperate man can be when he doesn't want to lose his woman."

"You think Napoleon will try and stop me from leaving?"

"He was here that night, wasn't he? The night you were assaulted, right?"

Johnnie nodded.

"He risked taking you to the hospital and everything, which is why I have to go through with what Meade wants. It protects everybody; you, me, our plans, Santino, and Napoleon. The last thing you want to do is put him in a position to have to kill you. Believe me, if he has to, he will."

"I don't understand. How would it put Napoleon in that position?"

"If I don't give Meade what he wants, he arrests Santino."

"So what? He didn't rape me. I'll tell the police that."

A little frustrated, Sadie exhaled before saying, "Johnnie, don't you see? If I don't do this, Meade arrests Santino, and he'll of course say he didn't do it too. He'll have to say what he was doing here and if anybody else was here. He'll say you, me, and Napoleon. And Mob guys can't afford to be in the newspapers. With Napoleon's involvement, don't you know this thing would be huge? It would expose the whole Mafia underworld. The same underworld J. Edgar Hoover says doesn't exist. Then the FBI would have to get involved, just to prove their hands are clean. Do you really *think* the Mafia is going to let itself be exposed because one of its leaders fell in love with a seventeen-year-old Negress? No, they won't. They'll kill us all before they let that happen. So you see, I have to do this now, and we'll leave town when they least expect it, okay? We'll plan it all out later, okay?"

Johnnie smiled, admiring her friend's sagacious mind.

Someone knocked hard on the back door.

"Are you expecting anybody?" Sadie asked.

"No, but it's probably Napoleon sneaking over."

They laughed.

"I'll see if it's him," Sadie said and went to the door. She pushed the curtain aside and saw Detective Meade.

"Let's go," he demanded.

Sadie opened the door.

Meade said, "I hope you know how to suck cock." Then he snatched her out of the house like he owned her—and he did, for the night anyway.

Chapter 28

"You're free now."

After Sadie downed two shots of scotch, they went upstairs to her bedroom and undressed. Seeing Sadie's tears didn't bother Meade one bit. He had come to Ashland Estates to get laid by one of the fancy Negro women he'd heard about all his life, and that's exactly what he was going to get—laid—several times. The women who lived in Ashland Estates were regularly talked about in the police station he worked in. Now he had brokered a deal to try one out.

Meade sat on the edge of the bed, his erection tall, pointing northward.

Sadie stood before him, completely nude, yet covering herself, humiliated beyond measure, thoroughly ashamed, feeling like a slave girl who had to bend to her master's will, indulging his debauched mind.

When Meade heard her sniff, he became angry. He stood up, slapped her, and yelled, "Dry up! You oughta be used to this by now. Now get tuh suckin'! I've been dreamin' about this for half my life." He ran his eyes over her marvelously sculpted body, taking in the rich mahogany, seeing how truly flawless it was. His eyes slowly rose to her face and penetrated her soft eyes. "Um, you sure are a pretty thang. Not as good-looking as your friend next door, but you'll do for my purposes tonight. Too bad she had that surgery. I would've fucked her instead of you."

Slowly, reluctantly, Sadie got down on her knees and did what she was told, silently weeping, fearing he would beat her if he heard her useless lamentations. Afterward, when he was satisfied, he threw her on the bed like she was his vassal to do with as he willed, and climbed on top of her wantonly, recklessly. She was dry, but that didn't stop him. He just forced the tip in and rammed in the rest.

She wanted to cry out, but clamped her mouth shut when she felt his long, burgeoning tool plow through her closed sheath, breaking and entering her store, committing grand larceny, taking her best goods and services, forcing her to participate in the theft of them.

His was mind full of depraved yearnings as he pumped her hard until she began to lubricate. But Sadie was there in body only, lying there, vacant, yet the tears still dripped from the corners of her eyes. She suffered silently to avoid any further blows for having the nerve to be emotional about what she thought was the equivalent of rape.

Suddenly he was angry again. "Pump, bitch! I thought all you nigger whores knew how tuh fuck! Pump, goddamn you, pump!"

As ordered, she pumped him. And then a strange thing happened. She began to feel pleasure, and she didn't want to, not with this animal, not with any man who would stoop so low, but God help her, she did. A few minutes after she began to pump him like he had ordered, they found a rhythm they both enjoyed and they went at it savagely, howling in each other's ears like they were madly in love, when nothing could be further from the truth. Their thrusts were so violent that the headboard threatened to punch a hole in the wall. This went on for a couple of hours, both of them releasing several times during the intense romp.

When they finally finished, Meade dressed and prepared to leave. He was planning to return to the house he lived in with his mother. Feeling good about himself, Meade looked at her and said, "Am I as good as a nigger stud?"

That's when Sadie lost it and began to cry again. She covered her face with both hands, weeping uncontrollably because her answer was "Yes." But she didn't answer his question. She didn't want to tell the white man who had, for all intents and purposes, raped her that it was the best sex she had ever had, but it was true. God help her. It was true.

Shaking his head, believing that she was crying because of what he made her do, he said, "Fuck it! I did the best I could. I just wanted you to enjoy it too." Then he left her home hurriedly, like there was an emergency at the police station.

It took a half-hour to regain her composure; another twenty minutes before she could stop the tears from flowing. She took a long, hot bath, attempting to get the smell of him off her before going over to Johnnie's place to get her children. She figured her children were asleep by now, having no idea what their mother had to endure to make sure they were properly cared for by the man who helped create them. She had to be strong; she had to show Johnnie that what Meade had done to her was next to nothing, so she wouldn't feel like it was her fault. Sadie knew that if she presented the right face, her friend would assume that she was okay with what happened and that everyone was safe.

Sadie saw Johnnie through the glass. She had moved the curtains when Detective Meade came over. She could have walked in, but courtesy demanded that she knock.

Johnnie was sitting at the kitchen table, waiting for her, having heard Meade start his car and leave. "It's open."

Sadie walked in, forced a smiled and said, "Hey, keep this door locked at all times!"

Johnnie knew why she had made the comment, but said nothing.

"Are the kids asleep?"

"Yeah."

"Okay, I'll wake them up and take them home. I appreciate you taking care of them on such short notice."

"My pleasure," Johnnie said. She pushed a brown paper bag forward. "This is for you."

Sadie grabbed the bag. "What's in here? Cookies for the children?"

Johnnie remained quiet, staring into her soft eyes, offering an unrestrained smile that seemed to glow.

"Girl, what is this?" Sadie opened the bag and her mouth fell open when she saw all the money. "How much is this?"

"Fifty thousand," Johnnie said, beaming. "Now you won't have to worry for at least five years, and if you invest it right, you might be able to turn it into a million eventually."

Overwhelmed, the tears returned, sliding down Sadie's smooth, dark skin. "I can't take your money, sweetie."

"Yes, you can. You're free now. You can leave anytime you want now, Sadie. Be happy and use it wisely."

"Are you sure?"

"Quite sure."

The two women hugged each other and held on tight.

Johnnie pulled back and looked her in the eyes. "Pour yourself a cup of coffee and let's plan our escape from New Orleans!"

Chapter 29

"What did I do?"

The same night Sadie gave in to the demands of Detective Meade, Bubbles and several of the boys who worked for him at the Bayou were in Napoleon's old office, playing Five Card Stud when Billy Logan walked in. They had been waiting for him. It was time to dispense a bit of underworld justice; only Billy didn't know it. All Billy knew was that he had been promoted to Lucas' old position. He was making good money, and now he had been invited to play cards with the inner circle.

Like nearly everyone else in the parish, he had heard about the article in the *Sentinel*. He paid strict attention to what people were saying about the rape he had committed. At first, he was afraid the police would come and arrest him, but when a couple of days passed with no one even questioning his involvement, he grew less and less afraid. At first he believed he'd gotten away with it. During the brief time that passed, he convinced himself that he hadn't raped at all. She had wanted what he gave her. She enjoyed what he gave her. That's why she didn't tell the police. That's why he hadn't been arrested.

"Take a seat, Logan," Bubbles said. "Have you eaten, kid?"

He sat down in the empty seat eagerly. "No, sir."

Bubbles poured a shot of 80 proof Jack Daniels into a shot glass and slid it to him. "Have a drink." He looked at Fort Knox, the man who had been the MC the night Johnnie sang in the Bayou. He had gold for teeth. "Get the kid a nice juicy steak and a baked potato." He looked at Logan. "You like candied yams?"

Billy downed the shot, snarled, shook his head as the heat of the drink burned his insides. In a scratchy voice, he said, "Yeah, man. I love 'em."

"Good. You got all that, Fort Knox?"

"Got it," he said and left. He waited outside the door for what he thought was sufficient time to pass, and then reopened the door and returned to his seat. "The cook said it'll be about forty-five minutes, Billy. Can you wait that long?"

"Yeah, man. No problem." He looked at Bubbles. "Oh, here you go." He handed him a yellow envelope full of money.

"Do you know how to hold your liquor, Logan?" Bubbles said, poured him another shot and watched him drink it.

Feeling like he had to prove he was as much a man as they were, Billy said, "Yes," knowing full well that he had just had his first couple of drinks.

Bubbles poured a couple more shots and watched him drink those too. One hour later, Billy's eyes were glassy, and he became talkative as they let him win, keeping him happy, keeping him relaxed and unsuspecting. Bubbles looked at Fort Knox, nodded slightly, signaling him to start the charade.

"Hey, Bubbles, my man, you still seein' Lee Shepard?"

"Yeah, why?" Bubbles said, playing along.

"No disrespect, man, but can I ask you a question?"

"Yeah, man, shoot."

"Lee Shepard is fine as hell, but um, how is she in bed? Do she know how to put it on you, or what?"

"Hell yeah! But she likes to play these games, ya know?"

"What do you mean?" Billy asked.

Fort Knox and Bubbles looked at each other, believing they had him right where they wanted him.

"She likes me to pretend like I'm a burglar and sneak into her house late at night. She discovers I'm there, and then I rape her."

Glassy-eyed, Billy said, "She wants you to rape her?"

"Yeah, but don't tell nobody I told you that shit. I don't want people thinkin' she's a nut, you know what I mean?"

"Yeah, man. I understand." Billy thought for a moment. "You think other women like that too, you know, want a man to break in and rape 'em?"

Fort Knox and Bubbles looked at each other and then at the other two men sitting at the table.

"Yeah, man," Fort Knox said. "I know women who like that shit."

The other two men agreed, saying, "Me too."

Bubbles looked at Billy. "So tell me, you ever been with a woman?"

"Yeah, man."

Fort Knox laughed. "Stop lyin'! You ain't never been with a woman, boy, please."

"Yes, I have," Billy said defiantly as he listened to the men laugh at him.

"Who?" Bubbles asked. "Anybody we know?"

"Yeah, as a matter of fact!"

"Who?" Fort Knox asked.

"You know who, Bubbles. I told you I was gon' fuck Johnnie over a month ago in this office."

The men stopped laughing.

"Wait a minute, man," Bubbles began. "The papers say Johnnie was raped. Was she raped or not?"

"Man, that bitch wasn't raped. I went over there a couple nights ago and we got tuh fuckin', man. Same as you and Lee Shepard."

The men looked at each other, their faces indefinable, no laughter, no smiles.

"Johnnie's a beautiful girl. And let's face it, you ain't the best looking man in New Orleans. Hell, you ain't even the best lookin' man in this room. So how were you able to get her to give it up?"

"I may not be that good-looking, but hey, she wanted me, man."

"Bullshit. Johnnie could have any man she wanted. Why the fuck would she choose you?"

"She told me that it turned her on when I kicked Lucas' ass at Walter Brickman's, so I went over, and she wanted to play that game Lee Shepard likes to play."

Bubbles said, "What game? Tell us about it."

"Okay, so I knock on her door, and right away, she starts the burglar game. So I kicked in the door and we got tuh tusslin' up in there. She grabbed a knife and told me she was gon' cut me every way but loose."

The men looked at each other.

"So I knocked the knife outta her hand and slapped her a

few times, dazed her a bit. Then she told me to lick her nipples. I said okay, and then I stuck it in her. We did it three times, man. It was great."

"Logan," Bubbles said, "you just described a rape."

"Naw, man. She wanted it."

"That's why she ended up in the fuckin' hospital? That's why she had to have emergency surgery on her pussy, man? Because she wanted it?"

"I got'a big dick, man! What can I say?" He laughed.

"And you think this shit is funny?" Bubbles backhanded him. "Lock the door, Fort Knox. We gon' kill this muthafucka right now!"

"Why, man? I didn't know nothin'."

"Johnnie is a friend of ours, fool!" Bubbles said. "And you raped her? We gon' kill you for that shit."

After they took turns with their fists, they took Billy Logan out back and beat him mercilessly with bats. As they beat him, he kept repeating, "What did I do?"

Chapter 30
Day 4

"A grand jury?"

Johnnie was in a deep, satisfying sleep when she heard loud knocking on her front door. *Bam! Bam! Bam!* She opened her eyes, looked around, and seeing her living room, realized where she was—on her couch. She closed her eyes again, planning to sleep a little longer, thinking the knocking was part of a dream. *Bam! Bam! Bam!* She opened her eyes again and yelled out, "Who is it?"

"It's Sheriff Paul Tate, Johnnie. I need to talk to you." Sheriff Tate was almost like family. He had been in love with Marguerite until the day Richard Goode blew her brains out.

Johnnie looked at the clock sitting on the fireplace mantle. It was nine in the morning. She and Sadie stayed up talking, planning their clandestine escape until four in the morning.

"Just a minute, Sheriff, okay? Let me get something on."

"Take your time."

A few minutes later, after cleaning up in her bathroom, she opened the door and let the beer guzzling peace officer in. She smelled whatever brand he drank before knocking on her door as he entered her home.

"What's this all about, Sheriff?"

"There's a storm comin' your way and it ain't gonna be pretty. Trouble's been brewing for three days now, ever since that damn article appeared in the *Sentinel*. That article done stirred up all kinds of trouble, legal and otherwise. I hoped that after a few days, people would move on, but they haven't. The white folks in the city are mad as hell at you. I'm afraid for your life."

"At me? For what? I didn't do anything, Sheriff. What's going on?"

"First let me say how sorry I am about what happened to you the other day. I wouldn't wish that on my worst enemy. But I gotta tell ya, Johnnie, you're in serious trouble." He handed her an official document.

Frowning, Johnnie said, "What's this?"

"A subpoena."

He handed it to her.

"A sub what?" she said, looking at the document.

It read: *YOU ARE HEREBY COMMANDED to appear and testify before the Grand Jury of the United States District Court at the place, date, and time specified below. YOU ARE ALSO COMMANDED to bring all documents, and correspondence having to do with Glenn and Webster Financial Services.*

"It's a legal document that says you must appear before a grand jury."

"A grand jury? Is that like a regular jury or something? I don't know what you mean, Sheriff.

"No, not at all. In some ways this is worse because they can investigate you. They can ask you anything they want. They can bring in witnesses and compel them to testify against you. The thing that makes them so dangerous is that they're not bound by evidentiary and constitutional restrictions. And you don't get to have a lawyer present to help you."

"What? No lawyer? Is that even legal, Sheriff?"

"Unfortunately for you, yes, it's legal."

"Well, what's this all about, Sheriff? Me being raped? They wanna know who raped me? Is that it?"

"I wish it were that simple, Johnnie. This is about something far more dangerous. This is about the Sharon Trudeau murder. The mayor read that article in the *Sentinel* the other day, and he near 'bout lost his mind. I'm surprised he didn't have you arrested while you were in the hospital."

"Why? Because they think I killed Sharon?"

"Yes, but the district attorney told him he needed evidence."

Knowing she had an ironclad alibi, she forcefully asked, "What possible evidence could they have, Sheriff?"

Sheriff Tate lowered his head and exhaled before saying, "It's like the *Sentinel* said. The amount of money still missing is the two hundred and fifty thousand you lost. The documents were in one of Sharon's suitcases."

"But that doesn't mean I killed her, Sheriff!"

"I know, but that article done stirred up a hornet's nest."

"I'm callin' my lawyer, Sheriff!"

"That's a good idea, honey. That's a damn good idea."

Johnnie picked up the phone and called Parker Jamieson's office. "This is Johnnie Wise. May I speak to Parker Jamieson, please? Yes, I'll hold." She put her hand over the transmitter.

"This is so crazy, Sheriff. I didn't do—Mr. Jamieson? I've been subpoenaed by the grand jury for the murder of Sharon Trudeau. They say I can't have a lawyer in there with me. Is that right?"

Sheriff Tate stood there listening as they talked.

"Yes, it is," Parker said. "But you can still take the Fifth Amendment. You don't have to incriminate yourself."

"Will they let me go if I don't say anything?"

"In all likelihood, no. They'll put you in jail for an undetermined amount of time to try and get you to talk. When do you have to appear?"

She looked at the subpoena. "In two hours. What are you going to do? I told you I'm not going to jail over this."

"Johnnie, are you alone?"

"No, Sheriff Tate is here with me."

"Be careful what you say to and around the sheriff. He can be compelled to testify against you too. And you've already said way too much. If he puts together what you just said, it could damage our case to free you."

She flashed her eyes at Sheriff Tate for a fleeting second, and then said, "What am I supposed to do then? I don't wanna go to jail."

"I'll meet you at the courthouse. What we want them to do is indict you."

"Indict me?"

"You know, charge you with Sharon's murder. I'll get them to set bail and get you out. Don't worry, I'll get you out. I promise."

"Don't they have to have some evidence or something?"

"No, they don't."

"That ain't right!"

"I know, but it's the law. The district attorney can ask you anything, but say nothing and take no documents with you. I'll be there, but I can't come in with you. If you have a question, you come out and ask me before you say one word, understand?"

"Yes. Don't say anything without speaking to you first."

Part 3

Ill Gotten Gains

Chapter 31

Fond Memories of Sharon Trudeau

Three hours later, after being grilled by the grand jury for thirty minutes, Sheriff Tate arrested Johnnie for the murder of Sharon Trudeau. On the advice of Parker Jamieson, she refused to answer all their questions, forcing them to take action against her, fearing that another blistering article would appear in the *Sentinel* if they let her go due to insufficient evidence. Sheriff Tate personally escorted her to jail. He wanted to make sure nothing happened to her, given the building volatile situation. The fears of whites were being realized. They believed that if they didn't do something about Johnnie, other Negroes would think they could kill Whites too. There had been plenty of talk about Whites being murdered ever since Colored and white men successfully defended Baroque Parish on an extremely hot night during the past summer.

When the *Sentinel* learned that the grand jury had indicted seventeen-year-old Johnnie Wise for murdering her white female stockbroker and an unsuspecting bellhop, they blew the story up bigger than before, using their own articles as sources, as if the words came from the mouth of God. Pictures of Sharon Trudeau made the front page, and suddenly her crimes against Whites were forgotten. They resuscitated Sharon to the point that the white citizenry of New Orleans only talked about how beautiful she was. They even conjured up a cocaine habit that she didn't have and then named Lucas Matthews as the supplier for her fictional addiction. Sensationalism was the order of the day, and it whipped Whites into a frenzy.

Sheriff Tate knew what was brewing and decided to get some help to protect Johnnie, just in case things got out of control. He'd overheard the men talking about lynching her the previous night while he was out on patrol. The more the men drank, the more they talked about Sharon Trudeau like she was Helen of Troy and not the woman who'd stolen nearly a million dollars from them. Soon the men began to make up stories about Sharon saving kitten from trees, buying poor children ice cream, and visiting aged widows. The liquor made their tall tales detailed and authentic. Two men actually fought over her, both of them declaring Sharon to be their first love. Truth be told, Sharon Trudeau never dated either man. She didn't even know who they were.

Tate promised Johnnie he'd return as soon as possible. He believed she'd be safe alone in broad daylight. Lynching generally occurred at night, so he felt comfortable leaving her. He didn't have the heart to tell her that in addition to recruiting more men to protect her, he was also issued a court order to search her home and car to find the missing two hundred and fifty thousand. He didn't want to do it, but it was his job.

Sheriff Tate had sat in his squad car and watched a murder unfold the night Marguerite met with Richard Goode to collect her blackmail money. Cowardice demanded that he watch Goode beat the woman he loved. He watched him kick her like she was an animal. He watched Goode put a gun to her forehead and blow her brains out. Guilt ridden, Tate knew he was culpable for everything that was happening at present. He knew that if he'd had a morsel of courage, he could have stopped Goode from killing Marguerite. Had he done what he was sworn to do, Napoleon would not have killed Goode. Richard Goode's death is what started it all. The riot would not have happened and Johnnie wouldn't be sitting in his jail cell.

Even when he slept, he dreamed about it. Night after night, he relived the murder, seeing himself sit there like the cowardly lion from *The Wizard of Oz*, having the strength to stop it, but lacking the intestinal fortitude to act upon his convictions. But this time things would be different. This time he'd do for Johnnie what he was too weak to do for her mother. He owed it to Marguerite's memory, which was why he personally delivered the subpoena himself and conducted the search of her premises.

Chapter 32

Eventually I want to be a wife

In her cell all alone with nothing to do except think, Johnnie lay on her cot quietly, wondering why God kept ruining her life. She wondered why he couldn't leave her alone, why he had to continuously keep all kinds of drama going on. She had forgotten that she was in charge of her life. She had forgotten that she made her own decisions. She had conveniently forgotten that her mother, at the Savoy hotel, had told her that if she wanted to be an Evangelist, she could still be one. She had dismissed Sadie's sisterly advice and continued down a dark path that led to unwanted pregnancy, and brought her to the cell she now occupied.

In spite of the subpoena, in spite of the rape she'd suffered, in spite of all that had befallen her, she had survived someway, somehow, and for that reason, she wasn't worried because with every trial, God had offered her a way of escape. In this case, she believed Parker Jamieson would get her out of the latest drama she had created. After all, he promised. Getting arrested was all a part of his plan, she remembered. As a matter of fact, Parker was arguing her case at that very moment, getting a reasonable bail set so she wouldn't have to spend a single night in Sheriff Tate's jail, which only had two cells.

I am so glad me and Sadie are getting out of here. This is the last straw! I've had enough! I've had nothing but bad luck in this city. Maybe this is all a blessing in disguise. I'm definitely getting out of town after this one. I can't wait to see Benny, Brenda, and my little nephew, Jericho. I bet he's gotten so much bigger since they came to New Orleans.

I guess I might as well forget about Lucas like he asked me to. I really miss him and could use his company now. I could always depend on him, no matter what. Now even he's done with me. I wonder if Marla is still trying to communicate with him. I wonder if she writes him. I bet she does. She wouldn't give up that easily, especially since she's about to get a divorce. Maybe that's the real reason he dumped me on Christmas Day! Maybe she has wormed her way back into his life.

I was so proud of Lucas when he told me he had given her up, even though she was lying in his bed, naked. She tried her best to take my man from me. She told him everything Napoleon did to me, to make me want to do it again with him. But he chose me over her. Maybe I shouldn't let him go so easily. What can I have with Napoleon besides sex? Eventually I want to be a wife—a good one, and have some children. I prefer to have them with Lucas. That way, if we have boys, they'll be big and tall and strong like him. If we have girls, they'll be pretty like me and smart as a whip. No, I'm not giving up on my man. No, not. Not ever. We're going to be joined at the hip and leave all this craziness behind. I'm sure of it!

Suddenly, she heard the click-click-click-click of high heels coming toward her.

Johnnie turned her head to see who was coming toward her cell.

It was Earl Shamus' wife, Meredith.

Chapter 33

"They're not going to believe that, Mrs. Shamus."

Five days ago, on Christmas Eve, Meredith Shamus had sat in her turquoise Cadillac and watched Earl come out of his former mistress' home, a house he bought for her with money he embezzled from Meredith's deceased father's insurance company. She suspected that Earl was up to something when he made the plausible excuse to leave their home, telling her he'd forgotten a present he had purchased for her at the office. Meredith followed her wayward husband downtown to the tall Buchanan Insurance building, where he went in and came back out in no more than five minutes. She was relieved to learn that he *really* had forgotten the present.

But relief turned into curiosity when, on the way home, Earl detoured toward Baroque Parish. That could only mean one thing as far as Meredith was concerned: Earl was going to see Johnnie Wise again. When Earl turned onto Vision Drive and pulled into Johnnie's driveway, Meredith's suspicions became an all too familiar reality. She started to pull off and go on home, but her curiosity got the better of her, and so she sat behind the wheel and waited, hoping he wouldn't be in there long. If he only stayed a moment or two, she would have reasoned he was only there to finally confront Johnnie about her betrayal with his best friend and stockbroker, Martin Winters. After all, he didn't take the present in the house with him.

She watched Earl get out of his car and approach the house she had confronted Johnnie in a few months earlier. The memory of confidently entering the modest dwelling and telling the young temptress that she knew all about the illicit affair and the cold-blooded murder of her mother flooded her consciousness and awakened her jealous, vengeful mind. She had told Johnnie she didn't want Earl and the Shamus family name involved. She had paid handsomely for Johnnie's silence. She had even given Johnnie excellent advice, telling her to take some of the money she'd given her and educate herself.

Ever since that day, Meredith wondered what Johnnie had been doing. She kept Tony Hatcher, her private detective, on retainer. He had been watching Johnnie since August to ensure the dalliance was over. Earl and Johnnie hadn't seen each other since the day Meredith paid Johnnie a visit and initiated a power play that was supposed to put an end to the affair permanently. But on Christmas Eve, her husband was back at her house again. She also learned from Hatcher that Johnnie was leading a tremendously risky lifestyle. Not only was Hatcher following Johnnie daily, he had wired her house and telephone, and had recordings of everything. He knew about the affair with Napoleon, the relationship Lucas was having with Marla, the Sharon Trudeau murder, the Las Vegas trip, Lucas' involvement with drugs and his subsequent arrest, his deal to go into the Army, Napoleon's plan to take over New Orleans, the abortion, and what really happened at the Beauregard mansion that infamous Thanksgiving Day. Meredith had listened to every single word.

Less than ten minutes after Earl entered Johnnie's home, Meredith saw Earl coming out of the house. She watched him turn around to say something to the young woman, but she slammed the door in his face. At first Meredith felt a sense of relief, believing that Johnnie was merely keeping the agreement for which she had been paid fifty thousand dollars. As far as Meredith was concerned, if the sexual relationship ended, the woman had to end it, otherwise, the man would keep being led by the flesh below his waist forever.

However, when she saw a pathetic Earl standing on his former mistress porch, staring at the door, weeping, his shoulders hunching uncontrollably as he wept, her jealousy turned into a blazing inferno. She started her Cadillac and headed home. On the way, she thought about the riots and remembered that it was a distinct possibility that Johnnie had known all along that Earl had nothing to do with her mother's murder. She began to believe that Johnnie had duped her out of the money she offered for her silence. The tapes Hatcher had given her offered irrefutable proof that her theory had been sound. Guided skillfully by a cauldron of heated jealousy, she was now implementing an idea to exact a measure of revenge.

"Hello, Johnnie," Meredith said in a well-defined, well-educated tone.

Shocked to see her, Johnnie nervously said, "What are you doing here, Mrs. Shamus?"

"I'm here to protect my investment," Meredith said matter-of-factly.

Frowning, Johnnie said, "What do you mean?"

"Why, that fifty thousand I paid you to keep our family name out of your business. Now . . . you do plan to keep our agreement, yes?"

Johnnie thought for a brief moment before saying, "They arrested me for a murder I didn't commit. Why do you think your family name will come up at all?"

"You never know with these matters. If you have to take the witness stand, the district attorney may ask you where you got your money to invest with Sharon in the first place."

"And you don't want me to say where the money came from, huh?"

"That's was our agreement, was it not?"

Flippantly, Johnnie said, "I don't think it will even get that far, but if it does, I'm telling you now, I'll try and keep your names out of it, but I'm not going to jail for something I didn't do. If the truth comes out, hey, it comes out."

"Just so you know, I'm not the only one who has something to hide. Keep your mouth shut about where you got that money. If you don't, and I get called to the stand, I'll do some talking too. And believe me . . . I have quite a bit to talk about. When I'm done telling all your secrets, who do you think they're going to believe; a rich white woman who's never had any trouble with the law or a Negress being tried for murder, whose pedigree is rife with whores?"

Rattled by the threats she'd heard, Johnnie began to understand just how dangerous her situation was. Until now, all the lying and conniving she'd done were a game that she had been winning. Men had used her body, and for that privilege, she had gotten seriously paid. This seemed fair to her because she had learned to use others just as she had been used. But it all became surreal the moment Sheriff Tate arrested her for murder. Besides, Meredith was right, she knew, because this wouldn't be the first time a Negro had been arrested for someone else's crime.

She looked at Meredith and said, "What am I supposed to say if for some reason it does go to trial?"

"Johnnie, believe me, this is going to trial. You're probably the only person in the country who doesn't know it. Since that article appeared in the *Sentinel* a couple days ago, all hell has broken loose. If your arrest hits the news wire services, this trial, the one you don't think is going to happen, will be covered by every newspaper from New York to Los Angeles. You're going to be famous. Or should I say *infamous*?"

Johnnie stood up and began to pace the cell floor, suddenly serious, suddenly scared beyond measure. She remembered what Sadie said about the Mafia and how they would never allow their underworld activities to surface. She knew she could be killed if it did go to trial, if Meredith was telling the truth about the trial being covered nationally.

Meredith watched Johnnie's defiance turn into horror instantly. Smiling within, she savored every moment of it. She wouldn't miss a minute of this, which is why she took the chance to speak to Johnnie face to face. She wanted to see her fear of going to prison for the rest of her life; smell the fear, too, if it were possible. *That's right, squirm, you black bitch! Squirm!*

"If I say you loaned the money to me, would you say the same thing on the witness stand? That way we protect each other."

"Why would I loan you fifty thousand dollars, Johnnie? Who's going to believe that? I'm a businesswoman. Wouldn't I have loan papers?"

After hearing that, Johnnie paced faster. Everything was happening so fast, incredibly fast.

"I'll tell you what, Johnnie . . . let's tell them I gave you extra money when Buchanan Mutual paid off your mother's insurance policy. Let's tell them that I felt sorry for you because you had no other family in New Orleans. That's what we'll say if you have to take the stand, okay?"

"They're not going to believe that, Mrs. Shamus."

"They don't have to. If we say the same thing, who can prove otherwise? Now, I have to go before the sheriff gets back. If he sees me here, he could testify that he saw us talking, and they would have reason not to believe us, deal?"

"Deal."

Meredith triumphantly walked out of the city jail, knowing she wasn't going to keep her end of the bargain if she was called to the stand. She was going to bury Johnnie; jealousy demanded it.

Chapter 34

The same day, somewhere in Manhattan

"What's so fuckin' important I gotta come all the way to New York, Joe?" Chicago Sam demanded as he walked into the room full of Mob bosses.

Calmly, Joe Russo, Kingpin of New York, said, "I got a package from our FBI stooge. He says Hoover expects us to handle this situation immediately or he'll have to. He says if he has to handle it, he'll have to handle everybody—personally."

Murmuring filled the room.

"Pipe down," Sam yelled.

The bosses quieted themselves.

"Now . . . what's in the package?" Sam asked Russo.

"Tapes and photographs of Napoleon Bentley," Russo said. "We're gonna have to whack him."

Russo walked over to the stereo system, hit a button, and the reel to reel began playing the conversation of a man and woman talking about doing nasty things to each other.

The man was talking. "I enjoyed licking you down there."

"So you did get something out of it, huh?"

"Well, to be honest, I'd much rather give than receive. It's more blessed, they say."

Frank De Luca, Boss of Kansas City, said, "I'd know Bentley's voice anywhere. Who's the broad?"

"It's the nigger broad," Russo said and passed out the photographs of Johnnie. "I tell ya, this fuckin' guy has gone ape shit over her. The cocksucker is eatin' the broad's snatch for Christ's sake! Listen to this shit!"

Upon seeing the pictures, one by one, all the bosses made lewd remarks about Johnnie and what they wanted to do to her.

"No way this broad's seventeen," one boss said.

"Look at the knockers on her," said another.

"No wonder Bentley didn't want to give it up. I wouldn't want to either."

"I want to hear it now," Johnnie was saying.

"Right now?" Napoleon asked.

"Right now."

"Are you wet?"

"Very."

The bosses laughed hysterically.

"So what?" Sam said. "He's fuckin' a nigger. Who hasn't? And which one of you cocksuckers wouldn't ride her into the sunset?"

Russo said, "It's bigger than fuckin' the spade, Sam. This is the broad all the papers are talking about. All of our livelihoods are on the line now. The girl is gonna be tried for killing the stockbroker."

"So what?" Sam said again. "It's her neck on the line. Hers and Bentley's. She knows nothing about this thing of ours, and Bentley knows to keep his fuckin' mouth shut."

"Do we know for sure that Bentley killed Trudeau?" Sam asked.

"Christ, Sam! How much fuckin' evidence do you need?" Russo asked rhetorically. "Bentley's fuckin' the black broad. Her money is stolen by Trudeau. Trudeau is hit, not killed in the heat of passion; she's hit professionally, Sam. Now, I ask you, who would have the juice to track her down, pop her and the bellhop, take the money, and not leave a trail a blind man could follow? Bentley, that's who. What's the matter, Sam? Afraid you're gonna lose your cut if we take Bentley out?"

The bosses murmured and nodded in agreement.

Sam practically leapt out of his skin. "Which one of you bastards would give up your end so easily? Which one of you would give up your skim of the Las Vegas casinos if the same thing happened to you? I don't think you'd so easily give up your share."

"Look at the fuckin' photographs, Sam," one of the bosses said, sliding him a photo. "What is Bentley doing sitting in a nigger café with his button man, Bubbles? Did he or did he not agree to keep those people out of our thing? Look at this one, Sam." He slid him another photo. "Isn't that Bentley putting the Colored girl in his car? Here's another one of him carrying her into the Colored hospital. Look at this one. He's going to the hospital to visit the broad every fuckin' night. The cocksucker must have steel for balls. What more do you need, Sam? We oughta kill 'im for eatin' pussy alone, if you ask me!"

"Why risk it all, Sam?" De Luca asked. "Besides, Bentley was stupid enough to discuss the murder of the Trudeau woman and the Klansman with the spade on the fuckin' phone. If he's stupid enough to do that, who knows? He could talk to the cops about us. I say we put it to a vote."

The bosses nodded in agreement. Each man cast his vote, and by the time they had finished, Sam was out-voted. Bentley was marked for death.

Russo said, "Then it's all settled. We take Bentley out. But we gotta get that big nigger first."

They then decided how and when it would be done.

Chapter 35

New Orleans, later that night.

"Good evening, Sheriff," a well-dressed man began. "I'm Jay Goldstein, and these are my associates." He gestured in their direction, but made no introductions.

"Goldstein? What are you, one of them there Jews? My daddy fought in WWII. And—"

The astute attorney cut him off. "By the way, Sheriff, I think it was smart of you to deputize men of color to protect Miss Wise. I think there's going to be trouble. We overheard some townsmen threatening to come over here and dispense justice the old fashioned way."

Frowning, Sheriff Tate said, "I figured as much. What did you say your name was again?"

"Jay Goldstein. I'm an attorney from Chicago. We're here to see Johnnie Wise."

"Does she know you're comin'?"

"No, but trust me, she's going to want to see us."

Tate looked toward the cell she was in and said, "Johnnie, you wanna see these people?"

"No harm in hearing what they have to say, Sheriff."

Tate opened a drawer and took out a set of skeleton keys. "Right this way. I sure hope you can help her. I knew her mother. Been knowin' Johnnie since she was born—her brother, too."

They all walked over to her cell. The iron door creaked when the Sheriff swung it open. They all went in.

Goldstein offered his hand. "I'm Jay, and these are my associates, Dee Dee Wellington and Cleo Steele."

Johnnie looked at the Colored woman and skeptically said, "You're a lawyer?"

"Yes," Cleo said, smiling, knowing exactly what the young woman was thinking. "I'm a real lawyer, Johnnie. Jay and Dee Dee are my friends. We're going to represent you if you don't have a lawyer."

"I have a lawyer, but he hasn't been in to see me since they locked me up at twelve this afternoon."

The attorneys looked at each other, subtly shaking their heads in disbelief.

Sheriff Tate, who was standing there the entire time, said, "She's got the same lawyer as Ethel Beauregard. Name's Parker Jamieson. He's the best in New Orleans."

"I'm sure he is," Goldstein said, looking at Johnnie, "but I have to question how he could defend you when he has a client we may have to cross examine. It's a conflict of interest. And the fact that he hasn't been here today tells me he's probably been preparing Ethel Beauregard just in case we have to put her on the stand. You need your own attorney, Johnnie. Someone who's going to look out for your best interests."

Johnnie looked at Cleo as if she needed her to approve, even though she had just met her too. Cleo nodded. Being a Negro, she knew Johnnie needed another black face to agree.

"Who hired you, Mr. Goldstein?" Johnnie asked.

"Our client, your benefactor, prefers to remain anonymous," Goldstein replied.

Johnnie smiled, knowing in her heart that Napoleon had arranged it all. If Napoleon was in on it, she knew to stop asking questions and to accept the gift being offered. "Anonymous, huh? Okay, Mr. Goldstein. You don't have to tell me who hired you, but I know who he is. I also know you guys know what you're doing, too."

While Johnnie was still speaking, the door opened and Parker Jamieson came in. When he saw the people in the cell were wearing business attire and holding briefcases, he knew they were attorneys trying to move in on his client. He fast-walked over to the cell and said, "I'm Parker Jamieson, Miss Wise's attorney. I'll thank you all to leave me and my client alone."

"Where have you been, Mr. Jamieson?" Johnnie demanded. "You told me I wouldn't have to spend a day in jail. It's dark out now."

"I tried to get the judge to grant you bail, but he considers you a flight risk."

"Based on what?" Goldstein asked.

"The girl's got two hundred and fifty thousand dollars. She can get lost for a very long time with that kind of money. I did the best I could."

"I'll just bet you did," Goldstein said, frowning. "Where is this alleged money, Jamieson? Have you even seen it?"

"No, but—"

Goldstein looked at Johnnie. "Did you tell him you had the money?"

"No, sir."

He looked at Sheriff Tate. "Did you search her house and car?"

"Yeah, but I didn't find any money, if that's where you're going."

Goldstein looked at Johnnie. "Do you have that much money in your bank account?"

"No, sir."

He looked at Jamieson again. "What two hundred and fifty thousand dollars are you talking about, counselor? You mean the missing money that Sheriff Tate hasn't found yet? For all we know, Sharon Trudeau's killer has the money and is long gone by now."

Jamieson looked at Johnnie. "Tell these people you prefer me as your attorney, so they can leave us alone to discuss your plea."

"The plea is not guilty, counselor," Dee Dee said. "This girl didn't kill anyone and you know it, don't you?"

"Of course she didn't," Jamieson said.

"Then why don't you act like it?" Dee Dee demanded.

Cleo said, "Who do you want to represent you, Miss Wise, us or him?"

"I think I want you three to represent me. Can you get me out of here?"

"We'll get you out first thing in the morning," Goldstein said. "Jamieson, you're done here."

"Johnnie, I'm offering my services for free. Can you afford to pay for your own defense?"

"It's not going to cost her a dime, counselor," Goldstein said.

"I think I'm in good hands, Mr. Jamieson," Johnnie added. "But I appreciate everything you tried to do for me."

Desperate, he said, "Are you sure, Johnnie? You need to be absolutely sure on these matters."

"I'm sure, Mr. Jamieson. The truth of it is Ethel Beauregard is rich and I'm not. Who's more important to you, me or her?"

Jamieson didn't respond.

"That's why I chose them over you. They're from Chicago and they got here before you did, Mr. Jamieson. You live here, sir. Where have you been?"

"I wish you the best," Jamieson said. Then he left the jail and went straight over to the Beauregard mansion, where he'd been most of the day.

Chapter 36

Later at the Beauregard mansion

It was all starting to fall apart. In the beginning, cheating Johnnie out of her rightful inheritance seemed to be as easy as taking candy from a baby. Even with the article in the *Sentinel*, Jamieson thought the case against Johnnie was weak at best and easy to overcome, even with her being a Negro during Jim Crow. Unfortunately, he made a huge mistake by leaving Johnnie in jail all day, and now he was in the middle of what could become a scandal of gargantuan proportions if it got out that he and Ethel had changed Nathaniel's Will.

It was supposed to be simple. He was supposed to be set for life with the seventeen million he had received. If Johnnie mentioned the inheritance, the attorneys would want to see the Will. If the attorneys asked the right questions and requested a routine check of all of Nathaniel's money transfers, and learned that seventeen million dollars was missing, they would want to know what happened to it. If they did enough digging, they might find out what really happened, and Jamieson didn't want to take any chances.

From the brief exchange he'd had with Goldstein, Jamieson believed he was more than capable of figuring out what really happened. He also believed that even if he couldn't prove anything, an attorney of Goldstein's caliber would certainly use the information to benefit his client during the trial, just to stir things up and eventually point an accusatory finger at him. He and Ethel had to discuss a contingency plan.

Using the brass knocker, he let them know someone was at the front door. A few minutes later, Katherine, who was now living in the mansion, opened the door.

Jamieson barged in, saying, "Wake Ethel up. It's an emergency."

"What's the matter, sir?"

"Just get her up and down here immediately. I'll be in the library."

Katherine hurried up the stairs and told Ethel that Jamieson was downstairs waiting for her.

Twenty minutes later, a fully dressed Ethel walked into the library. "What's the emergency, Parker?"

"Johnnie fired me forty-five minutes ago. She's got her own attorneys now and they are sharp as razors. I didn't let on that I was worried, but I've heard of Goldstein. He has a reputation for tripping up witnesses and then butchering them once he gets them on the stand. This guy is like a surgeon with a double-edged scalpel. He will filet you if we don't prepare, and I mean right now, Ethel."

Ethel maintained her composure and sat in a chair across from Jamieson. "What does that mean for us?"

"It means we've got to assume the worst. We've got to assume Johnnie's going to tell them all about you attempting to kill her. We can assume she's going to tell them about her inheritance money, and—"

"Doesn't that help us?"

"At first, maybe, but if her attorneys start asking questions, they may want to see the Will. Once they do that, they're going want to examine its authenticity, Ethel. Do you understand what I'm telling you? They'll want to see bank statements. When they see that you transfered seventeen million to my account, they're going to want to know why. They won't be able to prove we changed the Will, but it would look bad for us, like we are in cahoots against *her*. If she says you tried to kill her and the jury believes her, they might believe we changed the Will. And if they believe that, I'll be disbarred and you'll be indicted for murdering Eric and probably the attempted murder of Johnnie Wise."

"But you told me rich people don't go to jail, Parker. You promised me this wouldn't happen."

"Rich people, particularly rich women, don't usually go to jail, but you killed your husband, Ethel. You calmly, coldly, and deliberately shot him in the back of the head. Why? Because he was bedding your cook. And Johnnie knows about it. She could testify to all of this."

"But she's on trial for murdering Sharon Trudeau, Parker."

"It doesn't matter what she's on trial for. Her attorneys are going to use everything they can to sway the jury. I doubt the jury would believe her, but with all the press coverage the trial is going to get, the way these guys portray things in the papers could prove compelling. I can tell you right now that there's no way she's going to get convicted for killing Sharon Trudeau.

She wasn't even there. Besides that, it was a professional hit. Johnnie may be a lot of things, but she's no killer. Also, she's beautiful, Ethel. No white man, and I don't care if they're all members of the Klan, is ever going to believe a beautiful girl like her, a teenager, a Negro, would ever have the smarts to kill two white people and leave no trace, no evidence she did it. The girl has only been out of New Orleans one time, and that was after Sharon had been murdered."

"What are we going to do?"

"You're going to make nice with her. That's what you're going to do."

"No, I am not!"

"Yes, you are! If you don't, she could bury you, and she will. Why wouldn't she? She's on trial for her life."

"Why don't we throw some mud on the pretty Colored girl? Why don't we make her look bad? She was responsible for what happened here on Thanksgiving Day. That's the truth of it. As a matter of fact, she may have been responsible for the riots. I say we put everything on her. There's not a white man in New Orleans who'll believe her over me. I can get Katherine to back me up. She's my friend, and she hates Johnnie too."

"Why not pay her off and be done with it, Ethel?"

"Pay *her*?"

"Yes. She'll quietly go away. She won't say a word because she doesn't have to take the stand. The prosecution doesn't have much of anything. I don't think they have a chance in hell to convict. This is a ruse to make it look like the district attorney is taking the allegations in the *Sentinel* seriously. Let's not risk it all because you hate her, Ethel."

"How many people am I supposed to pay, Parker?"

"As many as you need to pay."

"I paid you seventeen million; Morgan cleaned the family safe out. Who knows what he got away with? Now you want me to pay the little bitch that caused all of this mess in the first place? No! No! No! A thousand times, no!"

"Fine, Ethel. You just make sure Katherine is prepared to back you up all the way. If she doesn't, we may end up in prison ourselves."

Parker and Ethel didn't know it, but Katherine was right outside the door, listening to every word they said.

Chapter 37
Day 5

"I'll tell you everything."

The next day, Johnnie was released on bail, just as her attorneys had promised. She was supposed to meet her attorneys at Walter Brickman's for breakfast, but needed a long, hot bath first. She asked Cleo to take her home. After she bathed and put on a new outfit, they went to the restaurant to discuss legal strategy. Jay Goldstein and Dee Dee Wellington were already there waiting for them.

Cleo helped Johnnie to the table. It was still a struggle to walk because of the surgery she'd had four days ago. Neither woman could help noticing how much attention they were getting from the other patrons. It reminded Johnnie of the last time she'd been there with Lucas, the day Billy Logan had confronted them. Billy had sucker-punched Lucas and promised him he would be next to bed his girl; a promise he carried out, albeit via rape. She wondered how Lucas was doing as she eased into her seat. She had forgiven him for breaking off the relationship. She missed him and wondered if he missed her too.

Now that there was definitely going to be a trial, Johnnie was starting to feel the pressure. So much was at stake; the Mafia's livelihood, her own life and the lives of those closest to her were on the line. She couldn't wait to get out of town. As soon as the case was behind her, she and Sadie were leaving New Orleans—forever.

"Are you okay, Johnnie?" Goldstein asked.

Rather than complain or remind them of what happened to her, she forced a quick smile and said, "I'm okay. I'm just having a little trouble this morning, is all."

"What are y'all havin' this mornin'?" their waitress asked.

They all ordered and the waitress left them alone.

"Jay, I think we oughta make a motion to change venues," Cleo said.

"No need. We're going to get justice right here in New Orleans with the jury they want. That's the one smart thing Jamieson did. He got the Fort Lauderdale people to let you be tried here instead of having you extradited down there. The Fort Lauderdale people know the case is a loser and refused to get involved. They told the district attorney here that if they wanted you to be tried, they'd have to try you here. I talked to the DA this morning, and even he doesn't want to try the case, but that article in paper made it impossible to ignore. I don't suspect he'll put up much of a fight."

Johnnie said, "Sir, do you really believe white men will believe I didn't do this?"

"Of course they'll believe you didn't do it. The problem is getting them to vote not guilty when they get together in the jury room. We need to present a case that compels them to do the right thing. And we will."

"I guess I have to trust you, Mr. Goldstein. My life is in your hands."

Dee Dee said, "We'll just need to know where you were the night Sharon Trudeau was murdered."

Johnnie knew she couldn't tell them the whole truth. Abortion was illegal. She didn't want to be exonerated for Sharon Trudeau's murder only to be rearrested for another crime she actually committed. She said, "I was in Bayou Cane, Louisiana, that night."

"Can anybody corroborate that, Johnnie?" Cleo asked.

"What do you mean, ma'am?"

"Was anyone with you who could testify on your behalf?"

"Yes. My friend and next-door neighbor, Sadie. Madame DeMille can corroborate for me too."

"Madame DeMille? Who's that?" Cleo asked.

Before Johnnie could answer, Dee Dee said, "Have you ever been to Fort Lauderdale?"

"No, ma'am," Johnnie said, ignoring Cleo's question deliberately. She didn't mean to mention Madame DeMille, but it slipped out. If it came down to it, she'd tell them she was there to get her fortune told like any other customer who visited a psychic.

"But you did have money invested with Sharon Trudeau, right?" Goldstein asked.

"Yes."

"Where'd you get the money?" Goldstein asked. "We may not have to deal with that, but just in case, I'd like to know. Do you mind telling me?"

"I do mind, sir."

The attorneys looked at each other, a little stunned.

"Why won't you tell us, Johnnie?"

"Because it's embarrassing."

"We're your lawyers," Cleo offered. "You can tell us anything and it won't go any further. Also, the district attorney may already have that information and use it against us. If you tell us how you got the money to invest, we can strategize and protect you if we have to put you on the stand. We believe you're going to have to get on the stand and tell your side of the story and prove you didn't commit the crime they're accusing you of."

After a long pause, Johnnie said, "It all started on Christmas Eve, when my mother sold my virginity to Earl Shamus."

The attorneys looked at each other.

Dee Dee said, "Shamus, huh? What a fitting name for the bastard."

Goldstein said, "Excuse me. How old did you say you were? Seventeen?"

"Yes, sir. I'm seventeen now, but I was only fifteen when he did it to me in my mother's bed."

Cleo lowered her eyelids and shook her head. "They're still doing that shit down here? You'd think the bastards would just find a prostitute for that sort of thing. But I guess that's asking too much. They have to go after innocent little girls and ruin their lives before their lives even begin."

Goldstein said, "And you say your own mother sold you to him?"

"Yes, sir."

The waitress came back with their breakfast and served them. "Enjoy," she said. "Are you all comin' to the meetin' at the Sepia Theater tonight? There's supposed to be some folks from up north talkin' about makin' things better for the Negro."

"Yes, were planning to be there," Cleo said. "Where's the Sepia?"

"Right across the street. I hope to see y'all there tonight."

The waitress left them alone again.

Dee Dee looked at Johnnie and with genuine curiosity asked, "Why did your mother sell you to him?"

Johnnie kind of laughed and said, "You know, I asked her that myself one day. And she told me she was trying to show me how men were." She stopped laughing and became suddenly serious. "The sad thing about it all is how right my mother was."

"Surely you don't believe that?" Cleo asked.

"Can I ask you a question, ma'am?" Johnnie said, looking at the black woman sitting next to her. "I don't mean no harm, but there's something I have to ask you. Were you serious yesterday when you told me you were a real lawyer like them?"

Cleo smiled. "Yes, I am. You may find what I'm about to say difficult to believe, but the first female lawyer in the country, black or white, was a Negress named Lutie A. Lytle in 1897. She graduated from Central Tennessee College that year. She didn't practice, though. She taught criminal law, evidence, real property, and domestic relations at her alma mater."

Upon hearing that, Johnnie was positively beaming with pride. She couldn't restrain the bright, wide smile that burst forth. "For real?"

"For real," Cleo said, smiling, understanding how shocking that must have seemed to the young woman who had once been in sexual bondage. "That's one of the reasons we came down here, Johnnie—to free your mind, to make that which was *thought* to be impossible not only possible, but tangible. I am the personification of this."

Completely overwhelmed by what she had just learned, Johnnie's eyes welled. Tears fell. She now knew and had evidence of a better life, where a Negro woman didn't have to sell herself or compromise herself to be somebody as she, Sadie, and perhaps hundreds of thousands of Negro women had done, even in 1953 New Orleans. It was at that critical moment that she began to realize she could've been something more, but she still thought, still believed it was too late, having made so many mistakes already.

Cleo put her hand on Johnnie's shoulder. "Are you okay, Johnnie?"

"Yes, ma'am. I'm just happy to know what you told me. We don't have many Negro women examples where I live. Not good examples anyway. Most give the white man what he wants, just so they can live a good life. It's good to know you didn't have to do it, is all."

Goldstein cut back in. "Johnnie, I hate to ask, but is there any truth to the article I read about you and the Beauregard family?"

"Mr. Goldstein, I keep hearing about that article, but I haven't read it. If it says I'm related to them, I am. And I have proof of it. My white granddaddy died and left me and my brother five thousand dollars each."

"You mean he put you in his Will?"

"Yes, sir."

"Have you actually seen this Will?"

"No, I haven't, but here's my check." She opened her purse, pulled it out, and handed it to him.

Goldstein looked the check over then handed it to Dee Dee, who then passed it on to Cleo after looking at it. Goldstein was already planning to work this information into the case he would build to get Johnnie acquitted. "So what happened at the mansion before the killing began?"

Before she could answer, Detective Meade came up to their table, sat down, and slammed the day's *Sentinel* on the table. The newspaper was open to an article with a headline that read: WHAT DID BILLY LOGAN DO TO DESERVE THIS? On the same page was a picture of a severely beaten Logan, his face and head battered and swollen. He was nearly unrecognizable. In fact, if the caption didn't tell the reader it was Logan, perhaps his mother might recognize him, but few others would.

"Billy Logan raped you, didn't he, Johnnie?" Meade screamed so loudly the entire restaurant stood still, frozen in time, looking, listening.

"Don't answer that, Johnnie," Goldstein said.

"And who the hell are you?" Meade said.

"We're her attorneys. Who the hell are you?"

Meade flipped open his wallet, showing his badge. "I'm a detective with the New Orleans Police Department. People around your client tend to die, counselor."

"Are you here to arrest my client?"

"Not at this time, but I would like to ask her some questions."

"Go ahead."

"Did Logan rape you?"

"Don't answer that," Goldstein said, smiling broadly at the detective.

"He did, didn't he? And you had him killed, didn't you?"

"You're being absurd, detective," Goldstein said forcefully.

"Am I, counselor? Let me paint a picture for you. Sharon Trudeau steals her money, and she ends up dead. Richard Goode probably killed her mother and he ends up dead. She gets raped, and Logan ends up dead, beaten with bats, the coroner says, and he had a cue stick stuck up his ass. This . . . a couple days after Miss Wise here is raped."

"So what, detective? My client was in jail last night. She can barely walk, let alone beat a man Logan's size to death. Even if she could walk, or run, for that matter, there's no evidence of my client doing anything to this man. Judging by the picture, it would've taken several men to do that to him. Only the men who killed him know why they did it. For all you know, he could have been having an affair with a married woman and her husband found out. He and a couple of friends could have found him and exacted revenge."

Meade pointed his finger in Johnnie's face, nearly touching her nose. "I'm gonna get you. I know you had something to do with this."

"That's it, detective. Unless you have a warrant for her arrest, please leave. And, detective, you've threatened my client in front of a restaurant full of people. Anything happens to her, we'll be coming after you."

Meade stood up. Looking down at Johnnie, he said, "You can keep the paper. I don't know how you live with yourself." Then he turned and walked toward the door.

Angry, Johnnie called out to him, "I don't know how you can live with yourself, detective, after blackmailing my friend Sadie into sucking your dick two nights ago. Only God knows what else you made her do."

Meade pretended he didn't hear her blistering comments and continued out the door.

Cleo said, "Johnnie, you need to tell us absolutely everything that's been going on down here so we can help defend you."

Still angry, she said, "I will, Cleo. I'll tell you everything."

Chapter 38
Day 5

Sepia Theater
Later that evening

Sadie stopped the car, helped Johnnie to the sidewalk. Then she got back in and parked a few blocks away because there were no spaces near the theater. Given all the cars surrounding the building, she assumed the place was packed, which wasn't all that surprising because one of the topics of discussion was voting rights. She exited the car and walked four blocks to the theater in the cool December air. She opened one of the glass doors and entered the elegant lobby to the smell of freshly popped buttered corn. Johnnie was waiting to be served at the concession stand.

"Oh, and did I tell you about Lutie A. Lytle?" Johnnie asked when Sadie approached the concession stand, eager to share the latest bit of knowledge acquired from listening.

She had been talking nonstop about her new attorneys all the way over to the theater, particularly about Jay Goldstein, who had impressed her with his legal expertise and his desire to protect her from Detective Meade and Parker Jamieson. But the thing that had her walking on air was learning of Lutie A. Lytle's amazing accomplishment before the turn of the century, thirty years after the Confederacy was defeated.

"No, you didn't," Sadie said, grinning, glad her friend was embracing knowledge, not shunning it. "Tell me all about her." As Johnnie excitedly talked about Lutie, Sadie was inspired as well.

"Well, Cleo says she was the first female lawyer in the country, black or white; graduated from college way back in 1897. Can you believe that?"

"Yes, I can. I told you there's so much more out there for you. I hope you're planning to do something with your life when we leave New Orleans, Johnnie."

"I'm going to do something for sure. I just don't know what right now."

They couldn't wait to leave New Orleans, which would be in about two weeks, right after the trial. Goldstein's confidence had become contagious.

By the time Johnnie and Sadie opened the auditorium door, Negro millionaire Walker Tresvant III was on the stage, standing behind a podium, patiently listening to another man speak about the coming grass roots Civil Rights Movement. The two women quickly found seats in the back, embarrassed to be late.

Tresvant patiently waited for his opponent to finish his persuasive arguments for integrating with Whites and how it would help the Negro secure voting rights, before responding to him. He carefully listened to Reverend Settlefore, who was in league with the National Association for the Advancement of Colored People.

Settlefore replaced Reverend Staples, who had been killed during the August riot. When he read the article in the *Sentinel*, he contacted the NAACP and requested their assistance. The NAACP leadership was more than happy to help, and believed it was necessary to rally black folk to their cause. They suspected that Johnnie would be found guilty of a murder no one, even the district attorney, believed she committed. If Goldstein hadn't stepped in to defend Johnnie, they would have—at no cost, of course.

When the Reverend finished, Tresvant spoke thusly: "To the esteemed Reverend Settlefore, to the Negro Chamber of Commerce, to the wonderful attorneys of the NAACP, and to the men and women of Sable and Baroque Parishes, hear me and hear me well. Let me began by stating unequivocally that I do not hate Whites, and I'm all for integration, but not now and certainly not at the expense of life, limb, and property. I think our distinguished guests have forgotten that in 1789, the Constitution thought of the Negro as three-fifths of a person. This was the thinking at that time, and it hasn't changed much since.

"To prove this, I point to the Fifteenth Amendment of the same Constitution, which says that the Negro already has the right to vote and yet, here we are one hundred and eighty-eight years later, still unable to do the thing they are offering you." Applause erupted. "Now, to be fair, I must point out that when the Fifteenth Amendment was first enacted, Negroes voted and put record numbers of Blacks in office at the federal, state, and local levels. But shortly afterward, white Democrats in the South became violent and scared us away from the voting polls. These same white Democrats then administered literacy tests they probably couldn't pass themselves had someone else developed the tests, and yet they continue to deny us a right we already have." Applause again. "Then they instituted Jim Crow—separate but so-called equal—to keep us subservient, to keep us dependent, to keep our minds in shackles . . . but we broke free, didn't we, y'all? Our minds are free! Free to think for ourselves. Free to do for ourselves. Free to do commerce by ourselves." Thunderous applause.

"Look around you and see the splendor of your own hands by your own developer. This place is a palace compared to the white theater they don't want you to sit in. We built this place, not Whites. Everybody involved, from the architect to the plumber to the electrician to the interior decorator, all were Negroes. Industrious, studious, imaginative, sagacious Negroes." Applause. He extended his arm toward Reverend Settlefore and the members of the NAACP sitting on the stage behind him and continued, "Sure, they'll take your hard-earned dollars and let you sit up in the balcony, but here, in our own town, in our own parish, we have it better than them.

"I don't care what they say . . . white folk started the riot last summer because we have it better than them. To prove this, ask yourself why the rich Whites, who have it better than us, didn't riot with the poor Whites? Why? I'll tell you why. When you have wealth, you aren't angry. When you have wealth, you aren't jealous of your neighbor because you have the same things he has. When you have wealth, you don't have pent-up anger and resentment. When you have wealth, you are satisfied." Applause.

"Look again, I say, at what we've accomplished without the right to vote. Did you hear me? I said without the right to vote and without the help of Whites. I say let the Northern white man fight the Southern white man all he wants. While they fight and slaughter each other politically, the Negro will quietly, almost imperceptibly, grow economically. The evidence is all around you, my friends. We have become a replica of the

Greenwood community in Tulsa, Oklahoma, before jealous Whites burned it down. Black Wall Street, they called it. They set the blueprint we follow to this day. But we accomplished this by having unwavering faith in our God. If we continue on this path, if we continue to trust in God, twenty years from now, by 1973, we will be an economic force in the land of our former slave masters. Do you hear me? I said an economic force! We will have risen from the ashes, as it were, excelling to heights previously unimaginable.

"The evidence is right in front of you, my friends. We have already surpassed them intellectually—right now, in this time—in 1953. Our teachers are better than theirs. Our students are ahead of theirs—even now. We are inventors and artists, hard workers at whatever we set our hands to do. The only thing the Negro lacks in 1953 is the white man's respect. Hear me well, friends. We will never, ever get the respect we have earned if we get involved with white Southern Democrats. If we get involved in this thing now, before we're ready economically, if we allow ourselves to be deceived by the likes of Lucifer himself, if we close our eyes to their chicanery, their serpentine grasp, they will choke the life out of our ambitious spirit with extreme prejudice. Fifty years from today, in the year 2003, we will be a lost and desolate people, nomads—a people that no nation will ever respect, not even our own African bothers and sisters." Applause. "And remember, my friends, that the Bible says the serpent was more subtle than any beast of the field, which means we won't even know we've been bamboozled for fifty years, when it would be too late to reverse course. It's up to us to stop this insipid invasion and leave a legacy of wealth our posterity can build on."

The people stood to their feet and clapped their hands and

cheered like they were at a football game and the home team had just scored a touchdown. The audience began murmuring, talking to each other about Tresvant's inspirational oratory. But Reverend Settlefore suspected that something like this could happen, having heard of the Tresvant family and how they acquired their enormous wealth. To thwart and nullify what he knew would be a stirring speech, he planted certain Negroes around the auditorium to incite the crowd by slinging malicious mud at Tresvant's family.

Someone from the audience yelled, "Don't listen to him. His family owned slaves!"

Tresvant tried to respond, but the Negroes shouted him down, saying, "We wanna sleep in white hotels!"

And just like that, they had forgotten every word he said. The deception had begun and prevailed. Other Negroes who weren't planted joined in, saying, "Yeah! And we wanna eat at white restaurants too!"

"Amen! And we want our children to go to white schools!"

When Walker attempted to speak to them again, to tell them how his grandfather, the first Walker Tresvant, had purchased his freedom by working hard on the weekends and being trustworthy, and that he had both black and white slaves, they booed and covered their ears and said, "He's gotten rich off the backs of blacks, and he doesn't care about us. He doesn't want us to have the best that life has to offer."

Reverend Settlefore didn't have to respond to Tresvant's stirring commentary. He just looked triumphantly at his opponent and smiled.

Chapter 39
Day 5

The same night

While the Negroes were having a meeting, infuriated Whites were having a meeting of their own at Grace Holiness Church of God in Christ, all Bible-believing Christians. They had all read or heard about the article in the *Sentinel*, which resurrected their sense of injustice because not one Negro had been arrested after the riot. The thing that really riled them up was the fact that the Wise name had been interjected again, just as it was before the riot. They believed it was Johnnie's fault the moment word got out that she was there when the fabled Beauregard family tragically met disaster.

After singing hymns and loudly praising God, the church members sat in their pews as their minister stepped up to the lectern. He raised his closed Bible above his head and said, "The Lord our God told the children of Israel not to intermarry with heathen nations because if they did, they would turn their hearts away from him. He told them to go in and possess the land; to kill them all; man, woman, child, and beast! And that's what we have to do too. The Bible says that's how you put evil away from among you!"

Applause.

One of the members stood up and said, "I say we go over there right now, preacher. I say we give 'em what we owe 'em—a prolonged lashing."

"That's what they deserve, all right," the minister said. "But this time we're going to be smart. We're not going to go into their town acting like undisciplined looters like we did the last time. No! We're going to organize this time, plan. We're going to keep this thing quiet. We're going to wait until they least expect it, and then we will swoop down on them like a hawk does its prey and crush them like the vermin they are." Applause. "When they try the pickaninny, that Johnnie Wise girl, that's when we'll make our move. All the Negroes will likely attend the trial. The rest'll probably be at work in their shops on Main Street. When they come back to their homes, there'll only be ashes left. This time we won't bother with the poor niggers.

"This time we will destroy the strong, and in so doing, we'll automatically destroy the weak. By destroying their wealth, we take away their ability to rebuild. This time we start in Ashland Estates, where rich white men have their black nigger whores and black bastard children right out in the open for all to see. God is not pleased with that! We won't kill them, though. We will humble them for the next fifty years or more, which is better than killing them. They'll have to live with the humiliation of being destroyed. Then they'll turn on each other and prove to themselves that they are nothing more than animals that need to be caged. That's what animals do, kill and maim each other. And we'll watch and laugh at their foolishness." Thunderous applause.

Someone shouted, "I'm with you, Reverend!"

"Yeah, me too!" another shouted.

And so said they all—even the women and children.

Chapter 40

"I was starting to."

"Goin' somewhere, boss?" Napoleon heard one of his bodyguards ask when he quietly exited his master bedroom through the French doors that led to the terrace. He was planning to visit Johnnie again. He had been sneaking over to her house every other night for two weeks, waiting on her hand and foot, doing whatever she needed, making life easy for her. He turned toward the man and said, "Yeah, I was just—"

Thud! A blackjack came crashing down hard on the base of his skull. Napoleon's six-foot-four frame collapsed and fell hard to the ground.

"Grab his legs," the bodyguard said, lifting the upper body of his former boss.

An hour later, Napoleon awoke to the splash of ice-cold water being pitched in his face from a large silver pail. He shook himself, shivering from the chill. He was blindfolded; his hands were tied with rope to the back of his chair. His bare feet were in hardening cement. He knew he was on a ship and they were moving. He could feel it. When he heard a steamship's whistle blow, he knew he was all done, and he knew why. The fact that his own people were waiting for him to leave through his bedroom let him know Don Russo, Boss of New York, and quite possibly Chicago Sam, were in on it.

As he thought about other possibilities, he heard water splashing. His bodyguard had tossed water in the face of someone else who was sitting next to him. He hoped it wasn't Johnnie. The last thing he wanted to do was get her killed because he wasn't careful. His captors snatched off his blindfold. He looked to the left. It was Bubbles. He assumed Johnnie was safe since she wasn't in the room with them. The bodyguard snatched Bubbles' blindfold off. His face looked like he'd gone a couple of rounds with Sugar Ray Robinson. His face was swollen and bleeding. He looked like he'd taken a fierce beating before being subdued.

"Sorry we had tuh rough you up, pal," the bodyguard said. "It was either that, or we would've had tuh blast Miss Shepard too. Stray bullets and all. Sweet piece of ass ya had there, pal. Sweet indeed. They told us you were as tough as they come. Now we know too." He looked at Napoleon. "It took five of us tuh take him down."

"Are you gonna talk all night, Ritchie?" Napoleon asked. "Get on with it."

"You satisfied now, Napoleon?" Bubbles asked, breathing heavily. He had been struggling to free himself as they transported him to the ship. "I saw this comin' six months ago. Why couldn't you listen to me, man?"

"If it's any consolation, I'm real sorry I got you into this, ol' friend. But you knew what you were doing. You wanted the money too."

"I was told to give ya a choice," Ritchie said, holding a loaded submachine gun.

"Yeah? Let's hear 'em," Napoleon said.

"You can go into the water alive, or you can go in dead. It's up to you."

"Who's behind the hit, Ritchie?" Napoleon asked. "New York?"

"And Chicago . . . but Sam fought for you, I'm told. He said to give you a message."

"Yeah? What is it?"

"He says that if we kill you before we toss you over the side, we gotta do the broad too."

"What broad?" Napoleon asked, hoping Ritchie wasn't referring to Johnnie.

"This broad."

He held up the picture of Napoleon carrying Johnnie to his Cadillac. Ritchie shuffled through about ten pictures, each more incriminating than the one before. Then he walked over to a table and began playing Napoleon and Johnnie's sexually explicit conversation.

"The bosses wanted you to know exactly why they had to kill you."

"I'm on pins and needles over here," Napoleon said sarcastically.

"Yeah, the suspense is killin' me," Bubbles said.

Ritchie looked at the men with him and laughed. "Ya gotta love these guys. Brass balls. The both of them."

Napoleon said, "Are you gonna tell me or are you gonna keep flapping your lips?"

"Nobody wanted to do it, I'm told. They figure you oughta know that before we toss ya over. Now, how you wanna go out?"

"Answer me something, Ritchie. How come the bosses didn't give me a chance to fix it?"

"They did. The trial starts tomorrow. You had plenty of opportunities tuh take her out and didn't. I've been watching you leave the mansion, Napoleon, c'mon. You didn't pop the broad, so they told me I had tuh pop you, or I get popped. It's not personal, ya know? If the broad fingers you, it ends with you, not them."

"What if she doesn't name anybody, Ritchie? The cops don't have a case against her. Nothing solid anyway."

"The bosses don't wanna take no chances, her bein' Colored and all. They figure no matter what, they're gonna pin the murder on her and when they do, she's gonna squeal on you two guys. Besides, you started the whole damned thing when you killed the Klansman and Trudeau. Now fuckin' Hoover's threatenin' tuh take action against the bosses. It's you or them. And you know it's not gonna be them."

"I see. Can you do me one last favor?" Napoleon asked.

"Sure, if I can."

"Can you kill me and then toss me in? I don't much like the idea of drowning."

"Sorry, Napoleon. No can do. They wanted you to think about how you fucked yourself over for a broad while you gurgle seawater. Besides, they sent those guys." He tilted his head toward the men with him. "They're here to make sure you got the choice. They're hoping you choose to let the girl live and if you do, they don't want me doin' you no favors like pluggin' you before you go in."

Bubbles said, "What about me? Can you shoot me first?"

"Sure."

Ritchie raised the gun and immediately squeezed the trigger. The end of the barrel lit up as bullet after bullet ripped into Bubbles' flesh, turning it into Swiss cheese. The men pick up Bubbles' bloody body and the chair he was tied to, and carried him out the door. Then they tossed him into the sea. When he hit the water, they heard a big splash.

"Thanks for doing that, Ritchie. It wasn't his fault."

"Thanks, but I didn't do it for either of you. The bosses wanted you to see your Colored friend die first. He never had a choice." He paused momentarily. "Tell me something, Napoleon. How did a smart guy like you let it get this far? You had everything. Did you love her, or what?"

"I was starting to."

"I'll let the bosses know that." He looked at the men. "Boys . . . toss 'im over."

And that was the end of Napoleon Bentley.

Chapter 41

"You knew about it all along?"

Nearly two weeks had passed since Lucas received the letter from Colonel Strong, offering him the opportunity to play football for him in Europe. A free man now, he and Marla Bentley were in an out-of-the-way spot called the Red River Motel. The motel was about ten miles from the gas station where Preston Truman worked before Bubbles put several bullet holes in him. Napoleon had used Preston to set up Lucas for the prison term he had served.

Upon receiving Lucas' letter detailing his early release and desire to see her, Marla meticulously planned the whole trip and checked in earlier as a single occupant. She knew they couldn't be seen together, so she wired him two bus tickets; one to Alexandria, the other to New Orleans, where he would pick up one of his cars.

Marla had sat in her Cadillac and watched the bus pull up to the stop. It was dark out, and fortunately, Lucas was the only passenger who got off the bus. When the driver pulled off, she flashed her lights to get his attention. When she saw him walking over to the car, she got out of the front seat and into the back to hide their affair.

"Hi, stranger," Marla said to him sweetly, lustfully. "God, how I missed you."

They made love ferociously for hours, like it would be their last time ever, panting deliciously as their carnality controlled them. They acted as if they had been apart for years, not weeks. Finally, after Lucas had spilled his seed in her for the fourth time, they breathed heavily and embraced each other in the sweat-soaked sheets.

"I see you missed me too, huh?" Marla said.

"A little."

"A little?" Marla laughed. "That didn't feel like a little to me. That felt like you missed me quite a bit."

Changing the subject, he said, "You drove all the way down here by yourself?"

"Yes."

"But I thought you couldn't drive, Marla."

"I can, I just don't like to anymore."

"So you drove all the way down here just for me?"

"Hard to believe I'd get behind the wheel of a car again just for adorable you, huh?"

"Kinda, yeah. So how was Chicago?"

"The same. Ever been there?"

"No. I'd like to see it someday, though."

"I wish I could show it to you, but all we can do is what we just did unless we leave the country. How would you like to live in Canada? It's almost like living here, I suspect."

Lucas frowned. "Canada?"

"Yeah. I could take you to see Niagara Falls. Ever hear of it?"

"Yeah, but I've got three long years to give the Army. Are you going to wait that long, Marla?"

"When boot camp is over, why not try to get assigned overseas? Germany or something. I can meet you over there. What about that?"

"You'd do that?"

"Yes. I have plenty of money now that Napoleon and I are done."

"Hmm, let me think on it some, okay?" he said, lying, having no plans to tell her he'd already been offered the opportunity to travel overseas, because after he left Louisiana, he was leaving all the past behind. He liked Marla, but she was being very unrealistic. He was through taking chances with his life and was ready to move on, but he still enjoyed sex with her, and it had been a while since he'd been fulfilled.

"So have you heard about your friend?" Marla asked.

"What friend?"

"Your girlfriend, Lucas. You know who I mean. And don't tell me she didn't write you every day, either. I know she did. If I was writing you regularly, I know she was too."

"She didn't write me. Not one time."

"You don't have to lie to me, baby. I know you *think* you love her."

"I'm not lying. I'm telling you the truth."

Marla raised her head and looked down into his eyes. "You're serious, aren't you?"

"Well, she did come and visit me on Christmas. I don't think she had the address."

"She didn't have the address, but she came and visited you on Christmas, Lucas? C'mon. Why do you keep making excuses for her? If I found the address, she could've found the address too—and before Christmas Day."

Lucas thought for a moment and said, "She did the best she could, Marla. I appreciate what little she did, but I broke it off with her when she visited me."

"Really?" Marla asked skeptically.

"Really. She didn't want to end it, and truthfully, I didn't either. But I think it's for the best. We both need to move on with our lives. It just wouldn't have worked out."

Marla smiled flirtatiously. "So you were afraid she was going to send you a Dear John letter, huh?"

Lucas looked at her. "Like I told you the first day we met, you're a very smart lady."

She laughed. "Somebody's been working on his English, I see."

"Yeah, I have. I'm not stupid. But back to what I was saying. Breaking it off was the best thing to do. Like I said, I still owe the Army three years. It would have happened sooner or later."

"Hmmm, I see you're maturing also."

"A little, I guess. I read those books you sent me. Can't you tell?"

"Sounds like it."

"I loved them both but, I'm partial to *The Negro in the American Rebellion: His Heroism and His Fidelity*, seeing that I have to go into the Army. After reading about all the Negro heroes, officers and enlisted, I thought, man, one day that could be me. Did you know the first man to die in the rebellion was a Negro named Crispus Attucks?"

"Yes, I knew. I read the book too. And one of those heroic Negroes could be you, if that's what you want. You can do whatever you want to do in this country as long as you don't let anybody stop you. If they won't let you ride the bus, walk. It'll take longer, but you'll eventually get to your destination, which is why I selected those particular books and sent them to you." She kissed him. "Can I tell you something? It's really been bothering me and I need to get it off my chest."

"Sure, you can tell me what's been bothering you, but first, tell me what happened to my friend, as you call her."

Marla remained silent for a few seconds before saying, "Johnnie's been arrested for murdering some woman named Sharon Trudeau."

Lucas bolted forward like he had been shot out of a canon, surprised by what he'd heard. "What? Johnnie wouldn't kill anybody."

"The papers say she was Johnnie's stockbroker."

"She was my stockbroker, too, but I didn't kill her either. Any number of people could have. She stole our money, Marla. Johnnie didn't do it. I know she didn't!"

"Well, the trial starts tomorrow. She's got the best lawyer in Chicago on her side; a man named Jay Goldstein. She'll be fine, I'm sure."

"Are you *serious*, Marla?" Lucas asked, stunned by her nonchalant attitude. "She'll be *fine*? In the fuckin' South? Accused of killin' a white woman?"

"Hey, Goldstein is excellent, okay? He tries these kinds of cases all the time and he wins them."

"Are you tellin' me he can get her outta this mess?"

"If anybody can, Goldstein can. I oughta know. I hired him to help her. It was the least I could do."

"Well, I've gotta get back there tomorrow. I've gotta make sure she's okay."

"May I ask you something, Lucas?"

"Sure, go ahead."

"What do you see in her? I mean really. I know she's a beautiful girl and all, but after that, what is it about her that makes you so crazy for her?"

"I love her."

"You mean you *think* you love her."

"I do love her, Marla."

"*Really*," she said like she knew his feelings better than he did. "What do you base that on?"

"Well, she's really smart, for one."

"If she's so smart, why couldn't she find a simple address to the prison you were in? It seems to me that if she *really* loved you, she would have gone to hell and back to get that address, especially being as *smart* as you say she is. So that's one mark for me, since I found the address quicker, and another mark for caring enough to write you regularly. Now . . . what else do you base your *love* for her on?"

"Why?"

"Because frankly, I don't think you have a reason to love her. I think you're in love with the idea of who you *think* she is, not who she really is, because if you knew who she *really* was, you'd be angry, and I doubt you'd love her as you say you do now."

"What do you mean, the idea of who I *think* she is?"

"You, like most men, *think* that if a woman's beautiful, she must be an angel sent from heaven just for them, when in most cases, nothing could be further from the truth. Take it from me, an expert; a woman is a woman is a woman, okay? She's a human being, not some celestial being who can do no wrong. As a matter of fact, because she's a woman, she can do plenty wrong and saps like *you* blind yourselves to her wicked ambitions. You guys come up with a million excuses for her conniving ways, even though it's right in front of your eyes. Why? Because she's beautiful, that's why."

"What do you mean?"

Marla laughed. "What do I mean? Lucas, are you *serious?* Jesus!"

"Yeah, I'm serious. What do you mean? I'm listening. Explain it to me."

"But will you believe me? That's the question, Lucas."

"I might."

"Okay, I'll make it plain and simple. If she were butt ugly, there's no way you wouldn't see her treachery, and you know it, right?"

"Probably not."

"And there you have it. Truth prevails again, at least for now." She kissed him. "Let me ask you something. Did you ever confront her after I told you about her and Napoleon and how much she enjoyed it?"

Solemnly, he said, "Yeah. I did."

"And?"

"And what?"

"Did she admit it? Yes or no?"

"She didn't have to admit it, Marla."

"Why not?"

"Because I knew it all along."

"Before I told you?"

"Yeah. I knew the night we killed Richard Goode at his farm."

"How? What tipped you off?"

"I saw her looking at Napoleon like he was a god or something. That shit fucked with me too. I mean it really did. So I confronted her at her place the night we came back from Shreveport."

"I remember her lying to you."

"I know. After you convinced me she had lied, I told her I knew what she had done and we agreed to move on."

Puzzled, Marla said, "And that was that?"

"Yeah. I thought about what she'd done *one* time and what I'd done with you *dozens* of times. She had her reasons for doing what she did. They were far more honorable than mine. Me, I just wanted to get up in you and you know . . ."

"Get off?"

"Well, yeah."

She laughed and said, "So did I. Now, what were her honorable reasons?"

"Napoleon threatened to kill me if she didn't."

"Do you believe her?"

"I guess so, but honestly, what difference does it make? The truth of it is this; if I hadn't been doing what I was doing with you, he wouldn't have been in a position to threaten her, would he, Marla?"

"I guess. . . . If you say so."

"What do you mean by that?"

"He wanted her, which means he was going to get her one way or the other. If he did threaten her, he took the most convenient route. That tells me he only wanted to get a piece and move on. The fact that he still wants her tells me he thoroughly enjoyed it too, probably more than her."

"Wait a minute. Are you saying he's still after her or what?"

She looked away and didn't respond.

"Tell me what you know, Marla. I know you know something. What is it?"

She rolled over onto her left side and reached back for his powerful arm. Having found it, she wrapped it around her waist and sighed heavily. "Do you think I'm the kind of person that would lie to you, Lucas?"

"No. I mean, you've told me the truth right down the line. You even told me the truth when I didn't want to hear the truth. So based on that, I guess I can trust you. Now, tell me what you know."

"So you believe I've told you the truth, and you know for certain your girlfriend—"

"Ex-girlfriend."

"Fine. Ex-girlfriend lied to you, right?"

"Right."

"Okay. I'm going to tell you some more truth about your ex, and it's not pretty, okay? Do you want to hear it?"

Lucas rolled onto his back and looked up at the ceiling, strenuously debating whether he wanted to know more dirt about the only woman he had ever loved. He wondered how much truth he could take and still be in love with her. He also wondered what she had done this time, and what excuse he could make on her behalf. Everything in him screamed no, but he found himself saying, "Yes, I want to hear it."

"Are you absolutely certain you want to know?"

Another long pause filled the air.

"Well, you obviously don't want to know, Lucas, so I won't bother telling you."

"Tell me," he said quickly, almost as if he was answering her challenge.

"Johnnie and Napoleon went to Las Vegas together."

He bolted forward again and screamed, "What?"

"Well . . . not alone."

Relieved, he said, "Oh."

"*Oh*? Are you shitting me or what, Lucas? You act like that's not a big deal or something. Jesus!"

"Who did they go with? Sadie? Bubbles?"

"Yes."

"So there. No big deal. But, um, why did they go?"

"Her brother was fighting at the Sands."

"Oh, Benny?" He let his body flop down on the mattress and resumed looking at the ceiling. "Yeah, okay, I met him. Again, no big deal."

Infuriated by his trusting attitude, she rolled over, looked down into his eyes and said, "He fucked her again that night, Lucas! Jesus! Do I have to spell everything out for you?"

He closed his eyes slowly and exhaled hard. "How do you know?"

"I know because it was his plan all along. He wanted her to be his permanently."

He sprung forward again. "What?"

"Yeah. That was his plan all along."

"Tell me about it, Marla," he demanded. "And I wanna know every single detail. Don't leave nothin' out."

She turned her body toward his, propped herself up on her elbow, and looked down at him again. "Finally, some anger. It's about time! Napoleon wanted to take over all of New Orleans, did you know that?"

"I heard talk about some business with the Chicago people, but that's about it."

"Okay, well, the Mafia doesn't like Coloreds in their La Cosa Nostra thing."

"La what?"

"La Cosa Nostra. It's Italian. It means 'this thing of ours.' Anyway, Napoleon used our relationship to set up the Don of New Orleans."

"You mean you and me? Our relationship?"

"Yes. I told John Stefano about our affair like Napoleon told me to. Stefano ran to the New York people, and they had a sit-down—a meeting concerning what to do about Napoleon. At the meeting, like we knew he would, Stefano told them all about our relationship, and they thought Napoleon was weak for your girlfriend, so they tried to kill him in Las Vegas, but John Stefano was killed instead."

"You mean he risked Johnnie's life? He put her in danger?"

"He put us all in danger, Lucas. Everybody."

Lucas thought for a moment. "You said *we*. What did you mean by that? Were you in on it?"

"To a degree, yes."

Frowning, he said, "What degree?"

"He knew all about our relationship when he caught us together in the pool, remember? He just didn't let on. He confronted me about it later, and that's when he told me he was going to have Johnnie even if he had to kill you. I could either help him, or he'd kill you for what we did that first time. He told me if I helped him, he'd let me go."

"So Johnnie told the truth, huh? He did threaten to kill me. That's why she did it with him that first time, and that's one reason I love her."

"That's not all. He also set you up with Preston Truman."

"What? How?"

"Preston's brother owed Bubbles money he couldn't pay, so they decided to send us to Shreveport to get you a new car, knowing you would either stop at the station or I would tell you to pull in there. You stopped on your own, which made the con all the more authentic. Preston had agreed to go along to keep his brother from being beaten to a pulp."

"So Bubbles knew who Preston was all along, huh? He came to my cell telling me to give up the name of the guy who put me in prison, when him and Napoleon knew who he was. So it was a set-up from the beginning. He had made up his mind the night he met Johnnie. Ruthless!"

"Not from the beginning. Bubbles warned Napoleon to stay away from Johnnie, but when he heard her sing, he fell for her. I was there that night. I saw it in his eyes when he came to my table after you and Johnnie left. You were in the way, so he had to get rid of you without killing you."

"Why couldn't he kill me, Marla?"

"If he killed you, Johnnie would never have anything to do with him. So he had to get you that car and give you a raise in pay, all to give Johnnie the impression that he was doing everything he could to be nice to you, so when you fell into his trap, she couldn't blame him for what you yourself decided to do. The night we all went to Walter Brickman's, Bubbles warned you not to get involved in drugs, right?"

"Right."

"He knew you had already agreed to the deal Preston offered you."

"How did he know I agreed?"

"I told him. It was part of the deal. Before we left the filling station, Preston nodded to me, which was the signal that you two had made the deal."

"So then that must mean the other part of the deal was to get me to sell the smack too, right?"

"Right, but you had to decide to do it on your own."

Furious now, Lucas said, "And Napoleon is the one who called the cops on me?"

"Napoleon owns the fucking cops, Lucas! He owns the judge who sentenced you, too. You didn't have to do one damn day in prison, or in the Army, for that matter. But it was that or the grave. He was going to have Johnnie no matter what. He even had Sharon Trudeau steal Johnnie's money, and killed her for her trouble. That's how determined he was to have her. Given the choices before me, I thought it better that you live, because I liked you. Besides, I didn't think it would last between you two anyway. You were both so young, with your whole lives ahead of you."

It occurred to him that Marla was just as much a part of what happened to him as Bubbles and Napoleon. Suddenly, intense anger gripped him without warning—temporary insanity. Before he knew it, his powerful hands were around her delicate throat, squeezing the life out her. "You knew about it all along? Why didn't you tell me, Marla? Huh? Why didn't you tell me?" With each word, his grip tightened, until he heard what sounded like a twig snap. He looked into her vacant eyes. Marla was gone, just that quick.

Chapter 42

"I'm sorry, Marla."

When Lucas realized Marla was dead, he panicked. He didn't mean to kill her. It was an accident. He had lost control for only a few seconds and had killed a white woman. He knew they were going to give him the electric chair for that, accident or not. He paced the room, trying to figure out what to do next, shaking his head. *Why me?* It had happened so fast. One minute she was alive, giving him invaluable information. The next minute she was dead and gone. He knew he had to get rid of the body somehow.

He looked at his watch. It was three in the morning. He had a couple of hours at best to get rid of Marla's remains, he knew. Otherwise, he was all done. He remembered parking the car with the trunk facing the room they were to stay in for the night. He grabbed her keys off the nightstand and opening the door, he looked to the left and to the right. All the lights were out in all the rooms. He'd caught a break, but he still had to get her in the trunk, grab all her things, and get into the car without being seen.

Nervously, he stepped out and quickly opened the trunk then returned to the room. He then picked up Marla and went back to the doorway. His heart was pounding, knowing that if anyone saw what he was doing, if anyone saw that he was a Negro carrying a dead white woman, they would kill him first and ask questions later. His only chance was to get her in the trunk and close it as quickly as he could. That way, if anyone saw him afterward, they might wonder what he was doing there, but that would be about it, because they would not have seen him put her into the trunk.

At the doorway now, he looked to the left then swiveled his head to the right. No one was there. As quickly as he could, he rushed to the car, put Marla in the trunk and closed it. Then just as quickly, he stepped back inside the room and shut the door in case a curious guest looked out the window after hearing the trunk slam shut. His heart was pounding so hard that it felt like it was going to explode. He sat on the bed, trying to keep from hyperventilating. It took a while, but eventually his breathing returned to normal. But he was still nervous, still shocked, still blown away by Napoleon and Bubbles' diabolical betrayal. All of a sudden, he remembered that Johnnie had warned him to stay away from Marla. She had done everything she could do to get him away from her.

What am I going to do now? I've got her in the trunk, but I can't just leave a Cadillac with Illinois plates out in the open, and I can't drive it around either. Cracker cops will pull me over in a second just to ask me stupid-ass questions. "How can you afford a brand new Cadillac, boy? Open up the trunk. Let's see if you got smack in the trunk. Maybe that's how you can afford a Cadillac." They'd take my ass to jail on suspicion alone. That means I can't drive my brand new Chevy to boot camp in South Carolina either. I've gotta drive my souped up 1941 Chevy Special just to have a chance of not being pulled over. I'll let Johnnie keep the 1954 model. But what am I going to do with the body?

He looked out the window to see if any lights were on. He didn't see any. Quickly, he grabbed Marla's suitcase and tossed it on the bed. He opened it and put the dress she'd worn in it, her shoes, her toiletry items, everything. Then he looked under the bed for anything he might have missed. He searched the bed for earrings or jewelry that might have fallen off while they were making love, but found nothing.

He began pacing the room again, trying to think of what to do as precious time dwindled, but his heart was beating so fast he could barely think. For all he knew, a guest or two might have been planning to leave early to beat traffic. He felt himself losing control again, panic setting in. His breathing grew erratic. Then he saw it. There it was on the nightstand. His salvation, if he could get out of there now. The key to the room was the key that was going to set him free. The motel key had a red plastic attachment with RED RIVER MOTEL stenciled on it in bold white letters. That's when it occurred to him that Alexandria was situated right on Red River. All he had to do was grab their things, put them in the back seat and drive to the riverbank. Once there, he would put the car in neutral and push it into the river.

He turned out the light and cracked open the door. This time he saw a couple of lights on. People were up, probably preparing to leave. It was now or never, he thought, his heart thudding feverishly. Just as he stepped out, he saw a man across the courtyard open his door. Lucas stepped back in his dark room, but kept the door cracked, watching to see what the man was going to do, and if anyone else came out of the room.

The man came out, opened the trunk of his car and put luggage in it. "How much longer, honey?" The man called into the room he had come out of.

"Ten more minutes, dear."

"Get a move on! I wanna make it to Roswell by nightfall," the man was saying as he went back into his room and closed the door.

Lucas opened his door again, peeked out. This time he saw more lights on. He could hear the people in the rooms adjacent to his moving around, talking, and showers running. *I gotta get the hell outta here. Now! Or risk being caught!* He opened the door all the way, picked up the luggage, and fast-walked to the car. He threw the luggage in the back seat and got in the front. Before starting the car, he looked in the rearview mirror and realized he had left the room door wide open. *Fuck! I don't want someone snooping around. I've gotta close that door and put the do not disturb sign on the doorknob.*

He looked around, scanning the area. Seeing no one, he opened his car door, raced back to the room, put the sign on the door and got back into the car before anyone saw him. He took a deep breath. *Calm down, man. We're almost home. Take your time. Drive slowly, but get the hell outta here.* He started the car and pulled off slowly, heading for the riverbank. Once there, he grabbed his bag, put the car in neutral, and pushed it into Red River. He watched it slowly descend until finally, it disappeared, gurgling as it went into the deep.

When it disappeared, he said, "I'm sorry, Marla. It was an accident. I hope you know I didn't mean to kill you." And with that, he walked back to Alexandria. It was 4:45 A.M. by the time he made it to the dark, sleeping town. He had gotten there just in time to catch the first bus to New Orleans.

Chapter 43

The Trial
Opening Statements

"New Orleans!" the bus driver called out. "Last stop!"

Lucas' eyes jerked themselves open when he heard the bus driver's bellowing voice. He had been reliving the nightmare of killing Marla in his dreams. Her pleading eyes looked into his and begged him not to kill her. A vacant look in her eyes followed the sudden snap of her neck. He sighed deeply, wishing he could go back in time and undo what could not be undone. He looked out the window while stretching his long arms toward the bus' roof. After picking up his bag, he walked down the narrow aisle, got off the bus, and made his way over to the courthouse, which was only two blocks away. The street was lined corner to corner with cars.

Are all these people at the trial?

Lucas didn't know it, but when the story of a young Negro female being tried for the murder of a beautiful white woman hit the wire services, reporters from New York, Boston, Washington, DC, Chicago, Fort Lauderdale, Texas, and even California boarded planes, and swarmed into New Orleans like starved locusts to be witnesses of what was being billed as the biggest trial with a Negro defendant since the Scottsboro Boys case nearly twenty years earlier. Due to the sudden influx of people, businesses boomed. Every hotel was booked, every restaurant was filled. The French Quarter taverns poured as much whiskey as they poured during Mardi Gras, which was rapidly approaching, and why the normal judicial bureaucracy was nonexistent. After all, this was an open and shut case.

The nigger did it.

Lucas climbed the stairs of the courthouse and entered the building. A police officer was sitting in a chair, reading a copy of the *Sentinel*. "Excuse me, sir. Which room is Johnnie Wise in?"

He tilted his head to the left. "This one right here. You're late, boy. I don't think there are any seats left."

"Thank you, sir," Lucas said and attempted to go in.

"Where you from, boy? Niggers can't sit on the first floor with Whites. Read the sign. Ya can read, can't ya?"

"Yes, sir," Lucas said, looking at a sign that read: COLOREDS SIT IN THE BALCONY. There was an arrow pointing the way.

"Y'all oughta know that by now. Go on upstairs and sit in the balcony if you can find a seat."

Lucas hid his desire to beat the police officer over the head with his own nightstick. He turned around and made his way down the long hallway. He had never been in the courthouse before, and marveled at all the ivory marble. He reached out and touched it, letting his hands glide along the smooth walls and up the stairs, where the rest of the Negroes were supposed to sit. The balcony was full of people and only offered standing room. From what he could tell, it was the same way downstairs, only it was full of Whites.

As his eyes took in the courtroom and its officers, he was amazed by it all. The judge was a gray-haired white man, dressed in a full-length black robe, sitting high up like he was a king on a throne. There was a table on the right and another on the left, where his beautiful Johnnie sat. She was wearing a lavender and black skirt suit. Johnnie's hair was shining black, and draped her shoulders. A man and two women, one of them Colored, sat with her.

"Mr. Madigan," the judge began, "your opening statement."

Madigan stood up. "The prosecution waives opening, Your Honor."

The judge frowned. "That's highly irregular, counselor. Are you certain you have no opening statement for the jury?"

"Yes, Your Honor."

"Very well. Mr. Goldstein, do you have an opening statement, or should we dispense with the trial altogether and move right into the sentencing phase?"

Mock laughter filled the courtroom.

Goldstein stood up. "Yes, Your Honor. I do have an opening statement." He walked over the jury and said, "Ladies and gentlemen of the jury, are you stunned?" He paused for about ten seconds to allow the question to penetrate. He knew most of the jurors had already made up their minds; Johnnie Wise was guilty, and the trial was just a formality. Even the judge jokingly mentioned sentencing before a single witness had been called.

"I've been trying cases for more than twenty years, and never has a prosecutor waived his opening statement in a murder trial. Why now? I'll tell you why, ladies and gentlemen of the jury . . . because the prosecution doesn't have a case against my client. He has no evidence whatsoever. He doesn't have the weapon. He doesn't have plane tickets, bus tickets, or even train tickets to prove my client went to Fort Lauderdale.

"If she didn't fly there, if she didn't take the train there, if she didn't take a bus there, did she drive Fort Lauderdale? Let's assume she did. Now, Fort Lauderdale is 840 miles from New Orleans. That's about a twelve-hour drive. Twenty-four hours round trip. Ask yourselves this, ladies and gentlemen of the jury; have you ever driven for twenty-four hours nonstop without falling asleep at the wheel? That's what my client would have had to do, because she was in Bayou Cane, Louisiana the night Sharon Trudeau was murdered. My client will tell you this under oath, and so will two other witnesses.

"Did she get a hotel then? If she did, why hasn't the prosecution said so? I'll tell you why he hasn't. Mr. Madigan hasn't offered you this possibility because he'd then have to produce hotel receipts, or at least my client's name on a hotel registry. Perhaps Mr. Madigan didn't consider this possibility and didn't bother checking." Goldstein put a blown-up map of the United States on an easel. "Assuming my client did drive to Fort Lauderdale, it makes sense that she would have taken the shortest route, which would have taken her through Gulf Port, Biloxi, Pensacola, Panama City, Gainesville, Orlando, West Palm Beach, and finally Fort Lauderdale. We investigated, and not one hotel has my client's name on the registry. So what did she do? Sleep on the side of the road? Maybe. But don't forget, ladies and gentlemen of the jury that we have not one, but two witnesses who will swear that Johnnie Wise was in Bayou Cane, Louisiana the night of the murder.

"I'm also stunned that this trial is even being tried in New Orleans when the murder took place in Florida. It's not taking place down there because the district attorney's office knew they had no case against my client. Yet here in Louisiana, a few states away from Florida, 840 miles away, we're trying a seventeen-year-old girl for a murder she didn't commit. Does it make sense to you, ladies and gentlemen of the jury, to pursue a case that the DA in the city where the murder took place refuses to even indict my client? No, it doesn't. Why, then, are we pursuing it? Could it have something to do with the article in the *Sentinel*?

"I think something far more scandalous is going on, ladies and gentlemen. I expect to prove beyond a shadow of a doubt that Johnnie Wise is not only innocent of the charges levied against her, but that she has an ironclad alibi. For the third time, I've got witnesses who will tell you where she was on the night in question. Not only that, ladies and gentlemen, I can tell you that the real murderers are in this room right now. Who they are, I won't say at this time, but they are here. I say 'murderers' because other people have been killed; people other than Sharon Trudeau and the bellhop who just happened to be in the wrong place at the wrong time.

"As a matter of fact, ladies and gentlemen of the jury, I can say for certain that Miss Trudeau and the bellhop were killed by professionals. My client is seventeen years old. She didn't even know where Fort Lauderdale was until I showed her on a map. Ladies and gentlemen, the prosecution is asking you to believe that a seventeen-year-old Negro girl . . . a mere child . .

. somehow knew how to do what other investors didn't. The prosecution is asking you to believe that a child could do what the police couldn't. The prosecution is asking you to believe that a child could not only track down a woman smart enough to dupe and elude the police, but upon finding Miss Trudeau, she was capable of killing her.

"Let's not forget why my client would have tracked her down in the first place. If my client tracked Sharon Trudeau down and killed her, where's the money?" He paused for a few moments and let the jury consider the question. "Again, where is the money? The cops didn't find it at her house, in her car, or in her bank account. So where's the money she allegedly killed for? If it was about money, why did she have to kill Miss Trudeau? Why couldn't she have just taken what belonged to her? Furthermore, if Sharon Trudeau's murder was about stolen money, why not take all the money? Why only take a portion of it? Could it be that someone was trying to frame my client?" He paused and watched them think about what he was saying. "Somebody else wanted Sharon Trudeau dead for other reasons, and that somebody is in this room right now."

And with that, Goldstein returned to his seat.

Chapter 44

"May we approach, Your Honor?"

"Call your first witness, Mr. Madigan," the judge said.

"Thank you, Your Honor. The prosecution calls Martin Winters to the stand."

A tall, thin white man wearing a gray pinstriped suit walked through a pair of swinging double doors and over to the stand where the bailiff waited.

"Place your left hand on the Bible and raise your right hand," the bailiff said. "Do you swear to tell the truth, the whole truth, and nothing but the truth, so help you God?"

"I do."

"You may be seated."

"Mr. Winters, what's your occupation?"

"I'm a broker over at Glenn and Webster's Financial Services."

"Did you have occasion to meet the defendant?"

"Yes, sir, I did. I was her stockbroker for a while, before Sharon Trudeau took over her portfolio."

"So you knew the victim?"

"Yes. We worked together for a couple of years."

"How would you characterize Sharon Trudeau?"

"Beautiful, sharp, understood business."

"Mr. Winters, you say you were the defendant's stockbroker before the victim took over?"

"Yes."

"Why did Miss Trudeau take over?"

"It was at the request of the client."

Johnnie stood up and screamed, "That's a lie, Martin, and you know it!"

Spectators murmured loudly after her sudden outburst.

The judge picked up his mallet and slammed it down hard on the gavel several times. "Order in the court! Mr. Goldstein, get your client under control or I'll have her bound and gagged."

Goldstein stood up and said, "Yes, Your Honor."

The judge looked at Mr. Madigan. "Proceed."

"I have nothing further, Your Honor," Madigan said. He then looked at Goldstein. "Your witness."

"Mr. Winters, do you know what perjury is?"

"Yes."

"And do you maintain that Sharon Trudeau took over my client's stock portfolio because my client wanted her specifically?"

"Well, she didn't ask for Sharon specifically, no."

"So my client just wanted any stockbroker, as long as it wasn't you? Would that be a fair statement?"

Martin Winters remained quiet, thinking, knowing he was in trouble already.

"Shall I repeat the question, Mr. Winters?"

"I wouldn't put it that way, no."

"Okay, Mr. Winters. Now . . . have you ever had any clients make the same request? A client that for no specific reason . . . no longer wanted you to handle their portfolio?"

Shit! You Jew bastard! "No, I have not. That's why it was so puzzling. I had made Johnnie quite a bit of money."

Goldstein smiled. He had him now. "You called my client by her first name. Were you two friends?"

"Objection, Your Honor! Beyond the scope."

"Your Honor, Mr. Winters called my client by her first name, which suggests that he knew her on a more personal level. He also called the victim, who he's worked with for years, by her first name suggesting the same thing. I'd like a little latitude."

"Very little, Mr. Goldstein. Proceed."

"So were you and my client friends?"

"No."

"And you say you made money for her?"

"Yes."

"How much money?"

"Uh, I'm not sure."

Goldstein already knew the answer. All he had to do was reel him in. "My client's only seventeen years old. How much did she invest? A couple hundred? A thousand, maybe?"

Winters' face reddened. He mumbled, "Over a hundred thousand."

"Could you speak up, Mr. Winters? I don't think anyone heard you."

"Over a hundred thousand."

Loud murmuring filled the courtroom.

"Order!" the judge demanded and tapped the gavel.

"How much did she start with? What was her first investment amount, Mr. Winters?"

"Four thousand."

"Four thousand? Dollars, Mr. Winters?" Goldstein asked, looking at the jury.

"Yes."

Loud murmuring again, followed by the judge tapping the gavel.

"That's a lot of money for a sixteen-year-old Colored girl, don't you think, Mr. Winters? That's how old she was when she walked into your office, right?"

"Your Honor, is this going somewhere?" Madigan asked.

"Is there a point to all of this, Mr. Goldstein?" the judge asked.

"I'm getting there, Your Honor."

"Get there. Don't indulge the court's patience any longer."

"Yes, Your Honor." Goldstein looked at Martin Winters, who looked incredibly uncomfortable. "Tell us this, sir. Why would she leave the broker who had made her money for an unproven broker she didn't even know?"

"I have no idea."

"Did you two have a falling out?"

"No."

Goldstein walked over to the jury and stared at them. "Mr. Winters, would you say my client is a beautiful woman?"

"Objection!"

"May we approach, Your Honor?" Goldstein asked.

The judge nodded, and the attorneys walked up to the bench.

Goldstein continued, "I have reason to believe that Mr. Winters and my client had an illicit but brief affair. My client broke it off. When this child molester wouldn't leave her alone, she threatened to tell his wife, and that's the real reason he passed her off to Miss Trudeau."

Madigan said, "Your Honor, even if he did have an affair with the defendant, he's not on trial for Miss Trudeau's murder."

"Yes, Your Honor, but if the witness did have an affair with my client and he lies about it, he would have a credibility problem. The jury needs to be made aware of it. Besides that, we know Sharon Trudeau stole money from a lot of people. If she'd do that, she might blackmail Mr. Winters. If she did blackmail him, he could have killed her himself. My client is on trial for her life."

"Mr. Goldstein, can you prove they had an affair or that Miss Trudeau was blackmailing him?"

"No, Your Honor, but I should be allowed to explore—"

"Stick to the facts of the case, Mr. Goldstein."

"But Your Honor, this is a bombshell!"

"Step back."

Madigan returned to his seat, but Goldstein angrily walked over to the jury and said, "Okay, Mr. Winters, just another question or two. Isn't it true that your wife found out that you were having an adulterous affair with my client, who was only sixteen years old at the time, and only then did you pass her off to Sharon Trudeau?"

Loud murmuring filled the courtroom. The judge slammed his mallet on the gavel several times and said, "Mr. Goldstein, Mr. Madigan, in my chambers. Now!"

Chapter 45

"Lucas!"

When Lucas learned of Johnnie having yet another affair behind his back, it crushed him. Marla had tried to tell him about her, but he wouldn't hear of it—not his Johnnie. She would never do such a thing, he thought. Not a second time. Napoleon, he could understand. She was being threatened. Earl Shamus, he could understand to some degree because at least she had been forced into that situation. But another white man? Somebody named Martin Winters? And it had happened a year ago?

His wife knew about it, but I didn't?

He walked down the stairs to the balcony railing and stared unflinchingly at Johnnie as she talked with the two women at her table. He couldn't tell what they were saying, but there was a lot of nodding and smiling going back and forth between the women. Suddenly, as if she could sense his presence, as if she could sense him staring at her, he saw her head swivel to the right and look up into the balcony. Their eyes met, locked, and the rest of the world stood still as he watched the realization of a deep secret revealed surge through her mind. He could tell she had no idea he was there until that very moment, and he had heard it all. He shook his head, their eyes still locked, neither saying anything, both knowing their relationship had come to a swift and decisive end. He turned around and climbed the stairs to leave.

Desperate, shaken, and incredibly sorry for what she'd done to him, Johnnie stood up and shouted, "Lucas!" Her words echoed in the large room and in her mind. Flashes of the wrong she'd done with Martin, Earl, and Napoleon forced their way into her conscience and condemned her to a fiery hell.

When Lucas heard the anguish in her voice, he stopped momentarily. As much as he wanted to turn around, as much as he wanted to forgive and forget, he couldn't. What he'd heard was the last straw, the final nail in their relationship coffin. Marla had been right all along. He knew that now. As he walked out the door, Marla and the watery grave she didn't deserve came to mind. It was time to leave New Orleans. And he would, that very hour.

Chapter 46

No more excuses

When Johnnie saw Lucas walkout of the balcony, when she saw him refuse to turn around and look at her, she knew she had lost him forever. There would be no more reprieves, no explanations, no magnificent lies she could tell to undo the destruction she had done a second time. As she thought about what he must have been thinking of her in those precious few seconds when they stared at each other, she remembered what he'd said to her when he learned of her dalliance with Napoleon. He'd looked at her and said, "Maybe you are a whore." Until now, she'd never seen herself as anything other than a good Christian girl. Sure, she had slept around a bit, but she could always blame her mother; she could always blame Earl Shamus or Napoleon Bentley; she could even blame God for her own choices.

However, she couldn't blame anyone but herself for sleeping with Martin Winters. She had convinced herself that she had to sleep with him to learn about the stock market. It was a business transaction. Now she knew that it was an act born out of laziness and unrestrained greed. She knew she had taken the easy road to riches that laying on one's back brings. She knew that what she had done offered no "real" rewards.

In short, she knew she had become her mother, and began to wonder if she would suffer her mother's fate. She wondered if she'd end up broke, used up, but still good-looking enough to sell the sweet heaven her body offered to desperate, depraved men. The strange thing about it all was that she realized she wasn't crying over the loss of the relationship; she wasn't even on the verge of tears. It had taken two years of sexual promiscuity to eradicate the softhearted girl who loved God and His law. That girl was gone now, perhaps for good, she thought.

Chapter 47

The brilliant light of truth

Lucas caught a bus out to Ashland Estates, which let him out at the entrance. No one was home. The adults were either working or at the trial, and the children were in school. He had the whole place to himself. With his belongings in tow, he walked the barren streets, still shaken by what he'd heard in the courtroom, still wounded by the Dear John letter he had hoped to evade. When he got to Johnnie's house, he lifted the garage door and saw his two automobiles parked next to each other like a set of twins. He hopped into his 1941 Chevy and was about to start it when an evil thought emerged and took root: *Burn it down. Burn the place to the ground.*

He told himself he was doing her a favor as he took out a container of gasoline he'd kept in the trunk in case he ever ran out on his drug runs to Grambling and Jackson State Universities. They both needed to get far away from New Orleans. Burning down her house would ensure that she had no reason to stay. He poured gasoline all through the house, up the stairs, and on her bed. He looked at the headboard and saw the carved-in angels blowing trumpets.

He remembered the first time they'd made love, and still drenched it with the rest of the gas. He grabbed a book of matches off her nightstand and ran the tip of a match across the sandpaper edge. A flame ignited. As he stared into the blaze for a fleeting moment, he seriously considered blowing it out and leaving. But he didn't change his mind. He couldn't, not after what he'd heard. It all had to end, and this was the way to do it, he believed. He dropped the flame. It looked like it was falling in slow motion.

Whoosh!

The fire seemed to gulp the oxygen like a thirsty wino drinking his favorite intoxicant. Lucas quietly watched the fire until it climbed the walls, listening to it crackle as it spread. Determined to finish what he'd started, he grabbed the matches off the nightstand and rushed downstairs. Room by room, he lit fire after fire to ensure the home's complete and utter destruction. As the fire raged out of control, he got into his Chevy, backed out of the garage, and headed to South Carolina, where he would be inducted into the Army.

As he was leaving the entrance of Ashland Estates, a caravan of cars and trucks full of angry Whites turned in. One of them yelled, "You best be on your way, boy. We gon' burn this wicked place to the ground." As each vehicle entered, more threats were shouted, but Lucas didn't even care. He was on his way to a better life in a different state. If all went well for him, he was going overseas to play football. He was going to be an officer and a gentleman someday. After the last car turned, he drove off and never looked back—not even in his rearview mirrors.

Chapter 48

"Tell the truth!"

After the judge threatened to put Goldstein in jail for contempt, the principals returned to the courtroom. When the Negroes saw Goldstein, they stood up and cheered. He looked up at them and nodded almost unnoticeably. The judge tapped the gavel a few times. "Order!" he demanded. Looking at the Negroes, he said, "If I hear another peep from you people up there, I'll clear the balcony." He looked at the jury. "You will disregard Mr. Goldstein's last question." He looked at Goldstein. "Are you through with this witness?"

"No, Your Honor. I have a few more questions."

"Proceed with caution, counselor. I won't warn you again."

"Yes, Your Honor," Goldstein said, looking in the eyes of a jury that was paying strict attention to him. "Now, Mr. Winters, can you tell us how you came to know my client and why you chose to do *business* with her?"

"She just walked in off the street one day."

"My client wasn't referred to you by Earl Shamus?"

"No."

"Earl Shamus didn't ask you to take care of his mistress' stock portfolio?"

"Objection! Asked and answered."

"Sustained."

"No further questions, Your Honor."

"You may step down," the judge said.

Martin walked past the defendant's table. As he passed Johnnie, he never even looked her way, like he didn't know who she was.

"Call your next witness, Mr. Madigan."

"The prosecution rests, Your Honor."

Goldstein stood up. "This is preposterous, Your Honor. Mr. Madigan waived his opening statement, and has only offered this jury one witness. Mr. Winters only told us that Sharon Trudeau and my client were in business together. He never made a case for her being the person who killed Miss Trudeau, and he certainly never placed my client at the scene of the crime. Mr. Madigan is making a mockery out of these proceedings. He's offered no evidence whatsoever, and yet here we are trying a case that should never have come to trial in the first place. He hasn't proven that my client was even in Fort Lauderdale on the night in question. He doesn't have the weapon, a shell casing, nothing. And most important, Your Honor, he doesn't even have the money she was supposed to have killed Sharon Trudeau to retrieve, which is the foundation of his case. We move for an immediate dismissal of the charges levied against my client."

"Denied. Proceed with your defense, counselor."

Goldstein went back to the table and picked up his witness list. "The defense calls Meredith Shamus to the stand."

Meredith commanded the attention of everyone in the courtroom when she stood and walked down the center aisle on her way to the witness stand. She wasn't much to look at, but she did look like someone of importance, someone who had money—lots of it. Her thin figure was easily hidden by a two-piece turquoise skirt suit, black belt, turquoise-and-black pumps. She wore a wide-brimmed turquoise veiled hat with a black ribbon around it. Her lips were red and full. After swearing to tell the truth, she sat in the witness chair.

"Miss Shamus, tell us what your educational background and occupation is."

"I have a bachelor's degree in English Literature, and I'm the president of Buchanan Mutual Insurance."

"And how did you come to be the president of an insurance company with a degree in literature?"

"It was my father's company, and he left it to me at his death."

"Are you married, Miss Shamus?"

"Yes."

"How long?"

"Eighteen years."

"Children?

"Yes, I have four beautiful children; three girls and one boy. However, my son died in a tragic accident last year."

"I'm sorry to hear that. I have children too, and if something happened to any of them, especially my daughters, I don't know what I'd do, which brings me to my next set of questions. I need to ask you how you would feel if one or all three of your daughters were molested by a man old enough to be their father?"

"I'd be sick about it."

"Would you be equally as sick if I told you my client had been molested by a man old enough to be her father?"

"I suppose."

"You suppose, Mrs. Shamus? I would think you'd be appalled like any other woman in this courtroom. Is that why you paid my client fifty thousand dollars to stop the affair your husband was having with her, knowing full well that she was only a fifteen-year-old child when he began having sex with her?"

Meredith shifted her eyes to Johnnie, realizing her scheme had failed, and that the young woman who had taken her husband had played her for a fool again. They had made an agreement in the city jail; an agreement she herself was going to break. Though she had hidden it well, she was on fire with an intense anger, having been outsmarted and double crossed first. Nevertheless, she took a deep but unnoticeable breath, and composed herself. She was still going to bury Johnnie by portraying herself as another victim in her rival's wake. The only thing that had changed was that Johnnie and her lawyers would not be caught off guard by her testimony. The story she planned to tell would be just as effective without the surprise.

Confidently, Meredith said, "She doesn't look like a child, does she, Mr. Goldstein? She looks like a full grown woman."

"So you saw a seventeen-year-old, a mere child, as a rival for your husband's affections, Mrs. Shamus? Is that what you're telling the jury?"

"I saw the little trollop as a threat to the security of my family and the sanctity of my marriage and every other marriage in the city, Mr. Goldstein. New Orleans is full of black whores like her who destroy white families and the very fabric of any civilized society. For proof of this, I urge you to drive over to Ashland Estates and take a look around for yourself. You'll see plenty of evidence there, I assure you. Given what I was up against, I did whatever I had to do to stop the affair. If fifty thousand dollars was the price I had to pay, that's what I did. I would have paid ten . . . a hundred times more to keep my family intact, sir."

Having been threatened with a gag, Johnnie sat there shaking her head as she listened to Meredith. Everything was going according to plan. Her lawyers told her that Meredith was the key to an acquittal. They didn't believe she was going to keep her side of the bargain. Even if she did, she'd still make a compelling witness for Johnnie if they went after her.

"You say you did whatever you had to do to stop the affair. Does that include murder, Mrs. Shamus?"

Surprised by the accusation, she shouted, "No! I would never kill anyone for any reason, Mr. Goldstein."

"Did the affair end when you paid the money?"

"Yes."

"How did you find out about the affair?"

"I hired a private detective."

"Tony Hatcher?"

Shocked that he knew the name, she said, "Yes."

"What evidence of the affair did he give you?"

"Photographs and his notes."

"And after the affair was over, did you end Mr. Hatcher's employment?"

"No."

"Why not, Mrs. Shamus? You knew all there was to know, didn't you?"

"I wanted to make sure the affair didn't start up again."

"What did you do with the photographs and notes and recordings?"

Meredith frowned, having been caught off guard again. "Recordings, Mr. Goldstein? I never said anything about recordings. What are you talking about?"

Goldstein looked into the faces of the jury and said, "You didn't have Mr. Hatcher bug my client's house?"

"No."

"I suppose he never gave you those tapes?"

"I have no idea what you're talking about."

Goldstein looked at his prey and said, "Really?"

"I most certainly don't, sir."

"You didn't know my client was seeing notorious Mob boss Napoleon Bentley?"

"No."

"You didn't know my client was related to the Beauregards?"

"Objection!"

"On what grounds, Mr. Madigan?"

"He's badgering his own witness."

"Your Honor, I request permission to treat Mrs. Shamus as a hostile witness. I have reason to believe she knows more than she's letting on."

"Overruled. Proceed, Mr. Goldstein."

Knowing she was on the verge of losing control, Goldstein walked up to Meredith and smirked. Then he screamed, "Well, Mrs. Shamus? Did you know?"

"No! I knew nothing about it until I read it in the *Sentinel*!" Meredith screamed.

Goldstein smiled again. He had her now. "You hated her, didn't you, Mrs. Shamus? You hated her for having duped you into giving her fifty thousand dollars for keeping your good for nothing husband out of the ensuing scandal concerning Richard

Goode and my client's mother, Marguerite Wise, didn't you? You wanted to teach her a lesson, didn't you, Mrs. Shamus? She had wronged you like no one ever wronged you. She had taken your husband! She had taken your money! And in so doing, she had taken your Buchanan dignity, hadn't she, Mrs. Shamus? To make matters worse, she was a child, and a Negro on top of that. As hard as you tried to let it go, you couldn't, could you, Mrs. Shamus, because your pride wouldn't allow you to, would it?"

"No!" she screamed, having lost control.

"Yes, you did, Mrs. Shamus. And you didn't stop there, did you? She had to pay for what she did, didn't she? You called the writer of the society page of the *Sentinel* newspaper and told him every detail, didn't you, Mrs. Shamus?"

"No!"

"You did, and I have two witnesses to prove it, Mrs. Shamus. Let's stop this farce now. Admit what you did! You hated my client, and you wanted everyone to believe she killed Sharon Trudeau, didn't you?"

"No!"

"Tell the truth! She deserved it, didn't she, Mrs. Shamus? She had wronged you, she had wronged your husband, and you knew what really happened in the Beauregard mansion Thanksgiving Day, didn't you? You knew about the murders because you had heard the recordings of my client and her neighbor Sadie discussing what really happened, didn't you? And you wanted to make sure she didn't get away with ruining another family, didn't you, Mrs. Shamus?"

"No!"

"No? My next witness is Ethel Beauregard. Do you really want to take her down with you? Have you no shame?"

Meredith Shamus left the witness stand and ran at Johnnie, screaming, “You little black bitch! You tricked me! I’ll kill you for this!”

All of sudden, shots rang out. Pow! Pow! Pow! Pow! Pow! Screams filled the courtroom—Pow!—as people ran in every direction.

Chapter 49

"You're right."

Several people were shot, including Goldstein, the judge, and Meredith Shamus, who lay dead at Johnnie's feet—a single bullethole in her forehead. Everything had happened so quickly, yet everything was moving in slow motion, just like it had the day the Beauregard men died. Johnnie stood up. She could hear the screams; she could see people running in all directions. She looked at Jay Goldstein. He had a bullet in his shoulder, blood was flowing, but he was trying to get to her before she was killed.

"Get down!" Goldstein shouted.

Johnnie heard him, but her mind was in a fog. It was happening again. People all around her were dying, falling at her feet. She felt someone staring at her. She swiveled her head to the right and saw Ethel Beauregard coming down the center aisle with a pistol in her hand. She was aiming it at Johnnie. This time Morgan wasn't there to save her, and Goldstein was too far away to help. It was all over this time. Not even God could save her this time, but she didn't care anymore. She didn't want to live anymore. After seeing the look on Lucas' face, after seeing his unguarded disgust, after realizing that she was a whore, just like her mother, she wanted to die. She welcomed oblivion. Death would be her angel of mercy, and she wasn't afraid of it.

Ethel pointed the gun at Johnnie and said, "You don't deserve to live another second after all you've done."

In a state of perfect peace, Johnnie said, "You're right."

She stood there looking at Ethel, looking down the barrel of the gun she was holding, waiting to be slaughtered like a sacrificial lamb. The police officer who had been outside the door rushed in, but it was too late.

Ethel squeezed the trigger. Nothing happened. No pop! No discharge. No nothing. Only the clicking of an empty chamber could be heard. And then, for some inexplicable reason, she put the gun to her own head, pulled the trigger and blew her brains clean out of her head. Her lifeless body crashed to the floor.

After seeing Ethel kill herself, Johnnie looked toward heaven and fell to her knees. She said, "Okay, Lord. I surrender." Then she began to sing, "Amazing Grace, how sweet the sound that saved a wretch like me, was blind, but now I see."

Chapter 50

Fire!

Before she left the courthouse, Cleo told Johnnie she was pretty much in the clear and that she would make sure it was over by securing an official dismissal. Johnnie thanked her and got into the car. Sadie pulled away from the curb and headed home. As they rode in silence, both of them were in deep thought, reliving the nightmare of bullets flying, whistling as they sought to sink into the flesh of their intended and unintended victims. This was the second such incident for Johnnie, and much like all experiences, it was easier the second time.

For some unknown reason, Johnnie's mind focused on Meredith Shamus' testimony and how upset she was about the affair she'd had with Earl, even though she knew it had been over for quite some time. It occurred to her that Meredith's death would usher in a whole new era for the Shamus family. Earl would finally take over Buchanan Mutual and all the wealth that came along with it. She found it ironic that he would end up with everything when he had married Meredith in hopes of getting his hands on her money from the beginning. Somehow that didn't seem right to her, that the wicked would prevail, at least for now.

As her thoughts deepened, she remembered how her defense team had learned of Meredith's involvement and how the *Sentinel* gathered its facts about the Beauregard secret. The whole thing with Meredith began to unravel the moment Johnnie told Goldstein everything that had happened to her, over breakfast at Walter Brickman's. She began by telling him what Earl Shamus and her mother had done to her when she was still innocent. She finished her gripping life story by telling Goldstein about the inheritance money she received from Grandpa Nathaniel.

Everyone who might have given the *Sentinel's* society page writer the story about Johnnie being a Beauregard by blood had something to lose, except for Earl and Meredith Shamus. The fifty thousand they had been duped out of, and the way Johnnie ripped into his heart were more than enough motivation to give the writer a juicy story that would get the attention of nearly everyone in New Orleans. However, there was no way Earl and Meredith would know the secret. It was so secret that it was rarely talked about on the black or the white side of the family.

As a matter of fact, the article in the society section was too specific for guesswork and innuendo, as it might appear to someone who didn't know the facts. To the casual reader, the article probably came off as juicy aristocratic prattle, embarrassing skeletons with no real substance to verify the story's veracity. After the Garden District's affluent had its brief amusement, the article would have become an urban legend of sorts, and that would have been the end of it. But since Johnnie knew the story was far more truth than speculation, she knew someone had told the *Sentinel* the facts about both sides of her family, which raised serious suspicions in her defense team's minds.

Led by Goldstein, the defense team began to suspect that someone had put listening devices in Johnnie's house. How else would the *Sentinel* know so much accurate information about the Beauregard family? Johnnie hadn't told the *Sentinel,* and Ethel certainly wouldn't have. They searched Johnnie's home and found microphones surreptitiously planted throughout the house. They believed it was the work of a professional who knew her schedule and came to retrieve the tapes when it was convenient. If they were right, that meant a private detective was likely involved.

With that morsel of information, they began to consider who, if they had the information, would take pleasure in seeing the story in print. Private detectives were expensive, so they knew it had to be someone who could actually pay for long hours of surveillance. Once they figured out that much, they knew, or rather believed it was Earl and Meredith Shamus. They had the money and the motivation to destroy Johnnie Wise with extreme prejudice. The Beauregards were unfortunate victims of the plot to devastate Johnnie—collateral damage.

There were a number of capable private detectives in New Orleans, and the defense team had two weeks to find the one hired by the Shamuses. Dee Dee Wellington was a good-looking blonde with enough curves to cause traffic pile-ups at a busy intersection when she wore a tight-fitting sweater. Her magnificent breasts would be more than enough of a distraction. So distracting were they that even a detective with high integrity might drop his guard if he was suspicious of her at the initial meeting.

Dee Dee had shown her delicious cleavage to a dozen or so private investigators before she entered the office of Tony Hatcher. Her cover story was simple but effective. She was married to a rich guy who ran around on her constantly, but she didn't have proof. Once Hatcher agreed to take her case, she asked for references, which he didn't hesitate to give her. The names and telephone numbers of at least five women were on the paper he gave her, and Meredith Shamus' name was at the top. Later, the defense team went back to Hatcher's office and threatened to have him arrested for breaking and entering. They also threatened to sue him for invasion of privacy. The lawsuit wouldn't have amounted to much, but the cost of the suit would have cleaned him out due to attorney fees. It wasn't long before he spilled his guts and told them everything.

However, Johnnie thought Goldstein's strategy had worked too well. She didn't want any more people to die—not because of her; but die they did. His plan was to slowly lead Meredith down a path, upset her, and then surprise her with the information Hatcher provided when she least expected it. No one expected her to try to attack Johnnie the way she had. They had no way of knowing that Ethel would lose touch with reality either.

Cleo had explained that when Ethel saw what Goldstein had done to Meredith, she probably knew she was the next turkey to be carved up and served to the jury—she was right, too. The destruction would have been complete, with zero opportunity for resuscitation. Ethel wasn't about to be publicly humiliated and later arrested for murdering her husband. She figured Goldstein was going to go after her and she would die in prison anyway. Having nothing to lose, she decided to kill the judge for allowing a white woman to be ripped to shreds publicly, Goldstein for being so good at cross examination, and Johnnie because if anybody deserved a bullet in the head, she did, since she was the cause of it all. The way she probably saw it, they could all play pinochle in the fiery flames of hell together—that very day.

"We got you niggers this time!" a white male screamed from a passing pickup truck.

Sadie and Johnnie had no idea what he was referring to until they neared Ashland Estates, which was engulfed in flames that seemed to reach the sky. The whole community would be lost because not a single fire truck came to put the blaze out. They later learned that their Fire Department had been set on fire too.

Chapter 51

"What are you going to do now, Johnnie?"

Main Street had been ransacked again, but this time the destruction was far worse. The landmark Sepia Theater, Walter Brickman's, the bank, every building was a shell of its former self. They were still erect, but burned out nevertheless. The affluent Negroes had lost it all—their homes, their businesses, and their money, absolutely everything—and they wept. The men, the women, and the children stood over the smoldering ashes that were once their privileged homes, and cried until they couldn't cry anymore.

Reverend Settlefore used the fire as an opportunity to get the citizens of Baroque and Sable Parishes behind the coming Civil Rights Movement. The people saw the NAACP as their saviors and got fully involved. Walker Tresvant III and his family were the only people in either parish who refused to cast their lot with the good Reverend. Tresvant had only lost his home and the Sepia Theater, but he was far from destroyed. The Tresvant family had lots of investments. They took a train to Manhattan while their property was still in flames. Prior to leaving, Walker vowed never to return.

Johnnie stood by all night with her neighbors and watched as yellow and red flames ate their way through wood and glass, until there was nothing left of what was once her palace and sanctuary. Now that the fire had finished wiping her out, she sifted through the ashes, hoping a little of the money was untouched by the hot conflagration, but there was nothing left of the fireplace, which was where she'd hid the remaining two hundred thousand Bubbles had retrieved for her. All she had left were the clothes on her back and the money in her purse, forty-five dollars and change. Ironically, that sum was a little more than what Earl Shamus had given her the first time he entered her unblemished body. She sighed heavily as the reality of being broke again washed over her. "I guess you were right after all, Sadie. I trusted in money, and now it's all gone."

"What are you going to do now, Johnnie?" Sadie asked, crying, shushing her children, who clung to her, their only means of refuge.

Johnnie exhaled like the wind had been knocked out of her and said, "Drive to East Saint Louis, I guess. My daddy told me I could stay with him when my mother was killed. If not him, I know my brother and sister-in-law will take me in. I've never been anywhere, and the world is so big. I'm still getting out of here. I'm still leaving New Orleans today. What about you? What are your plans?"

"I'm scared, Johnnie," Sadie said with a breaking heart. "I've got three mouths to feed. What can I do? The money you gave me is gone, burned up in the fire. Our plans to start over are a memory now. I'm stuck. If I had just left the moment you gave me my freedom, I could have returned the favor. Now I have to keep working for Mrs. Mancini. I have to depend on her generosity for the remainder of my life. And if something happens to Santino, I don't know what I'm going to do."

"Save your money, Sadie. Save every dime you can."

"I'll do what I can, but what about Lucas, Johnnie? Will you try and find him?"

"No. I hope he makes it in the Army. One of his cars is gone. Thank God he left before them crackers set the fire. He'll never have to see what we've seen. He'll never have the memory of seeing what was once a beautiful black community burned to the ground. Besides, I don't think he ever wants to see me again after what he heard in court yesterday. I don't know that I could ever face him, either. What lie could I tell him that would change what he heard?"

Still standing in what used to be her living room, she looked on the ground and saw what was left of her Bible. It was completely burned except for one page, and it had been nearly ruined by smoke. Only one passage on the page could be read. She picked up the page and read the following verse: "I will never leave you nor forsake you." After reading the passage, she shook her head and smiled.

"Why are you smiling, Johnnie? You've lost everything."

She looked at her best friend, handed her the passage, and said, "Not everything, Sadie. After all I've done, after all I've been through, the Lord still loves me."

Johnnie and Sadie embraced each other. They held on for a long time and wept bittersweet tears, knowing they might never see each other again.

"I gotta go, Sadie. Thanks for everything. Thanks for being a *true* friend."

"No, thank you, Johnnie. Thank you."

Johnnie got into her car and started it. Then she looked at Sadie one last time and said, "I love you. And I won't ever forget you."

"Don't forget that good grammar opens the doors bad grammar shuts."

Johnnie smiled and pulled off, looking at Sadie and her children in the rearview mirror. She heard her friend shout, "I love you too!" As she drove down the road, she promised herself that if she ever did well for herself again, she would find and take care of the woman who'd treated her better than the woman who had birthed her.

Epilogue

The author thought it best that I tell you all what became of me after I left my native New Orleans. I've read every single email, so I know you're dying to know. First, let me start by telling you I just had another birthday. It's hard to believe fifty-four years have passed since my fifteenth birthday. I'm sixty-nine years old, and I still look good. Tina Turner ain't got nothin' on me. Thanksgiving was last week, and the year is 2006. I live in a house that sits on 2.3 acres of land in Tiburon, California, right down the street from my favorite nephew, Sterling Wise. He's one of three sons my brother Benny and his wife Brenda had together.

Do you all remember the check that Parker Jamieson gave me in my hospital room? I thought I was broke when I left Sadie and her children standing in the middle of what used to be a beautiful area for Colored folk. Like many of you, I had forgotten all about my inheritance money until I was three hundred miles away from New Orleans. I stopped to get gas and discovered I wasn't totally broke after all. In those days, five thousand dollars was more like fifty thousand dollars. That amount was next to nothing when you compare it to the two hundred thousand that burned up, but it was still a lot of money. I remembered what stocks I had in my portfolio and bought some more, and they grew.

Eventually, I decided to take all the pearls of wisdom that had been offered me concerning education; the same pearls I'd rejected, which landed me in the mess I'd made of the early part of my life. I went on to college and earned my bachelor's degree in English Literature. Thanks to Sadie, I had discovered the pleasures of reading, and I stoked that fire by reading at least three books a week for the last fifty years or so. I also earned a master's degree in business and became a stockbroker. I lived lavishly in Manhattan, and had one baby—Karen, who I adore. I did not do to her what was done to me and my mother before me. You'll be happy to know that I broke the cycle forever! As a matter of fact, I made sure I didn't spoil Karen. I accomplished that feat by teaching her the value of work and earning everything from dollars to accolades. Praise the Lord!

I guess now is a good time to tell you what happened to all the people I met during my journey to self-discovery. I'll begin with Katherine, my nemesis, Ethel Beauregard's cook, friend, and confidant. Eleven years ago, in 1995, financially well-off, Katherine hired the Drew Perry Private Detective Agency to find me. She was eighty-four at the time. We talked of the old days and we laughed so. It was truly a blessed time. I don't think I've ever seen her happier. She said she had to find me and clear her conscience before the good Lord took her home. She went on to say that Ethel and Parker Jamieson had changed Grandpa Nathaniel's Will and cheated my brother and me out of two million dollars. By the time she told me the truth, Parker Jamieson was dead, and the Beauregard fortune had been given to a number of worthy charitable organizations.

After years of questioning why Ethel could cavalierly put a gun to her head and pull the trigger, Katherine finally shed a bit of light on the subject. It turns out that Ethel came from a long line of women with suicidal tendencies. Apparently, a public trial shoved her right over the edge. I found it interesting that her favorite son, Blue, had done the same thing without hesitation. I had seen both of them make a decision to end their lives in an instant. I guess what they say is true; the apple doesn't fall far from the tree. Ethel's DNA leaned toward suicide, I guess.

The promiscuity DNA from Nathaniel was passed on to me and Benny. Benny passed it on to his son, Sterling, just as Brenda had predicted five decades ago, long before DNA became so prevalent. Benny's other two sons, Jericho and William, are as monogamous as their mother. Now, that's something to think about.

Katherine was wealthy because the Beauregard mansion and the land surrounding it were bequeathed to her. According to her, Ethel had promised years earlier to leave it to her in her Will, which was why she saw me as a threat back in 1953. But the aristocracy in the Garden District told her that if she didn't sell it to their committee, they'd burn her out of it. She was smart enough to have the property appraised before selling. Interestingly enough, the committee gave her a fair price to abdicate the premises. She found herself a good man and married him.

As for my good friend Morgan, I got a letter from him around the same time Katherine tracked me down. It had been about twenty-five years since I'd seen or heard from him. Morgan was living in Quebec City, Canada with his family. He confirmed Katherine's story concerning the theft of my money, but I guess it's like the Bible says—you reap what you sow. As the young people say today, "It's all good," because I ain't broke. I live a very lavish life in an expensive home. What makes it "all good" is that all my money was earned legally. No more ill gotten gains for me; that ain't nothing but trouble, ladies. Anyway, Morgan also sent me a diary my grandmother had written, which was full of interesting entries.

Reading the dairy of Josephine Baptiste was like reading a very engrossing novel. Apparently, selling young, ripe nigrescent females was a time-honored tradition that went back well beyond my mother's mother. According to the diary, it appears as though it started with my great grandmother. Her name was Antoinette Jacqueline Gabrielle Baptiste. The diary included several pictures of Josephine and a few of Antoinette. They were both quite beautiful, as you might imagine. Looking at Josephine was like looking in a mirror. No wonder Grandpa Nathaniel was taken with me.

There were a number of references to the Tresvant family. Antoinette was engaged to Walker Tresvant I. To make a long story short, two weeks before her wedding nuptials, she was raped by a white man who owned a rival plantation. Unlike today, if a woman wasn't a virgin on her wedding night, she was said to be ruined. Needless to say, the marriage was off. To make matters worse, her rapist impregnated her. She was the victim, yet everyone, including her own parents, blamed her. In the process of time, she delivered a baby girl, Josephine. When the bastard child turned fifteen, Antoinette placed her with Nathaniel Beauregard. He promised to adhere to the old placage system, which meant he had to buy her a home and hire several servants. Inheritance money for any children he sired was a part of the deal.

My mother came along two years later, and all was going well between Josephine and Nathaniel until she had a brief affair with Francois Devereux, a handsome, but married Negro lawyer she'd met by chance at Woolworth's. Francois was a third generation quadroon who had been educated at the Sorbonne. He was also a linguist, able to fluently speak German, Spanish, Latin, and of course, French. My grandmother was terribly smitten after that initial meeting. His command of words awakened her mind as well as her body. Shortly after meeting him, in spite of Francois' marriage and her "arrangement" with Nathaniel, nature took its inevitable course.

When Nathaniel learned of the affair, he put Josephine out of the house and stopped supporting her and his daughter. Determined to exact a high price for her betrayal, Nathaniel, using his wealth and influence, ruined Francois' business. One by one, all of his white clients left him and before long, he had to leave New Orleans. Using the same formula, Nathaniel made it impossible for Josephine to find suitable employment. With opportunities being few, she swallowed her pride and went to a local brothel to "work." As Paul Harvey says, "Now you know the rest of the story."

I wish I could tell you my life had been an easy series of making the right choices, but it wasn't. The bottom line is I eventually started making better decisions, but that took a lifetime of learning, just as Reverend Staples had said fifty-four years ago. I still think about him from time to time, and the final sermon I heard him preach from the book of Jeremiah, chapter thirteen, verse nine—powerful stuff.

Upon leaving Ashland Estates, my original plan was to visit my father and his wife Jasmine, but on the way, I met my first husband, a man named Paul Masterson. He was an evangelist who traveled all over North America, preaching the Gospel of Jesus Christ. Paul was Caucasian, but don't hold that against him. I didn't, because he was probably the most loving husband I had of the three white men I married. He also made a darn good living preaching God's word. Paul and I had a marvelous time, going from church to church, singing praises to the Lord, helping build the kingdom of God, and seeing the lost being saved.

I suppose I would have stayed married to him for the remainder of my life if I hadn't caught him having sex with a white woman—the pastor's wife—in the pastor's church, in his study. They were lovers years earlier and didn't know they were still attracted to one another. That's what he told me anyway.

I never saw a man beg the way Paul begged me to stay with him. He apologized profusely and explained a thousand times, but I could never get the image of him and her thrusting wildly against each other like animals in heat. The thing hurt me because I really liked him. I suppose I had something to do with his cheating because I never loved him. If I'm being honest with you, and I am, I knew I could never really love another man, at least not the way I should because I never stopped loving my first love—Lucas Matthews. I'll get back to him later. Believe it or not, I wasn't destroyed by Paul's lack of self-control, nor was I destroyed by what many folks might describe as my own hypocrisy.

Over the years, after all of my own doings, after watching what was left of my house burn down, I learned not to be such a harsh judge of most matters. You live and you learn—hopefully. I've spent a lifetime fighting my own innate self-righteous attitude, which, I've learned over the course of nearly five decades, leads to self-destruction. Sometimes I wonder if I would have been better off being a blatant sinner with no hope of salvation. Perhaps then it would have been easier to come to terms with my own destructive nature, which was the love of money and doing what was right in my own eyes. But again, as they say, you live and you learn. All I can say is boy, have I learned.

However, with all my learning, with all that I've been through, I still don't like white women—well, there are two that I grew to respect and, to some degree, appreciate. One was my nephew William's wife, Terry Moretti. Italian girl, beautiful, voluptuous, had her own money and a Ph.D from Stanford, but she had a mouth on her. She put me in my place a couple times, too.

You'll figure out who the other person is during the course of reading this final chapter of my life. Perhaps there are more white women I can respect out there that I have yet to meet. Please don't hate me for being hypocritical at times; I'm just being honest with you. Maybe it's just American white women I don't like. I'm not sure. Those are the only ones I've had dealings with.

When I was fifteen, shortly after being sold to Earl Shamus, I remember being told by my mother that black women and white women don't like each other. At that time, I wasn't sure if she was right, but I've learned over the years that she was. It's funny now when I think about it, but I wonder how we're all going to get along in heaven. Heaven will probably be Jim Crow, white women on one side of heaven and black women on the other (smile). Perhaps we'll do better up there than we do down here.

Anyway, after divorcing Paul in 1963, I finally moved to San Francisco, where Benny and Brenda lived. I enrolled at the University of San Francisco and happened to see Lucas, who looked quite dashing in his green Army uniform. He had gold clusters on his shoulders, the rank of Major, and pretty medals all over his chest, like he had won some war somewhere on Mother Earth all by himself. I wasn't surprised. Lucas was a born warrior. He kind of reminds me of my nephew, Jericho, Benny and Brenda's firstborn son, who turned out to be a big-time drug dealer and gunrunner. He had connections inside the Central Intelligence Agency.

Anyway, Lucas was stationed at the Presidio, but was on campus visiting the ROTC Unit. President Kennedy had been assassinated, and there was talk of Lyndon B. Johnson committing forces to Vietnam, which was why Lucas was there. He'd told me he was going to be an advisor to the South Vietnamese and that he was leaving in two months. I hadn't seen him in years, yet when we saw each other, it was like we had never been apart. Everything was so perfect, and our lovemaking was wild and totally untamed. I love the Lord, but Lucas was my first love, so I sinned with him until he left for Vietnam.

We talked about the old days, Bubbles, Napoleon, Marla, the Beauregards, and the Bayou nightclub. I never found out what happened to Bubbles and Napoleon. No one ever saw them again. We assumed the Mob killed them. He told me what happened to Marla and what she'd told him before her death. I felt sorry for her because she had hired Jay Goldstein to defend me. But like Bubbles told us at Walter Brickman's one night, "What's done is done."

I'm not sure how long, but it took a while to forgive Marla for her part in what happened to me and Lucas. If it weren't for her and Napoleon, maybe Baroque Parish would still be a vibrant example of what black folk can accomplish when they put their minds to it. Napoleon sure was something else, wasn't he? To think, he had Sharon steal my money and then he had her killed to cover his tracks.

Lucas and I had planned to marry, but we never did. He was Special Forces, and he loved it. Clearly, he'd found a home in the Army. Nevertheless, when he left for Vietnam the first time, I was pregnant with Karen, and there was no way I was going to get another abortion. I regret the first one, even though it was Napoleon's.

Lucas was supposed to be in Vietnam for a year, but he ended up staying over there for six long years. He sent me a letter telling me he'd married a Vietnamese girl less than a year after he left me. Her name was Hanh, which means "has good conduct." He was shocked when I told him I was pregnant with his child. I thought it would bring him home to me, but it didn't. He sent me a monthly stipend from his Army pay, but it wasn't enough; thankfully, my stocks were still doing well, because I was accustomed to having whatever I wanted when I wanted it.

During the six years he was in Vietnam, Lucas and Hanh had five beautiful children together; three boys and two girls. He brought his family to America in the summer of 1969. He was stationed at the Presidio for a couple of years. I hate to admit it, but we had a torrid affair during those two years. That's when I knew my first husband, Paul, had told me the truth about the attraction he had for his former flame, the preacher's wife.

I had sent him numerous pictures of Karen, but I took such pleasure in seeing the expressions on their faces when father and daughter finally met. I had seen pictures of Hanh; she was a beautiful woman. When I met her in person, it was clear that even at thirty-two, she was somehow able to maintain a form of innocence. Her bright smile, her conservative manner of dress, her genuine loving attitude, everything about her was like the evil of this world had never touched her, like she was as close to perfection as any human being could ever be. That's when it occurred to me that Lucas had found the old me, the one he'd fallen in love with when we were teenagers, and married me—the young, sweet, innocent, virginal me. I knew then that what he heard in the courtroom so many years ago had killed the image he had of me.

But when I looked at Lucas, who was holding six-year-old Karen in his arms, I knew I still loved him. Our eyes met, and we communicated our love without saying a word. The next thing I knew, we were making plans to see each other. We tried, but we just couldn't keep our hands off each other. Eventually, Hanh found out about it, and the next thing I knew, Lucas had gotten orders to Fort Meade. He was going to Owings Mills, Maryland, to be a part of the National Security Agency.

Eventually, I met other men and moved on with my life. I married twice more; both men were white and wealthy. I didn't love either man, and please don't hate me for that. I'm not the first woman, nor will I be the last who married for financial security. Besides, I didn't go looking for white men; they came after me. Furthermore, any woman who doesn't consider a man's financial status prior to marriage isn't a saint; she's a fool! If she's wealthy already, I guess that's okay. I'm not saying a woman should marry for money. I'm saying there's nothing wrong with marrying a man who has his financial "stuff" together, okay? I certainly wasn't going to marry any man who had less than me, okay? It really bothers me to see so many women hanging on to losers. What really blows my mind is that there are lots of educated women out there settling for ignorant, broke, uneducated men, just to have a man.

Anyway, my second husband's name was Reginald Shore. He managed the brokerage firm his family owned. I met him at the firm. He was my interviewer. I saw his desire for me, and when the interview concluded, I had the job. He asked me to lunch, and nearly a year later, we were married, much to the chagrin of his adoring mother, Samantha. We lived in a plush apartment in Manhattan which offered a wonderful view of Central Park. We had gotten married in 1971. I was faithful to him for four years, which was when I literally bumped into Lucas at the World Trade Center in one of the restaurants; I can't remember which one it was.

The National Security Agency had offices in the Towers. Lucas was still happily married to Hanh. The year was 1975, and I had just seen handsome Robert Redford and Faye Dunaway in *Three Days of the Condor*. Much like before, we started seeing each other and didn't stop until Reginald's private investigator produced several very incriminating photos of Lucas and I doing some rather nasty things to each other. That was the end of marriage number two.

I was fired from the Shore brokerage firm shortly after the divorce papers were signed. I walked away with a nice severance package from the firm and the divorce. I wasn't hurting for money, and I knew how to make more. I moved back to San Francisco and bought the house where I currently live, which is where I met and married my third husband. His name was Charles Beauregard—no relation. Ironic, isn't it?

Charles was a sweet man, but he was fifteen years older than me. He was a widower and the owner of the house I'd purchased. The house was for sale by owner, so we did the deal over lunch at a seafood restaurant at Fisherman's Wharf. I remember eating the most succulent lobster ever. Six months later, we were married. Less than a year after that, we were divorced. I'm sure some of you think of me as a gold digger, and maybe I am. But as I said earlier, I wasn't about to marry a man who had fewer assets than me. Well, I would have married Lucas, but he wouldn't leave his wife and I wouldn't ask him to. Anyway, it made business sense to marry a man of means. Hate me if you like, but I'm not broke. Believe me, it's better to be rich!

As for Sadie, we've kept in touch over the years. She told me one of the most difficult things she had to do was go back to work for Mrs. Mancini. Santino's wife gave her the blues and treated her like she was nothing when her children weren't around. But when the children were on the Mancini grounds, she treated them like they were her own, spoiling them on birthdays and during Christmas. Sadie often wondered if Mrs. Mancini allowed her to stay in the small apartment over the garage so she could torture her.

Shortly after I divorced Paul Masterson, my first husband, I went to New Orleans and brought Sadie and her children to San Francisco. When her last child graduated from high school, I put her through college and she opened her own bakery. She realized that baking was the one thing she enjoyed and would do for nothing. Eventually, she met a man and fell in love for the first time. I was happy for her. Unfortunately, my friend Sadie died of a heart attack ten years ago. I still miss her.

Now for the very best news I can offer. Today is my wedding day. Lucas and I are finally getting married. He lost Hahn a year ago. I have always kept tabs on him. I kept hope alive for five decades. Think about that. When Hahn died, I entered his life once more; the right way this time. And now, in the twilight of our lives, we finally have each other exclusively forevermore, still hopelessly in love.

Book Club Discussion Questions

1) Militant feminist groups say rape is about power. Do you agree with them? What are your thoughts as to why Billy Logan became a rapist?

2) If Lucas hadn't broken it off with Johnnie on Christmas, would she have met Napoleon at the Bel Glades Hotel?

3) What two books did Marla send Lucas?

4) Why do you think the author chose those books?

5) What is the central theme of all three *Little Black Girl Lost* novels?

6) In this novel, the author alluded to wives knowing about extramarital affairs. Why didn't the women of that time period expose them, and why don't many women expose them today?

7) Did Napoleon love Johnnie? Explain your answer.

8) Did Marla love Lucas? Explain your answer.

9) In all three novels, there was lots of black/white sex going on, much like it was during the 1600s. It was dangerous then, and in many respects, it's dangerous now. Do you

believe it goes on so much because of the forbidden fruit analogy? Could there be other reasons? If so, cite them.

10) In the last two novels, God clearly protected Johnnie from murder. Why do you think he didn't show himself in the first novel? Or did he? If he did, in what ways?

11) Who was your most sympathetic character other than Johnnie and Lucas? Why?

12) What were your thoughts on Walker Tresvant's speech the night the NAACP came to recruit Negroes to join the grass roots Civil Rights Movement?

13) Was Walker Tresvant wrong? If so, support your position. Was he right? If so, support your position.

14) What message was the author attempting to convey with the Johnnie Wise character?

15) List whatever truths you garnered from all three novels and discuss them.